10/2/98

‖‖‖ ‖‖‖‖‖‖‖‖ ‖ ‖‖‖ ‖‖‖‖‖‖‖ ‖‖
S0-AHM-351

The Block
is an unqualified success!

THE BLOCK

Bob Litwin
Chip Silverman

Scribe ☐ 1994

A Hardcover edition of this novel appeared in 1994.
Trade Paperback edition 1997

Printed in the United States of America

ISBN# 1-880325-17-9

Cover art copyright © 1994 by Matt Dowling

Jacket design by Bob Litwin & Chip Silverman

Typesetting by Elizabeth E. Monteleone & Nevah Stevenson

2nd printing

Scribe Publishing is a division of Borderlands Press

ACKNOWLEDGMENTS

Special thanks to Renée Collins-Blumenfeld for her invaluable assistance in the typing and editing of the manuscript.

Thanks also to the following individuals for their contributions to the flavor and history of *The Block*: the late Pam Gail, Chick Sirota, the late Joe Finazzo, Tommy Bruno, E. Thomas Maxwell (former Baltimore Assistant State's Attorney), the staff of the Telephone Reference Service and the Maryland Desk at the Central Enoch Pratt Free Library in Baltimore, Harry Van Valin, Elena Suhomlin, Margo Perrera, and Harriet Silverman.

To Julie and Ted,
parents and friends

THE
BLOCK

Bob Litwin
Chip Silverman

Prologue

Charles Whittier

The big 727 dipped suddenly, and rolled lazily to one side as it panned the Baltimore skyline. Clouds filtered past and the view became clearer, giving Charles a straight shot of the Chesapeake Bay and its surrounding waterways. The stewardess leaned in to remove his ginger ale and deftly caught two stray peanuts as they wobbled toward the edge of his tray table. "We'll be landing soon, sir. Please place your seat in the upright position." Charles obliged and squirmed to readjust himself in the suddenly uncomfortable airline seat. The corduroy of his trousers was crushed against the back of his thighs and his boxers were riding up. He couldn't wait to get on the ground. Thank God for short flights. New York to Baltimore was palatable. But sitting on an airplane for more than an hour really sucked. Last month the trek out to Phoenix had been brutal, although once he got out of the airport, the warm, dry air had done wonders for his sinuses. He made a mental note to pop another Seldane when he got to the hotel.

Charles looked over at the yellowed newspaper on the vacant seat next to him and picked it up. Again, the headline jumped out at him. This Tennyson guy must have been some kind of king shit, he thought to himself as the seat belt sign glared red above him and the captain signaled the flight attendants for landing. He tucked the newspaper into the side compartment of his carry-on bag and fastened his belt. "The Lord," Charles muttered to himself, shaking his head. "Who the fuck did he think he was?"

BWI Airport was relatively quiet. He'd picked a good day to travel. The baggage claim was a piece of cake, nothing like JFK. Damn, you were lucky if *you* made it off the plane, let alone your luggage.

He dragged the oversized duffel off the conveyer belt and did a quick scan of the bags rounding the corner. He spotted his leather garment bag easing its way down the pike, so he ducked into the thick of the crowd, grabbed the handle and heaved it over his shoulder. Now all he needed was his rental, some decent directions, and he was on his way.

The Chevy Corsica wasn't exactly what he had in mind. It reeked of cigarettes and had those sorry-looking cloth seats he hated. If he ever decided to move out of the city, he had big plans in the four-wheel-drive department.

He pulled onto the Baltimore-Washington Parkway and headed north. This part was vaguely familiar. A native of Northern Virginia, Charles had ventured into Baltimore once or twice back in his high school days. He and the guys would catch an occasional Orioles game, then head back to the comfort of their parents' Great Falls digs with their swimming pools and the well-stocked bars. It never really occurred to him to "hang out" in Baltimore. Outside of baseball, what else was there to do? Georgetown had been a much more enticing prospect. Full of good-looking, underage girls, and bouncers who looked the other way when Charles and his sixteen-year-old cohorts flashed their fake IDs. He smiled at the memory. Even now, some fifteen years later, Charles still hadn't done much time in Baltimore. He'd been meaning to come check out the new stadium, but if he was home for a visit, he usually spent most of his time back with the folks.

Baltimore really had become an attractive city. As he sped along 95 North, he could make out the business district. The tall, streamlined buildings, though few in number compared to New York, stood stoic and secure. Charles caught the downtown exit and cruised west into the blaze-orange sunset and the heart of Baltimore. Bright-colored billboards were strung along the highway, singing the Orioles song, Baltimore's claim to fame. The magnificent Camden Yards stadium loomed ahead, a formidable, first-class structure with an ornate brick surface and hard-to-come-by tickets. As he rounded the bend and came upon the renovated Inner Harbor area, Charles could immediately see the appeal. You could almost feel it, actually. Alive with people on the move, but different from the Big Apple. Everything was immaculate. No street garbage. No bums, that he could see. Clean-cut-looking folks for the most part. Good ethnic mix. And the restaurants. Charles' buddy Terrance who lived in D.C. claimed Baltimore had enough fabulous restaurants to keep you fat and happy for weeks. Judging from the looks of the harbor area, with a beautiful sunset glinting off the water, you could probably say that Baltimore had arrived. The city had kind of an "open invitation" feel to it. You know, that arms extended, broad smile on the face, come on in and let me buy you a beer kind of warmth—a characteristic that was really more aligned with a small town. Baltimore had sure come a long way from the dirty, unwelcoming, working-class city he remembered.

The rental agent said the Stouffer was just down from Camden Yards on Pratt Street. He eased over into the far left lane and came to a stop at the light. It was dusk on a Friday afternoon in April and people were everywhere. Business suits. Tourists. Kids. Couples. Old folks pushing strollers. Maybe there was a game at the stadium tonight. He glanced at the digital car clock. Five-twenty. He still had time to take a hot shower and check in with Julia. Then he'd grab a quick bite and head down to The Block before the so-called action kicked in. He swung the Corsica into the Stouffer garage.

The room would suffice. Two double beds, small table for his laptop, telephone, TV, bathroom and room service. It would do until he figured out how long he'd be in town. If it looked like more than a couple of weeks, he'd check into renting a furnished apartment, show the big guy in the corner office he understood the value of a buck. He sank down on the bed and reached for the phone. His fingers flew rapidly over the buttons as he punched out his calling card code from memory and listened to the rings on the other end, counting. She picked up on the third ring as usual. "Hey, babe."

"Hi, honey," she said softly. "Where are you?"

"At the hotel. I just got in." Charles leaned back and kicked off his shoes, stretching his toes. "I miss you already."

"So hurry back." He heard the subtle irritation in her voice. But he knew she understood. If he was going to become a successful writer and reporter, it basically meant they would have to give up time together. They'd had their share of missed dates, last minute cancellations for the theatre, overcooked gourmet dinners at Julia's tiny East Side apartment. But Charles subscribed to the success ethic. Do what it takes to make it. In most instances, Julia understood his reasons. He was especially pleased with her attitude about the Baltimore stint. He had a June 1st deadline, which gave him six weeks to conduct his research, track down his subjects, and put together a hell of a piece. And even then he wasn't guaranteed it would print. His editor, Mosley, was a hardass. "I'm gonna be on you like stink on shit, Whittier," he'd bellowed from his corner office. "Give me something to make your mama proud."

"I'll make it as quick as I can, babe. You know that," Charles said.

"Yeah."

"Besides, you got a couple of days off coming to you, right? Maybe you could pop down for a long weekend."

"Sure. While you work 'round the clock, I'd be sitting around twiddling my thumbs wondering what the hell I was doing in Baltimore. Look, I told you, I understand this is a really big deal for you. I'm not about to get in the middle of you and the story of your life." Now that was the Julia he loved and admired. "I'll settle for a phone call at the end of the day."

"You got it. Oh, here's the number where I can be reached." He fumbled in the drawer for some hotel stationary and read it off to her. "I'm in room 215." He heard her take a deep breath and let it out. She missed him bad. "Hey, Jule."

"Yes, honey."

"Keep those home fires burning." He smiled into the phone, remembering last night and the incredible things she could do with her gorgeous body. He didn't deserve her.

"I love you, Charles."

"I know. I love you, too." He hung up and lay stretched out across the bed for a minute savoring the sound of her last words. He could picture her sitting on the couch in the little living room, probably still dressed in her suit blouse and stockings, beat up old house slippers on her feet. Right about now she'd be reaching over to pick up her glass of wine and click on the remote to tune in the news. He'd give anything to be there with her. But first things first.

Charles moved over to the table and popped open his briefcase. The stack of clippings stared back at him, the face of "The Lord" front and center on the front page. *Harry 'The Lord' Tennyson, club owner on Baltimore's infamous 'Block' indicted for racketeering.* Charles smelled scandal big time, but he had a lot of research to do. He pulled his sweater over his head and unbuttoned his shirt. He couldn't wait to get out of his corduroys and into a nice, hot shower. Then he'd see about scaring up some food.

Downstairs in the Stouffer, Charles asked the concierge for directions to The Block. But first he decided to cross the street to the Harborplace Pavilion where he was told there was a great food court. True enough. After milling about, taking stock of his choices, he picked up a crabcake sandwich and a cup of gourmet coffee with whipped cream. The temperature had dropped somewhat, but people, eager to exhibit that sense of freedom springtime brings about, braved the rather un-springlike bite in the air to munch their finger food outside along the promenade. Charles was surprised by the number of tourists, easily identifiable with their Nikons and disposable cameras, sensible shoes and Orioles paraphernalia. It was still early in the year, school wasn't even out, but already folks were flocking to Baltimore.

He strolled along the walkway that encompassed the harbor, and watched as a cruise boat featuring special group packages for dinner and dancing eased slowly out of its berth and pointed its nose toward the Bay Bridge. He made his way back across Pratt Street and started to walk north toward The Block. He headed up Calvert, crossing over Lombard. A wino loitered against a banged-up phone booth at the corner. A sign in a small liquor store advertised the lottery and numbers games. A surge of adrenalin worked its way up from somewhere deep in Charles' gut and gave his brain a momentary jolt. This was going to be fun. He'd covered prostitutes and pushers and hustlers before, but it was always smalltime for a back page, no byline story. He'd spent five years at the *Post* doing general assignment reporting, covering various beats, going nowhere. Then the job at *Esquire* came up and he'd lunged for it. Now he was guaranteed a shot at a story in every issue. But he worked his ass off for it, and so far had only been in print a couple of times. Once with a small piece on the homeless, and two months ago with a pretty beefy article on AIDS awareness among college kids. But this was a shot at something big. The magazine was looking to do a series on the age-old art of burlesque. Every city had its red-light district, but *Esquire*'s expense account pockets were only so deep. They weren't about to shuttle writers off to the top ten cities to do in-depth stories. A handful had been selected originally, and then they cut it down to just three. Charles had volunteered to take the Baltimore beat. The other two had gone to San Francisco (North Beach) and New Orleans. Charles saw this as a real opportunity to make his mark. May the best man win was the name of this game, and he hated to come in second. The very thought sickened him.

He rounded a corner and, suddenly, there it was. There wasn't a whole lot to it as far as he could tell. The name seemed to do it justice.

Barely more than a block long, it appeared that Baltimore's red-light district had seen better days. Charles squinted ahead of him, trying to make out just how many blocks it really was. One or two, tops. On each side of him loomed loud, tacky, neon billboards hyping the strippers, hoping to stir the basest desire.

Outside the clubs stood the standard bouncer types, although some of them didn't look like they could bounce much of anything. Thin, wiry guys mostly. Seedy-looking. Charles searched hard and finally found what he was looking for. A hooker. She was what you might call a bit of a stretch. Tired, too old, too soft, too pitiful. But there she stood, tight knit dress pressed against her ass, braless tits sagging beneath the cheap fabric, hair an astonishing electric red. She was mouthing off to some old guy on the threshold of a club. Something about the performance status of his manhood.

The last three barfronts on this side of the street had official-looking notices on the glass doors that announced they would be permanently closing in a few weeks to make way for a new city government office building. One of them was the storied Desert Club.

Charles decided to get the inside perspective, so he ducked into the Desert Club, and tried to appear inconspicuous. The air inside felt warm and thick, as if the heater had been on "high" for too long, and the smell of rancid beer and cigarette smoke invaded his sensitive nostrils. He suddenly remembered that he'd forgotten his sinus pill. Fuck. He felt the music before his auditory system could even register its sound. Deep, rhythmic thumps of a drum and the sound of a disco soundtrack came from beyond a partition ahead. A girl brushed past him wearing a bikini top and very tiny shorts. Kind of a hard-looking girl, not more than twenty or so, with a hideous dye job. But what he noticed most was the wedding band strung on a chain around her neck. A story within a story within a story. The words of a journalism professor at Northeastern came back to him suddenly. A little Jewish guy who swore that the real story was the one you weren't there to cover. The key to success was when you discovered that your story was really ten stories, just waiting to be told.

He moved ahead to the partition and peered around it. A long room stretched out before him. The bar, with stools all around, extended the full length of the room. The stage started midway down the bar. It was actually built up level with the customers' beer glasses. A guy would have to look up to see something. That was probably the general idea. The obligatory cloud of smoke hung in the air and a fairly hot-looking brunette was in the process of winding her ample self around a pole stuck through a hole in the middle of the bar. Charles held steady for a minute and tried to spot an open table along the outskirts. There was none. As he turned to see if anyone was behind him, he caught a familiar face in his gaze. Harry The Lord Tennyson's stone-cold eyes looked out at him from a frame hanging on the wall across the club's entry hall. Charles cocked his head momentarily, then turned back. Must have been his old stomping grounds. The girl had wriggled herself out of her top and revealed two heavy breasts. Working the scruffy-looking dude at the bar, she lowered herself so her breasts practically toppled his beer. Charles took a weighted breath and moved casually to the bar and pulled up a stool. "I'll take a Coors," he said to the bartender. The guy nodded and slid one across the bar. Charles took a long, slow drink and set the bottle down. The brunette had spied him and was picking up her pace with the scruffy guy, vying for the tip.

The dancing girl was skilled at the art of squeezing tips out of customers. If she had been sitting next to the guy at the bar, a couple of well-placed clutches at his crotch would locate his penis. Then some slow rubbing with her hand (and a few friendly squeezes) would have encouraged the customer to leave her a dollar or two tip on the bar. Sometimes a harder squeeze was necessary. On stage she used a different routine, one that she had rehearsed many times until it seemed smooth and looked natural. After the last dance of her set, which was usually three or four jukebox songs, she would kneel down and duck-walk over to the guy she had made the most eye contact with during her dance set. Charles watched with some interest as she moved in close to the guy a few stools down from him. When she was very close, she reached out and grabbed his head and pulled it between her breasts. The guy managed an embarrassed laugh and licked and nuzzled around her breasts and nipples, then put a dollar bill in the elastic band that kept her G-string tight. She stood up and moved back on the stage. So much for "up close and personal" on The Block, thought Charles as he watched the little routine play itself out.

Dollar in hand she shook back her hair and moved down

toward Charles. Amused, he turned his head to study the architecture of the far wall with the neon exit sign. He knew she wouldn't let him off that easy. Nice looking guy. Expensive shirt, Levi's, clean fingernails. Probably a "ten" in her book. A ten with a few twenties in his pocket. He could feel her movements as his fingers wrapped around his vibrating beer bottle. As she drew closer, Charles had to admit she did have nice tits. But the idea of leering at women in this situation really never appealed to him much. He reached into his left pocket and pulled out his wallet. Before she could even dip down to make eye contact, he had folded a couple of dollar bills and pressed them into her open palm. He looked up into her face and gave her a sideways nod. She moved down and around to the other side of the bar.

As the only black guy in the place, Charles figured he kind of stood out. But he was used to that. He'd grown up with that. It always fascinated him to watch how other people dealt with it, or didn't deal with it. In this case, no one was paying him much attention, except for the brunette who kept glancing his way across her shoulder as she pranced in front of some other poor sap. She probably thought she'd missed a good thing. Charles couldn't help but crack a smile. Julia wouldn't find this too amusing.

The bartender came back around with another beer and Charles threw a couple of bucks across to him. "What's with the guy in the picture on the wall?" he asked with a nod toward the entrance. "He the owner?"

"Used to be. Been gone for years." Charles took another swig. The beer tasted good.

"What do you know about him?"

"Just that he used to be big time around here back in the fifties. Then the guy just up and disappeared." The music stopped and the brunette slipped behind a dark red curtain. It felt kind of like a blanket had been tossed over the room. The smiles dimmed, eyes turned downward, the stage stood empty, and customers went about the business of consuming their beer.

ONE

HARRY TENNYSON

Little Marvin was coming in to collect his half mil', and Harry The Lord Tennyson didn't have it.

In 1956, half a million was more money than *God* had on hand . . .

And everybody knew Harry never had that much cash in a liquid condition. His money was tied up in real estate, boiler-room sales operations, and, of course, all the gambling shops. He was the only guy in town who never set limits on his customers. That's why if some schmuck wanted to bet a "dime" on a number straight up, he could always lose his money to The Lord.

But right about now Harry was thinking there were only two problems with his famous business policy: one, a schmuck could get lucky with his dumb bet, and two, The Lord would have to come up with the payoff.

Now, if the schmuck's name happens to be Little Marvin, Harry Tennyson was in deep shit. He would have to—

There was a light tapping on the door to Harry's office. It was a tap that reflected both familiarity and respect.

"Yeah?" said Harry.

The door opened just far enough to admit the bald head of Syd Daniloski, one of Harry's faithful lackeys.

"Just got the word that Little Marvin left the Shake & Bake on the Avenue. He's on his way."

Harry Tennyson nodded. He eased back from his desk and sunk a little lower in his leather executive chair. He thought about how to deal with this crazy little fuck who was driving his Coupe de Ville down to The Block right now.

"Tell Jerry to come in here a minute," he said.

Syd disappeared behind the door, leaving it open. Jerry tapped once and walked in. He was a tall, thin guy with broad shoulders. He always looked like he forgot to take the hanger out of his jacket before putting it on. He used to play football for the semi-pro league that played at Kirk Field, and he had that knocked-around face that told you not to mess with him. It was a face that said, I've seen it, done it, and it ain't no biggie—I'll do it again.

"Yeah, Harry?"

"I've been thinking about what to do with Marvin. You know I hate violence, but I might need you to be ready for anything."

Jerry tapped a fist into his open palm. It was a gesture he'd picked up in a bad movie. It would look silly on anybody but Jerry. "You got it."

"Got your piece?"

"Sure, Harry, I always got that."

"Okay, so I want you sitting over there in that chair. Hands in your pockets, holding iron, okay?"

"Can do." Jerry scratched his head, allowed himself a little chuckle. "So, look, what're we *really* going to do with this guy?"

"Not what you think," said Harry, wishing he had a real answer. " I got an idea, but in case the scene goes south, I want you to be ready."

"You know, I heard you don't wanna try anything funny with this little jerk. The saps say he carries two .45s around with him. And he uses them whenever he feels like it. Everybody's afraid of him. He gets away with it. And you can bet he ain't comin' here alone."

"I got a plan, don't worry about it."

Only Harry didn't have a plan. He didn't have shit, but he was going to have to think fast.

Harry got quiet again, which cued Jerry that the conversation was over. It wasn't the first time Harry had to function under pressure. He'd been in jackpots before and always made the right move. That's what business was all about—making the right move. Some of his longest and best friendships had developed this way. Only this time it was different. Harry didn't want Little Marvin as a friend, he just wanted him out of his hair.

Little Marvin Harper was too much trouble, thought Harry. Too much of a hot dog, no class. There's an unspoken code that you had to live by—don't try to impress people who know better. Always realize who you can learn from. That's how you get stronger—you never get so cocky you think there's nothing left to learn. 'Cause there always is. Little Marvin was riding high right now. He'd gotten lucky dealing on the Avenue and made a rep for himself among the blacks. He started making so much money he didn't know how to get rid of it. When he started playing his lucky numbers for big tickets, he said he was going to score with The Lord.

There weren't too many people in Baltimore who could piss away a thousand dollars a day, but Little Marvin was one of them.

It was a dumb play. Real dumb. But the little bastard got lucky and hit his number with a $700 bet!

Harry's concentration was broken when he heard some voices outside his office door.

"Nobody sees The Lord 'til I give you the once-over," boomed Syd.

"Man, I ain't got no heat. Only an asshole be here in whitey's spot with a gun."

The voice was unfamiliar yet recognizable at once.

Quietly and evenly, Syd repeated himself.

Although Syd had a reputation for being somewhat of a lunkhead, nobody messed with him and his 300 pounds. His dedication to The Lord was widely known. He'd do anything to protect Harry and that meant jumping in front of a bullet if he had to. The day he shielded Harry from Skippy Belinsky and his .38 revolver at Pimlico was a legend around the track. Syd was "The Real." And as long as The Lord was in business, Syd would have a job.

The familiar tapping came once again. Syd, at the threshold, announced Little Marvin's arrival. "He's here, boss. And he's clean."

Harry remained seated as the door swung open to reveal a wiry, little Negro dressed in a steel-gray sharkskin suit. It shined in the overhead lights like a new battleship being built down at Key Highway Yards. It occurred to Harry that a suit shouldn't shine. Marvin Harper stood in the doorway, legs spread apart, defiant, like a punk gunfighter looking for Doc Holliday. He wore a floppy, wide-brimmed hat and wide tie with yellow crescent moons on it.

"Mr. Harper, I presume," said Harry. He stood up and walked around his desk extending his hand. "You got lucky, eh?"

Little Marvin's expression gave him away. He was obviously taken aback, not used to a white man showing such courtesy. Harry was instantly reminded of the Last Supper. Judas and the Kiss.

"Luck ain't got nothin' to do with it," said Little Marvin. "I got me a system. I knew if I waited long enough, held my ground, it would all work out. See you gots to keeps your cards close to your chest so you don't tempts the fates."

Harry wasn't sure what he meant by this last statement, but he smiled graciously and gestured the little man to a chair in front of his big desk.

Marvin Harper sat down and leaned back, puffing out his chest and his garish tie like a peacock showing off his feathers.

"You aren't superstitious, are you, Mr. Harper?" Harry asked as he walked back around his desk and eased back into his leather executive chair.

"Let's say I likes to keep my fingers on top of everything. Believe in everything and nothing at the same time."

"You sound—"

Harper held up a hand like a traffic cop. "Hey look, man, I don't mean no disrespect, but I ain't here to talk, Mr. Tennyson. You tole me to come here to pick up the scratch, remember?"

Harry nodded. "Yes, I did say that, didn't I?"

Marvin looked at him, wary but still locked into his brazen routine. "I ain't got no time for socializing. I gots to go celebrate. I gots pussy to tend to."

"Don't be so vulgar, Mr. Harper. Respect, you need to show respect. You'll find that courtesy will get you a long way," Harry said as he directed a steely gaze at the Negro.

The bravado was getting Jerry hot under the collar, too. It was quite obvious to him that Little Marvin needed to be taught a lesson real bad. He started to make a move, but one glance from Harry and he knew to keep his cool and sit back down.

Harry needed to remind this little cocksucker who he was addressing.

"Good things come to those who wait, Marvin. May I call you that? Or do you prefer something less formal—just 'Little' or 'Mr. Little' . . . ?"

"You fuckin' with me, man? Don't you be fuckin' with me now. I can tell you right now, I came in here clean, 'cause everybody says you can be trusted."

"I can."

"So don't be fuckin' with Little Marvin, my man. If I was gonna get you, I'd be gettin' you on the street, when you wasn't expectin' it. Not here in your own crib, dig?"

Jerry stood up, hands still in his pockets. Harry told him to sit back down with a knowing glance.

"I quite understand," said Harry, lost in his thoughts for a way to deal with this loudmouthed, little brown turd.

"So, where's the money, Mr. Tennyson?"

"Why're you so anxious? I thought we could talk first. Get to know each other."

"Look, you either gots the money or you ain't. I ain't interested in socializing."

"But you have to socialize."

"Say what? Since when do the likes of you want to socialize

with the likes of me? If I was to be on the street I don't think you'd even look at me. I'd be your 'boy.' I ain't your boy today, is I? You owes me, don't you? And everybody knows it. I made sure everybody knows. How'd it look to everyone if you stiffed me, big man? You know, and I know, and your goons, and my mamas, all of Baltimore knows: you owe me, and you owe me big time."

Harry looked away in mock disgust.

"Enough of the sermon. I don't have time to listen to you. I wanted to talk to you because I thought you might have been a cut above the rest of your kind. I had big plans for you. I thought that you had it in you to take over . . . " Harry waved his hand in a gesture of dismissal. "Nah, never mind."

Marvin looked at him with a puzzled expression, but trying to conceal it, trying to stay cool, and doing a bad job of it.

Harry looked at his assistant. "Jerry, get me Benny the Bank. Let's pay this little guy and get on with the day's real business . . . "

Jerry stood up, wondering what was going on . . .

"Hey, wait a second! Take over *what*?" Little Marvin asked a little too anxiously.

Harry shrugged. "It doesn't really matter anymore, does it? You've proven yourself unfit to be in my circle."

"What makes you think I'd want to be in your circle?"

"Why wouldn't you?"

"I got my own scene." Marvin Harper was clearly angry, but unarmed as he was, he knew he must contain himself. Harry saw his chance to score heavily. He stood up, glared down at him over his desk.

"Little Marvin Harper," he said in a satiric voice. "He thinks he's on top, that Harry Tennyson doesn't know who he's fucking with. Just 'cause you got street smarts and a high school diploma from Douglass doesn't cut it with me! You want to play in the majors, Marvin, you gotta have respect and you gotta have some class. I was going to offer you a chance to step out and you're too stupid to catch the drift!"

Little Marvin crossed his arms against his chest, and suddenly out of character, spoke slowly, evenly: "Look, you ain't dealing with no sawmill nigger here! I knows the score. If you got something you want to say, just say it, man."

"Suddenly interested, are you?"

"Maybe."

"That's the first intelligent thing you said since you got here."

"I'm listening, Mr. Tennyson."

"Respect. Now you're showing it," said Harry. He had pulled out the chocks and was rolling now. What he had in mind might just work. "At least you're willing to pay attention. That's a good sign. Care for a smoke?"

Harry knew he could push this thing only so far. "Socializing" with a five-foot-four-inch lunatic was not how he wanted to spend his morning. But this little fucker was not as dumb as the rest of the big numbers players, thought Harry. He wasn't about to swap a half 'mil for a few nights getting his pipes cleaned with a white woman, not even Lola from the Gayety.

"Before we get started, I'd like for you to tell me a little about yourself."

"Say what? This ain't no interview, man. I didn't come here to tell you about myself." Marvin Harper smiled for the first time. He had a gold cap on one of his front teeth with a cutout in the shape of a star. Very tacky, thought Harry. "I came here for one reason and one reason only, and you know what? I think you're fucking with me."

"How so?"

"You ain't got the scratch, do you?"

Harry chuckled. "Mr. Harper, please don't insult me . . ."

"All right then, what is it, man? Tell me what's shakin' or pay me so I can get outta here. I ain't used to bein' around all these white people this long."

Harry knew he had him now.

"Mr. Harper, as you well know, I run a large operation. There is the point where one man can get too big, too greedy. That's a lesson those who've come before me never seemed to learn. They didn't know when to ease up, to let go. Spread the wealth, so to speak. So they ended up looking over their shoulders too much. Always worried that someone would try to fuck them. Not trusting anyone and trying to control too much by themselves. Know what I mean?"

Little Marvin sat there like a piece of amateur sculpture. Harry smiled inwardly. Maybe Marvin was keeping his cards to his chest and not tempting the fates. That stupid little piece of dreck, mused Harry.

Harry continued, "As a smart businessman, I know there has to come a time when I have to start trusting people and give others a chance to succeed, much in the same way I did and will continue to do so."

"I sees your lips flapping but so far I ain't hearing nothing of interest. Seems to me like you be show boatin'. What do you want, man? I'm in a hurry. I got the whole Avenue waiting for me! Shit, I gots all of Northwest waitin' to party with me."

Harry smiled. Yes, he thought, and that's all you think you've got. And that's your problem, little man—little thoughts to go along with your suit size.

"Well then, let's cut to the chase. Forget the money, Marvin. I'm going to give you an even better prize—the best prize of all. I'm going to give you all of East Baltimore, Marvin. Fuck the money. You want everything I run from the Fallsway east . . . It's yours for the taking."

Even Marvin couldn't contain the shock he was feeling. His eyes lit up like a cheap pinball machine, and a smile twitched to be born in the corners of his big lips.

"Think about it, Mr. Harper. An offer like this is a dream come true. No fighting or hassling over the turf. Just a nice clean business transaction."

Little Marvin fidgeted in his chair like a kid who just got called on in school and doesn't know the answer to the geography question. He looked down at his patent leather shoes, then at his hands, like he'd just noticed them for the first time. Finally he stood up, reached across Harry's desk and shook his hand.

"It's a deal . . . I'll take it!"

Harry The Lord Tennyson smiled broadly. He'd just saved himself a $490,000 payoff by giving Little Marvin Harper control of all the drug traffic in East Baltimore. And that was the sweetest part of the deal—Harry never controlled it in the first place.

Two

Katherine Louise

"See, it didn't matter to me if I had to shake off some clothes because the bottom line was, I needed to make it... you know?"

The interviewer watched intently as Katherine reached to the floor to retrieve her purse. She slid open the flap of her small leather bag and removed a pack of menthol cigarettes. It was practically full, and he could see the outline of a second pack stuffed into the compartment generally reserved for lipsticks and other small objects. She moved a cigarette to her lips in the offhand, yet studied manner of a woman who enjoys creating an effect, and flipped her little gold lighter twice. After a deep, rather indelicate draw, she slowly exhaled such a long stream of smoke that the interviewer's own lungs involuntarily expanded and contracted, keeping pace. Katherine shifted her weight, crossed her long legs and returned her reminiscent, blue-eyed gaze back to the unanswered question that hovered somewhere above in the recessed lights of the posh Prime Rib restaurant.

"Yes," she said slowly, hesitantly. "I suppose I thought about what my family would think. What all those people back

th⟨...⟩ ⟨...⟩ out to
do." She ⟨...⟩ ⟨...⟩tray and
seemed to focus mome⟨...⟩ ⟨...⟩ct, red lip print
she'd left on the filter.

The interviewer continued to watch and wait. He allowed his eyes to take in more closely what he'd initially only glanced over with a firm handshake and a polite head-to-toe. The graying, blond hair with the slightly mismatched highlights was elaborately done up in a hairstyle more appropriate after six. The widely-spaced, blue eyes seemed to glisten with the bright, wet look of an eager child, and were set on a broad, aging face that a man in his sixties would instinctively call attractive. She had a very full mouth that turned slightly downward and the interviewer noticed she had drawn the corners up with a dark red lip pencil, giving the faintest impression of a smile, even though now, she clearly was not smiling.

"I was in my late teens when I left and I knew what was sure to be coming if I stayed. I wanted to get the hell out of Blanning, West Virginia and on to the stage in the big city. Yeah, I guess I wanted to be a star, at least subconsciously. Consciously, I'd always thought being a secretary in a big city was glamorous."

Another deep drag on the cigarette and a tunnel of gray smoke sifted upward through the dust that hung on the sunbeam coming through the restaurant window.

"So maybe the big city stage wasn't Radio City Music Hall, but it was the closest I was gonna get. Come hell or high water, I was gonna make it. Besides, Charles, before I left, I fixed it so there was no turning back."

"What did you do?" asked Charles. He sensed he was about to become privy to the aging stripper's reason for being. Suddenly this assignment didn't seem so dull after all. His little interviewer ears perked up.

"It's kind of a long story . . . " she said apologetically. But Charles had done enough feature pieces to know when the subject was inwardly thrilled to the gills when presented with an opportunity to spill their guts. Katherine Louise, renowned striptease artist in the heyday of Baltimore's Block pulled herself up straight, ignited another cigarette and opened her pretty, red mouth to speak. "Blanning, West Virginia isn't anyplace to spend your life. I was one of seven kids living with my mama and pa in a broken-down farm house on a sorry little farm. My life consisted of tending babies, milking cows, house cleaning and farming. But that all changed. And, you wanna laugh? They called me Mabel."

"If you think I'm gonna watch those damn kids again while you go prancing into town you got another thing comin'. I got too many as it is and I ain't about to start in with your crazy offspring." The woman standing on the top step of the rotted-out porch was bellowing across the littered yard to a girl moving quickly toward the main road, blue print dress flapping in the spring breeze. Moments later a dusty, gray Ford screeched to a halt at the end of the gravel drive and the girl popped in and was gone. Eleanor McCallister scowled at the place where the car had been for a good minute, eyes cold, her full lips pressed into a hard, thin line.

"Mama?" A delicate hand touched her arm.

"What d'ya want?"

"Linette's just tryin' to find herself."

"Then she oughtta take a good look in the mirror." Eleanor turned to stare at her younger daughter and winced slightly. Sometimes the girl reminded her so much of herself at that age, it was scary. She had those same bright eyes, big blue ones, always watching. And a head filled with big ideas. Eleanor wished she had the courage to tell Mabel to get lost.

"Goddamn girl thinks just 'cause I got seven kids I want two more. And that Clyde is a devil. That boy just ain't like normal kids." Eleanor stooped to pick up a basket of unshelled peas and handed it to Mabel. "I done spent my life raisin' babies. It's all I know. You'd think maybe your sister woulda picked up a few tips is all. At the very least she could find a husband."

"I think that's what she's tryin' to do, Mama. Her kids don't got a daddy to speak of and Linette's still only a kid herself."

"Time I was her age I had four kids, so she ain't gettin' pity from me."

Mabel McCallister watched as her mother went into the house, slamming the battered screen door behind her. From somewhere upstairs baby Sara let out a hungry wail, and Mabel could hear her mother's heavy footsteps moving up and toward the back of the house. Out past the yard, Mabel could see the boys playing by the creek that ran parallel to the main mountain road. They were a rough bunch, always picking at each other and constantly turning up with a bloody nose or a black eye. The kids at school called them the Creepy Critters because the whole lot of them had come down with head lice last year. Danny, Jonas, Pete, and Willie were like four little steps, with Danny at the top at the wise old age of ten and the others falling in right under him at nine, eight, and five and a half. They'd been kind of cute when they were younger, but now they were just too much to handle. Mabel tried her best to discipline them in a way that wasn't mean and hurtful like Pa did, but it was no use. The boys were like a herd of wild horses, intent on destroying anything that got in their path.

Evening settled in as the sun had started its graceful descent, slowly dipping into the mountainside. Mabel finished shelling the peas and scraped the remains into a feed sack to take out to the horses later. Inside she could hear Mama clanging pots as she went about preparing supper, yet another variation of stew, using some of the deer meat from Pa's last kill. Mabel wasn't even hungry. She called out to Danny to wrap up their play and get inside. He hollered back that they were coming, then started the countdown for another round of hide-and-seek. Mabel could see little Willie's feet dangling from a tree branch, anxiously waving back and forth. She smiled. He always got found first.

She shut the screen door softly behind her and bent down to scoop up baby Sara. The little girl grinned broadly at Mabel, revealing her one lone tooth, front and center. She was a sweet child, although as the youngest, she probably didn't get nearly as much attention as she deserved. Once again, Mabel tried to pick up where Mama fell short, playing with Sara whenever time allowed, after her chores were finished and the boys were tended to. And then there were Linette's kids, Josh and Clyde. At five, Josh was a decent boy who pitched in around the farm with the older boys and spent the rest of his time trying to steer Clyde the Devil out of harm's way. Mama swore up and down that the child was truly evil. It was amazing that a four-year-old could be so spiteful. Last week he had dumped a bucket of pig slop on Willie's head while he was sleeping out back in the hammock. Willie had hopped up like a jack rabbit, howling and screeching. It was a pretty funny sight. Clyde was mad because Willie had borrowed his toy wheelbarrow to haul around some mangy-looking puppy he'd found. Instead of just taking the wheelbarrow back, Clyde waited for a more opportune moment to take revenge. The pig slop seemed to get his point across. Little Willie had promised in great earnest to stay away from Clyde until the day he died. Which might be soon if Clyde didn't watch it.

"Mabel, bring me those peas, will you?" Mama called out from the kitchen. "I can't make the stew until you bring me those damn peas."

"I'm coming, Mama. I'm coming."

Supper was a chaotic affair. The long, pine table had more nicks in it than it probably did as a tree, and the pitcher had already been tipped once, sending icy water sloshing into Jonas' lap and prompting boisterous laughter from the rest of the Creepy Critters. Mabel noticed Clyde the Devil laughed the hardest. It figured. Where in the world was that dumb Linette anyway?

Frank McCallister lumbered in just as the last of the water was mopped up and lowered himself into the chair at the head of the table. He cast a long look around the table and everyone fell silent and went about the business of eating. He was a large, angular man with a thin, rather handsome face, marred slightly by pockmarks from a skin allergy. He had deftly managed to make each and every one of his kids fear for their life when he entered a room, simply by fixing his icy, gray eyes on each of them at supper time. It was kind of a ritual with him, surveying his property, taking stock. Inevitably, if someone had done someone wrong, lied, cheated, skipped out on their chores, Pa knew about it. He always knew. It was amazing that he could spend all day in the fields or in town picking up supplies and still know what was going on at home.

"Everyone done their chores?"

A resounding, "Yes, Pa."

"Mabel this stew is cold. Warm it up a bit, will you?" Frank McCallister said without even tasting it. Mabel moved quickly to take the bowl away from his already outstretched hand and hurried over to the stove to spoon some hot stew into a new bowl. She handed it to him, her eyes taking a sudden interest in the grooves in the linoleum on the kitchen floor. "Look me in the eye, girl," he commanded, giving her arm a tug. Her eyes darted up and into the icy, gray domain of her father's. Her heart lurched momentarily, forcing her to suspend her breath as she held his gaze. The goal was to be the last to look away. So far she had never won. This was no exception. She felt her eyes drift downward even before they actually did, and relaxed slightly when the familiar linoleum came into view. "Thank you," he said simply as he picked up his fork. "Now go sit down." Mabel caught the pained look on Mama's face as she brushed past her chair. The word "weak" came to mind and stuck there as Mabel returned to her place and began to eat the abominable stew.

Later on, after the dishes were done and Sara had had her bath, Mabel stepped out onto the porch and took a deep breath of the crisp nighttime air. There was a slight breeze blowing and that comforting rustle in the trees that only tiny new leaves can make as they brush against one another. Spring was Mabel's favorite time of the year. She enjoyed the sense of renewal that presented itself both in nature and in her mind. At fifteen she felt almost as if she'd lived an entire lifetime. Yet, in a way, she hadn't really lived at all. She'd read about people in books who'd completely altered their lives just by picking up and moving to another town or another state. The heroine always finds a job in some big city as a store clerk or a secretary or a waitress. She gets a quaint little apartment or shares a room in a boarding house until she gets on her feet. Then along comes some fantastically handsome man who promises to help her get a leg up in the world. He buys her dinner and offers her a chance at a real life with some substance to it. One where she goes to parties and meets interesting people who enjoy talking about the world and great books and travel to faraway places.

Mabel moved to the porch steps and sat on the top step, stretching her long, slender legs out in front of her. It was okay if she couldn't move to a big city and get a job as a secretary. At this point she would settle for just getting off the mountain. But the image of a grander lifestyle was never far from thought. It sat patiently on a mental shelf, void of dust because it was pulled out and thumbed through so often.

Suddenly the sound of tires on gravel invaded the melody of night sounds, and the dusty, gray Ford rumbled into view and made its way down the road toward the house. Mabel was momentarily blinded as the car hit a rut and bounced up, then back down again. The driver swung up parallel to the porch and the passenger door flew open. A bare leg emerged, then lurched back in as a squeal erupted. "Luke, let me go! I got to go tuck in my kids!" Linette flung herself out of the car, straightening her flimsy blue dress and tucking her long, blond hair behind her ears. "Call me," she ordered as she strode to the steps, rear end switching absurdly.

"You bet I will!" came the enthusiastic reply.

Linette came to a halt at the bottom of the steps and looked at Mabel.

"Where's Pa?" she asked with a sudden frown and a glance at her watch.

Linette cocked her head upward to check the window of Mama and Pa's room. The light must have been out because she relaxed suddenly and leaned her body up against the rail of the steps and stretched.

"Damn, that man knows how to make me feel good!" she purred as a slow smile crept across her face. "You should see him in action, Mabel. Like a cat on the prowl. I swear if this ain't the man for me then I don't know who is!"

"The next guy in line, that's who," Mabel said absently.

"Mabel McCallister, you watch what you say, girl. I ain't like that and you know it. I've only been with two guys since Buddy and I split. And both times I thought I was gonna marry those boys. But Luke, well he's different. We really got something good, him and me." She ran her hands over her hips, smoothing her dress down, then bounded up the steps and plopped down beside Mabel.

"I think Luke's gonna ask me to marry him soon," she gushed. "We'll probably take the kids and move into his place on the other side of town. Mama'll be glad to get Clyde off her hands, I know."

"You really ought to pay more attention to those boys, Linette. They need lovin', you know."

"They get plenty of lovin'. They're just spoiled rotten is all. Mama lets 'em have the run of the place and she doesn't assign 'em chores like she does with all the rest of the kids."

"Linette, the point is, Josh and Clyde are your kids. Mama shouldn't have to make 'em mind her. That's your job."

"Yeah, I s'pose." Linette pulled at a weed that was poking its way through the slats in the stairs and tenderly touched her fingers to her lips. "Damn, my lips are near raw." She smiled again. It didn't take a genius to figure out what she'd spent the last three hours doing.

"Whatcha sittin' out here thinkin' about, Mabel? Dreamin' those silly dreams again about bein' some kind of secretary?"

Sometimes Mabel had a hard time believing her sister was almost twenty-two years old. Linette had to be one of the dimmest people around. Even Clyde could outsmart her. Listening was very difficult for Linette. She had the attention span of a flea. "I was just enjoying the night air before goin' up to bed."

"Yeah, and thinkin' about moving away again. Look, Mabel, there ain't no way you're gettin' outta here. It just don't make sense. Heck, you're so good with kids, you'll probably have one of your own in no time."

"Like hell."

"Well you're gonna have to fix yourself up a bit if you want a man. I mean a little lipstick wouldn't hurt." She reached out to touch Mabel's honey-blond hair. "And I know a real good hairstyle for you. You'd have to wear those rags in your hair overnight, but the curls would really suit you."

"I don't think so, Linette. But thanks. You go on to bed. I'm gonna sit out here for awhile." Linette got up slowly and shrugged her pretty shoulders.

"Suit yourself. I gotta say goodnight to the boys. I hope they're still up." She disappeared inside, leaving the putrid scent of her sticky, sweet perfume behind to mingle in the cool night air.

It must have been two or three in the morning when he appeared at her bedside. He wore his pajama bottoms and the sickening look of desire.

Wordlessly, he slid into bed and reached for her, catching her hand in his firm grip as she attempted to stop him from lifting her nightgown.

She closed her eyes and turned her face to the wall as he rolled over on top, crushing her breasts to her chest bone. There were no preliminaries. He just entered her, roughly, in one big thrust and groaned a deep, soft groan. For perhaps the hundredth time, Mabel marveled that Linette and the boys couldn't hear him through the thin partition wall that separated their sleeping quarters. No one ever heard a peep. He shifted his weight slightly and quickened his pace, raising up on one arm to grab a breast and fix his glassy-eyed stare on the wall behind her. She bit her lip hard to keep from crying out and waited for him to finish. When he began to throb inside her she felt his body tense up, her hip bones stinging with the weight of him. He let out a long, deep sigh and fell heavily against her. She wriggled free and gathered the sheet between her legs. Frank McCallister rolled from the bed to his feet and sauntered out of the room. Mabel, head still facing the wall, released her lower lip from its hold and quietly drifted off to sleep.

THREE

MARVIN HARPER

Little Marvin sat in Shorty's barbershop chair wanting to flat out *cry*. The lye Shorty used to straighten hair was killing him.

"Marvin, let it out. Ain't no use holding it in, man. Even Luther Johnson jumps and howls when I goes to conk his big ol' head," Shorty said with a chuckle. ". . . And he's a lot bigger an' tougher than your brown ass."

"My brother, I ain't got no need to let it out, 'cause you see it ain't the size of the man, it's the amount of his fortitude."

"Ooh wee! Usin' them big words, ain't you? You know what I . . ."

Marvin was really feeling it now. He could try and get his mind off the pain by conversatin' with Shorty, but it didn't really help much. Those nasty chemicals felt like they were eatin' holes in his nappy head, exposin' his nervous system to the air, makin' him uncontrollable. He could already feel his right leg startin' to jive around without his wantin' it to.

"Shorty! Ain't it time to rinse this shit?" he asked with a quiver in his voice.

"I thought you had fortitude."

"Fuck that, man. I want that stuff out NOW!"

Jumping up out of the chair like it was suddenly on fire, Marvin raced to the sink and ducked his head under the faucet. He groped helplessly for the cold water tap. Shorty chuckled as he reached around and turned the porcelain wrapped handle and the rinsing commenced.

"Mercy, mercy, mercy! That feels good . . . !"

"A lot better than that 'fortitude,' eh?" Shorty said under his breath.

"Shorty, I pays you to do a job. It ain't good to go insulting your customer. You got to show me respect."

Shorty wrapped a towel around Little Marvin's head and guided him back to the barber's chair—pink and gray speckled Naugahyde. As he unwrapped the towel and started to comb out Little Marvin's suddenly straightened hair, Shorty couldn't help but smile. And Marvin, of course, could see the barber's round, purple-black face in the mirror.

"Man, why you be smilin' like that? I ain't heard nothin' funny."

Shorty released a long, slick strand of Marvin's hair, leaned real close to the little man's face, and spoke softly.

"I knows you is a big man in the street, Marvin. I knows how you got a rep. And I also knows how you makes you money. But you gotta know somethin' about me. And that's that I ain't scared of you. I knowed you since you was a skinny, little runt in these back alleys. I've been watching you grow up. I've seen what you has become, and I . . . well, I guess I pity you."

"Don't need your pity! What's that trash you talkin'?"

Shorty kind of sighed. His face was as round as the moon, full of wrinkles and experience. "Just means to tell you, when I was your age, I was just like you . . . "

Little Marvin had heard enough. How could Shorty know who Little Marvin was? Or the deal he just cut with The Lord?

"Old man, you was never like me! So don't be sayin' that knowin'-me shit or that just-like-me shit . . . 'cause there ain't nobody really knows me and there sure as hell ain't nobody like me. If there was, then one of us be dead, 'cause there ain't room enough 'round here for two Marvins, you hear?"

"Take it easy, Marvin Harper . . . "

"*You* take it easy! You *don't* know me! You just an old nigger that lets The Man walk all over you. Yessir, nosir. Mr. White Man Sir. Ain't that how it goes, Shorty?"

"You don't have to be hurtful, Marvin."

Marvin smirked as he checked out his hair in the mirror. Long and black and shiny. It was lookin' good already.

"I can be anything I want, and that's the difference 'tween you and me. You never were nothing and you'll never be nothing. You gonna die a nothing nigger with nothing to show for having your brown ass here, so just turn this chair around and comb this thing out!"

Little Marvin saw something die in the old guy's eyes. As the chair slowly turned around and Marvin faced the mirror, he suddenly caught a glimpse of himself at Shorty's age. No way, he thought. No way I'm gonna end up in a dead-end job like this.

"You know, Marvin, I likes you," said Shorty as he went back to his work. "Always have. But you ain't got no right talkin' to me that way. You don't have to believe me but let me warn you. You is heading for big trouble and that would break your mama's heart."

"Now don't be bringin' any peoples' mamas into this thing, Shorty . . . especially mine! I hate it when you do that."

"Just be careful, Marvin. Just be careful."

A few more strokes of the comb and Shorty was finished.

Little Marvin checked himself out in the mirror from every angle. His hair was very straight. No sign of a nappy-headed kid there. If he had to suffer through a lye job every once in a while, it was worth it, 'cause Marvin sure did like what he saw.

"Shorty, you did such a mighty fine job, migh-tee fine. It was almost worth hearing your jive bullshit while you work."

Marvin pushed money into Shorty's hand, but Shorty pushed it back.

"No, Marvin. I don't wants it. I don't want your tainted money. It ain't no good here."

"Say what, you workin' for free now? Since when?"

41

Ignoring him, Shorty leaned a little closer. "So you think *I* bows down to whitey, eh?"

"Huh?"

Shorty took Marvin's face in his hand, forcing him to look in the mirror.

"Look, Marvin, what do you see?"

Marvin tried to push away but Shorty's grip was strong and firm.

"What're you talkin' about?" Marvin was getting concerned.

"Marvin, I sees an old, worn-out nigger, and I sees a young one straightening his hair like the white man. One of us is the fool. You tell me who that be."

Marvin straightened up and looked in the old man's dark eyes. His words had struck a chord in him. His mama always said the truth always hurt worse than a lie.

"Shorty, the world is changing, and I'm the one to change it. Maybe I have to look as much like The Man as I can so's that I can get on with the changin' without bein' noticed . . . "

"Marvin, that's the sorriest excuse I ever heard for a reason."

"We'll see about that." Marvin oozed out of the chair, heading for the door with as much style and soulful strutting that befitted someone in charge. Reaching the door, he stopped at the counter, dropping a twenty-dollar bill on the Formica.

"If it will make you feel better," he said without looking back, "you can give this twinsky to Reverend Blaylock C. Calhoun."

Once outside, Little Marvin dusted off his suit jacket and checked out his reflection. He was young, had plenty of money, the respect of his people, and all the 'tang he'd ever want. And if that wasn't enough, he'd just had the whole East Side of Baltimore handed him.

Whew . . . what could be sweeter?

The old man just didn't know . . . Marvin loved Shorty. He was like an uncle to him. Which was the only reason Marvin allowed him to talk to him that way. Anybody else would be gettin' their ticket punched.

He adjusted his porkpie hat, checked his Bulova watch, and decided it was time to collect his boys. As he strutted down the Avenue in his new maroon suit accented with a thick, long, gold pocket-watch chain, he passed another full-length plate glass shop window.

"Lookin' good," he said as he paused to do some serious profiling. "Ain't nobody messin' with Little Marvin Harper."

His gait had a commanding aspect and as he reached the next block, the first of his lieutenants caught up with him, falling into a choreographed rhythmic step behind him. For the next block, every storefront or two, another young man joined the formation until there were six of them, half marching, half dancing, down Pennsylvania Avenue like half-assed mourners in a French Quarter wake. No one spoke for five blocks, even when Marvin stopped in front of the Shake & Bake restaurant. They all knew the drill—-keep your mouth shut until the little big man decided to talk to you.

"Gentlemen," said Marvin with a big, gold-capped smile, "today is the day."

Sweet Sam (Sweets for short) opened the door and held it to allow Little Marvin and Shades in. The rest of his henchmen, Jimmy, Leroy, and Cutter stayed outside.

Little Marvin, Shades, and Sweet Sam looked almost comical standing at the doorway in James Cagney fashion. With deliberate hesitation, Little Marvin started to the back of the diner and noticed his usual corner table was occupied. The waitress, Dillcie, hurried over to the customers and whispered to them. They stood up like they'd rehearsed it, all together, without saying a word, and moved to the other side of the diner. The busboy wiped the table clean, and, within thirty seconds, Little Marvin and his associates were ordering lunch.

I'd like to see Shorty get this much attention, Marvin thought.

The diner was small and plain, but the chicken was spicy and crispy, and the ribs were so good that even white people had to come in and order them to go once in awhile. Of the fifteen tables, four were occupied, and Marvin noticed the diners trying to be discreet as they stared at the three men.

Sweet Sam spoke first. He got his name at the tender age of fifteen. By that time Samuel Elijah Jackson looked to be a man, and already had a reputation for being a sweet talker and smooth with the ladies. Some said he was lucky that at an early age he discovered that "hiding the salami" (getting laid), busting heads, and making a fast buck was his purpose in life. He wasn't too bright, but he was dedicated.

"How do you know The Lord ain't gonna cause no trouble when we goes down the East Side? What kind of guarantee did he give you?"

Shades spoke, "Sweets, the man can't go back on his word."

Sam ignored the comment. "But you ain't got no witnesses 'cepting those white men, and they could say anything."

"Sam . . . " and there was a definite edge in Shades' voice, "I done told you, Marvin here knows what he's doing. If The Lord goes back on his word, it would be real easy to off him."

"Off The Lord?" said Sweets. "Real smart. How long do you think it would take the cops to pin it on us?"

Marvin allowed his attention to drift in and out of the conversation. Like Sweet Sam, he too wondered if he had dreamt the deal he struck with The Lord. Was it too easy? He wondered. He knew everything hinged on him getting connected to the hookers—the white ones who worked Patterson Park. Most of 'em were ridin' the Horse, and if they weren't they knew plenty of chicks who did.

Someone dropped a tray and the clattering music of broken dishes brought Marvin's attention back to the conversation.

"Sweets," Marvin said, "don't worry. As a matter of fact, I don't want anybody worryin'. The Lord gave me this territory. He didn't have to. You shoulda seen the way he talked to me, man . . . ! Ain't no white man talked to me that way before. Yeah, it was bullshit, but he didn't have to do it. There was no reason to lie to me." Little Marvin looked from one of his lieutenants to the other. "Don't you think I know what I'm doing? Anybody question my decision don't have to hang with me."

Sweets and Shades jumped over each other to respond.

"No way, my man, I'm with you," said Sam.

"Ditt Toe, Boss."

Marvin nodded, dropped a few bucks on the table and moved towards the door. "Screw the food, man, let's get things scoped out."

Marvin's Coupe de Ville had every luxury, and when he got behind the wheel he was king. Shades sat shotgun and Sam spread out in the back seat.

They cruised towards Patterson Park around Eastern Avenue and all the streets that crisscrossed the neighborhood. They checked out the bars and schools to get a better grasp of the area. It was not their usual turf. In fact, if Marvin was in an admitting frame of mind, he might cop to it; he'd never been down the East Side during the day.

Too conspicuous. A Negro on Eastern Avenue stuck out like the hood ornament on an old LaSalle.

White people were not an uncommon sight, but Marvin marveled at how white everything looked there. Even the steps of each house glistened in pristine whiteness. There was no way to blend in.

"Ooh wee, it sho' be white around here," Shades said in mock slavery drawl. "I sho' hope the masser will be pleased to find us be helping their chillens."

Sweets tried to hold back a laugh from the back seat. As they drove around the neighborhood, little girls with their jump ropes stopped to stare, their mouths hanging open. It was obvious to Marvin that these children had never seen Negro men before. Some mothers actually scooped up their kids and ducked in their houses. Men just stopped in their tracks to glare at them and their outrageous land yacht of a car.

Little Marvin was no stranger to prejudice, but this display even impressed him.

"Marvin, I don't know about this," Sweet Sam said.

"If looks could kill, huh, Boss . . . ?" said Shades.

"Sam, it ain't like being on the Avenue. These people ain't got no soul, but we is gonna bring it to them. I got Sugar Bear working on getting us friendly-like with some of the chickens by the park."

"White meat?" asked Shades.

45

"Whaddya think?" Little Marvin smiled as he cut the wheel with one hand, glided past the fire station where three fat, white guys sat back in their chairs and jeered at them.

Marvin shook his head. This was so weird, man. Baltimore was a big, diverse city, but everyone stayed within their limits. Even if East Baltimore hadn't been a blue-collar neighborhood, it would still have been difficult for Marvin and his louies to blend in because of the glad rags they wore. Working-class *white* people didn't wear sharkskin suits and cuff links and tie tacks, so they definitely couldn't dig three spades in a Cadillac lookin' like a million.

Little Marvin figured it was time to add a little color and spice to the scene.

"What say we park the car and take a little walk around the neighborhood?"

"Marvin, I don't mean no disrespect," said Sweet Sam, "but in the words of my mama: Niggah, you crazy!"

"Uh, yeah, boss," said Shades. "We done cruised every street and there ain't nothing left to do, is there? We done did all that's getting done today." He hunched down in his seat, adjusted his sunglasses, then folded his arms across his chest.

Funny thing about Shades, it didn't matter what time of the day or night it was, he always wore his sunglasses. Some nights, Marvin wondered how that "blood" could see his own ass.

"What's the matter, boys?" Marvin smiled broadly, as he pulled to the curb near a corner bar called "Hap's Place."

"Let's go, Little Marvin," said Sweets. "I got me a few things to take care of, some collections, you know . . . "

Sweet Sam tried to look as bored of this scene as Shades was wary. That's why Marvin chose these two guys. One cautious and one cocky. Neither was afraid to speak his mind but both knew not to question a final decision. Marvin wondered if they knew just how much they helped him just by kicking in with their observations . . .

Better they never know.

"Look out the window and tell me what you see," he told them.

Shades shifted in his seat. "I see a lot of nasty-looking white people."

"Shades," Marvin was getting pissed off now. "Shades, that's your problem. You gots to see it as the Promised Land. The Lord *promised* it to us, and we gonna *land* ourselves a whup-ass mountain a cash!"

Little Marvin stepped out of the car and stood there in his best don't-even-*think*-about-fuckin'-with-me stance. Shades and Sweet Sam stood behind him . . . stone-faced and very straight. As Marvin started to walk, Sweet Sam and Shades fell into step. Their gait and demeanor spoke clearly to anyone who witnessed this scene.

They hadn't reached the end of the block when a cop on horseback circled the men twice and stopped in front of Little Marvin. Under the cop's gentle direction, the horse nuzzled very close to Marvin's shoulder. Man, fuck this, Marvin thought. I ain't movin'. Fuck this badge and swayback nag!

The horse nudged ever closer until Marvin could smell its sour-wet-hay breath. Just as Marvin looked up to confront its rider, the horse let loose with an explosive sneeze, sending a thick spray of mucous across Marvin's face with typhoon-like force. It caught him off guard and almost knocked him down.

"What the fuck!?" screamed Marvin and reflexively reached for his piece, stopped himself, and yanked his ivory, silk handkerchief from his suit pocket.

Sweets and Shades immediately pulled out their own finery to help Marvin clean up.

"Boy," said the cop, who had obviously seen the inside of a donut shop one too many times, "whatcha doing here? Whatcha want?"

Marvin wouldn't answer.

"I'm talking to you, boy." The cop shoved his nightstick into Little Marvin's shoulder.

"Cat got your tongue?" As he spoke, he kept poking Little Marvin and moving his horse closer and closer to the men.

Marvin didn't move.

"You're not going to talk? Boy, I suggest you answer me, or you could get into some real trouble. Now, you ain't broke

47

no laws yet, and I wanna make sure none get broken. So turn around, get back in your car. . . "

"I think you're gonna have to do better than that," said Marvin.

The cop smiled. "Oh, we can do a lot better than that, can't we, guys?"

Following the smiling gaze of the cop, Marvin turned to look back over his shoulder. He felt like a groom down to Pimlico. Suddenly there were horses and riders all around them, and Marvin never realized how damn big they were, or how hard a nightstick could feel when it caught you between the shoulders.

FOUR

The Article

Maybe we don't want to admit it, but somewhere deep down inside, most men know, as sure as the sun rises in the East, and tax day comes on April 15th, we simply can't ignore the magic and mystique of a beautiful woman about to disrobe. It goes beyond the power of the male psyche. It's one of those things we just accept. With pleasure.

Consequently, it doesn't take a Rhodes Scholar to deduce that the art of striptease was born out of pure primal instinct. It's been going on for centuries, all over the world. But burlesque American style is what we're after here. And believe it or not, in the first half of this century it didn't get any hotter than what you could see on Baltimore's "Block." That's right, Baltimore.

Mention Baltimore to a national or international traveler and inevitably The Block would be singled out along with steamed crabs, white marble steps, the Orioles, and the Colts. For almost three-quarters of a century The Block has been a part of Baltimore—from Prohibition to permissiveness—and it has become an integral part of the city because of its bars and its *women.*

From vaudeville to burlesque, from striptease to go-go dancing, from nickelodeons to massage parlors, this area on East Baltimore Street — now incongruously located between a refurbished City Hall and a gleaming police headquarters — has lived for over 75 years with little or no pretense. The Block has always enjoyed a national reputation for pleasure-seekers, like The Tenderloin in San Francisco, The Strip in Las Vegas, The Combat Zone in Boston, 42nd Street in New York, Bourbon Street in New Orleans . . .

"Mix 2 parts bourbon with 1 part woman, add the grinding thump of a bass drum, and dust with heavy cigarette smoke. That's the basic recipe for The Block."

This colorful description was recently applied to life on The Block by one old gentleman who used to frequent the businesses there. And "woman" is really the operative word. With tantalizing names like Irma the Body, Ineeda Man, and Cupcakes Cassidy, The Block was alive with sexy, class acts in its heyday. People traveled from far and wide to catch the shows.

At the turn of the 20th century, Baltimore emerged on the scene, bold and brassy; a hubbub of cultural and economic activity. The harbor was world renowned, bringing the city tremendous advantages for financial gain. But suddenly, in 1904, a devastating fire raged through the downtown district, leaving behind 140 acres of smoldering ash. The city was forced to rebuild, and in the process, three short blocks on East Baltimore Street rose up from the ash, a virtual entertainment Mecca. They called it The Block.

It was the place to go on a Saturday night, dressed to the nines, with your lady on your arm. Vaudeville acts, burlesque, restaurants and movie houses all came together to decorate those three short blocks, and people came from all over the city for a look. You could catch dinner and a show for next to nothing. Lubin's Theatre was the first film showcase in Baltimore. Other movie houses rapidly followed suit, and soon The Block was home to among others, The Grand, The Embassy, and the most famous, the fabulous Gayety Theatre.

In 1910, The Gayety was acquired by John "Hon" Nickel, who later parlayed his purchase into one of the best burlesque houses in the United States. Its buff-colored exterior provocatively sported a male and female holding the theatre name and promised enticing live acts inside.

Movie theatres on The Block in the twenties began to be called by a different, though not endearing, name — they were known as "scratch houses" since there were a number of fleas and other tiny creatures (best viewed under a microscope) that left people scratching as they walked out of the movies at The Grand, The Embassy, The Rivoli, etc.

A stroller on The Block would view people who pushed two-wheel carts that sold roasted peanuts at each end of the street, lunch rooms like the ones that operated on Coney Island, and even the familiar organ grinder with the polite monkey who would tip his hat for a coin or two. And overtop of the middle of the 400 block of Baltimore Street resided Dr. Louis Hamrick who was a specialist in the diagnosis and treatment of "social diseases."

Five

Katherine Louise

Katherine Louise nervously toyed with the sequin tassels dangling from the short skirt of her costume and started to count back slowly from twenty. Her nerves were knotted up inside her stomach and her palms felt clammy. She wiped them along her stockinged thighs and continued counting. The music was audible through the closed door of the dressing room and she realized her cue was fast approaching. A quick glance in the lighted mirror revealed a strikingly painted face surrounded by softly curled hair, pinned dramatically up in a twist. Two stray curls had found their way out of the coiffure and brushed lightly against her cheekbones. Katherine pressed her lips together and took a deep breath, trying hard to muster up the confidence and maturity she'd seen in some of the other acts. She wanted to make a strong impression. Her goal was to leave the audience breathless. The question was how to go about it since she was obviously an amateur. She thought about the advice Marlena had given her. Marlena Divine was every inch the professional entertainer, with eight years in the business, a fan club, and money to burn. She told

Katherine that above all else, maintain eye contact. She said it was like possessing the key to a man's soul. Translation: his wallet.

There was a knock at the door and Dave Witt, the stage hand, stuck his head in and whistled, "Sweetheart, you're on."

Katherine pulled herself up and stood before the mirror. The stiletto heels put her at a statuesque five-feet-nine-inches. Her honey hair sparkled with the gold glitter highlights she'd sprayed in, and her lips appeared full and sensuous beneath their bright red blanket of lipstick topped with petroleum jelly. She would smile seductively. She would peel with deliberate, taunting precision. She would move with grace and somehow manage to create the illusion of stripping bare, when in reality she would still be partially clothed.

The mechanics of it all overwhelmed her. She had practiced at home in front of the mirror in her one-room apartment. Twisting and gyrating, turning and seducing. She felt utterly ridiculous. But not so ridiculous that she wasn't willing to give it her best shot and take home a hundred or so to boot. She was out of money, and the electric bill was overdue.

"Hey, Katherine honey, let's go!" Dave bellowed from the hallway.

She turned and followed him past the light control panel to the stage entrance. The lights dimmed. "Ladies and gentlemen," the announcer began. "Allow me to introduce to you a sweet young lady who's traveled all the way from the hills of West Virginia to entertain you tonight. This young lady promises to dazzle you with charm and beauty. Let's hear a big round of applause for Miss Katherine Louise."

The sound of a smoldering saxophone opened up from the speakers above. Katherine felt a jolt of adrenalin surge through her and took a tentative step forward onto the stage.

The smoky barroom of the Desert Club lay before her, its small cocktail tables clustered around the stage, each filled with eager-eyed men, young and old. An occasional woman dotted the crowd, but most of them looked as if they worked the place. Katherine fastened her gaze on one particular gentleman at the table to her right. He was about thirty and incredibly handsome. His jet-black hair was slicked back fashionably with Brylcreem. He wore a swanky, pinstriped suit with a crisp white shirt, and smoked his slender cigarette with the elegance of a movie star. His eyes held Katherine's for a split second, then moved downward. A flash of attraction had sparked between them and she suddenly felt empowered.

The saxophone gave way to a thumping drum and her stilettoed foot took a more solid step as she threw back her head and smiled slowly. The frothy chiffon of her shoulder wrap brushed up goose bumps on her arms, and she shivered as the handsome man with the cigarette allowed his eyes to travel over her hips and legs. It was at that moment that Katherine decided she had what it took to be good, and she proceeded to seduce each and every man bold enough to meet her stare. She toyed with them like she toyed with her tassels and fringe, and it was irresistible. When the time came to slip off the chiffon shoulder wrap, she did so as if she were slipping off a layer of skin. She turned her back to the audience and let the garment fall like a cloud to the stage floor, and while the music drummed on, she stood there like a statue, milk-white shoulders bare and broad, slender hips blanketed by a short, black skirt that fluttered in the breeze created by the fans above. Whistles erupted from the crowd, and slowly Katherine turned to look over her shoulder at a fat, sweaty man in the front row. She gave him the kind of smile she knew a woman would give her lover after a particularly good romp. The kind of lusty smile her sister, Linette, used to use. The effect was phenomenal. The sweaty, fat man nearly toppled his drink, and the sick smile he wore faded quickly from his face. He was mesmerized. Katherine instinctively knew it was time to move in for the main thrill. Marlena Divine also said timing was everything. Wait until you have them drooling, then sock it to them.

Katherine reached behind and unclasped the eyehooks on her bra. She felt the pleasant sensation of her breasts expanding as they broke free of their captivity. Her nipples hardened instantly, and she wondered absurdly for a split second whether it was caused by the draft from the fan above or by the fifty pairs of eyes on her back. Then she turned to face her audience. She knew what kind of power her body could have over a man. She had heard it over and over again in the early hours of the morning back on the mountain.

"Mabel, you got a body to kill for," Papa always said.

But the response here was somehow different. The audience appeared somewhat stunned by her performance. Their silence confused and delighted her at the same time. She strolled to the edge of the stage and swayed her hips back and forth. In the mirrors dead ahead behind the bar, she caught sight of herself and was surprised by her image. The mirror revealed a woman who was every inch a woman, with full, supple breasts swaying with the music, hands fluttering over slender thighs. Whatever happened to sweet Mabel McCallister? she wondered with an inward laugh. The music came to an end and there was silence. The announcer piped up as Katherine turned and strolled quietly off the stage, leaving a lot of open mouths and her chiffon wrap in her wake.

"That, ladies and gentlemen, was not just any little girl from the hills! Let's hear it for the sizzling Katherine Louise." There was a thundering round of applause, the strains of which trailed down the hallway under the door and into the needy, desperate ears of the best thing to hit Baltimore's Block in years. Katherine heard it loud and clear as she sat at her dressing table and watched a fat tear roll down her face.

The night Katherine Louise had arrived in Baltimore was the night she left Mabel McCallister behind. The air had been warm and humid, and her suitcase with the fake leather handle weighed heavy in her sweaty hand. She stood on the platform watching the train pull away and felt a sense of relief. There was finally enough distance between her past and her future. Gone were the hazy West Virginia mountain ranges she'd grown up with. Gone was the dread of her father's sickening presence. Gone was her mother's weary voice of doom. And gone was the burden of responsibility for young kids that all but consumed her. She'd packed her bag in the middle of the night and slipped out before the sun was up. A bus had carried her to Wheeling and the train to Washington D.C. It was there in Union Station that she'd picked her new name, right off the cover of a fashion magazine featuring Katherine Hepburn, one of her favorite movie stars. Then she had asked for the fastest route to Baltimore and before she knew it, she was there, standing on the train platform, honey-blond hair pinned primly up under her hat, yellow cotton dress wrinkled beyond repair from the many hours of travel, and the name that was going to make things happen for her emblazoned in her mind. Katherine Louise.

She set herself up in a cheap room and bought a copy of the local paper in search of the perfect secretarial position. She spent a lot of time preparing for her interview, laying her clothes out on the chair the night before, rehearsing her responses. But still, interview after interview had ended in rejection. She had no experience. She was too young. She had just missed her chance, the position was already filled. There were a million excuses. There must have been at least fifteen interviews that all led down the same path to utter disappointment. Katherine started to really worry. After a week and a half, her money was just about gone, and her landlady was a cold-hearted witch. Desperate, Katherine took the advice of a dimwitted waitress near Baltimore's Block, and went to see about getting a job as a coat check girl at the Desert Club. The manager had taken one look at her and offered her a dancing job. Delighted, Katherine accepted before really thinking things through.

She still had hopes of becoming an office worker, perhaps in a legal firm or some sort of business. After all those many days she'd spent sitting on the steps back in West Virginia, dreaming of learning to type and take shorthand and draft letters, dancing had never even entered her conscious mind. Nobody got anywhere in life by dancing. Except maybe Fred Astaire. She had desperately searched her mind for confirmation that what she was doing was right. But in reality she knew that right now, what she was doing was simply necessity. She would still become a secretary. If she saved her money each week, she would be able to afford secretarial school. There she could really hone her skills and in no time at all, probably land a fantastic job. In the interim, she would dance.

There was a knock at the door of the dressing room and Katherine quickly reached for a tissue and wiped her tears away. Marlena bustled in and dropped her coat on the hook on the wall.

"Honey, that was one hell of a performance. What am I doing giving you advice? You damn near stole the show out from under me."

Wide-eyed, Katherine looked at her in disbelief. "What are you talking about, Marlena?"

"Honey, didn't you hear that applause? It was like rolls of thunder out there. Those people loved you. You were a sensation. In fact, Artie is already talking about booking you as a main act. It's Wednesday night. Nobody dances like that on Wednesday night. The good girls always get booked in prime time."

"I don't know if this is right for me."

"Hon, don't analyze the obvious. You got a certain magic up on that stage. You don't see it too often. Trust me. First of all, you're young. I know you ain't twenty-one, but I won't say anything. Men like young bodies. Plus, you got the face of an angel but the moves of the big, red guy down under. You know what I'm saying?" She slipped out of her street clothes and stood before Katherine in nothing but her panties. Her breasts were enormous. "So here's what you do. You definitely need the hours, right? I know you're short on cash. So when Artie comes around telling you what you're gonna do, you tell him what you want. Waitress hours during the week like I got. Prime time dancing Friday and Saturday nights, and Sundays off. Got it?" She hooked up a pair of fishnet stockings and stepped into her waitress uniform.

"Yeah, I've got it." Katherine still couldn't believe she had elevated herself to Marlena Divine's status with one simple dance and striptease. Perhaps Marlena was just offering encouragement so Katherine wouldn't quit. After all, one more waitress meant less work for Marlena. But the woman did seem sincere.

"You better get yourself into your uniform and take advantage of all those appreciative folks out there. See you."

Marlena breezed out, and Katherine pulled herself together. She was a hit? This was unbelievable. Maybe she really could muster up a few nice tips if she smiled and thanked the customers for coming to the show. She slid into the short cocktail waitress uniform and tugged on some sheer black stockings. Another dab of lipstick and she was out the door.

The stage was dark and music filtered through the sound system, settling above the quiet hum of conversation. Katherine cast a quick glance towards the front table where the handsome man had been seated, but he was gone. She wouldn't have minded getting to know him a little better. At the bar, she picked up a writing pad and pen and started to make the rounds. The first table she came to was alive with the laughter of two older men drinking beer. She stood quietly beside them, waiting for a break in their hysterics.

"Can I get you gentlemen something from the bar?"

Their eyes turned to her and instant recognition popped onto their faces. "Oh, it's the new girl, Frank!" one exclaimed. "Sweetheart, you were wonderful up there. Best I've seen."

"Well, thank you, sir."

"No, thank you," the other one piped up. He pressed a couple of dollars into her palm. His buddy followed suit. "We always enjoy a good show."

"Thank you again. Can I bring you another round of beer?"

"Sure, sweetheart. And some peanuts, too."

Katherine continued to work each table, and found the tips to be quite generous, just as Marlena had predicted. Everyone seemed to be singing the praises of Katherine Louise. It was, without question, an indescribable feeling. Her moral reservations aside, Katherine felt a certain sense of pride in her accomplishment up on stage. And she was moderately surprised at the eagerness inside her as she anticipated her next appearance. She was scheduled for tomorrow night.

Katherine Louise pulled on her coat and slung her bag of costumes over her shoulder. She had some alterations to make and a few accessories to buy, but basically, she was on the road to making it. Tonight she was heading home with thirty-five dollars in tips stuffed in her purse, and she felt good.

As she stepped into the blinking brilliance of East Baltimore Street, the neon signs intrigued her. The Gayety was just down the street, and the marquee said a comedian named Barry Thomas was appearing this week. And Pantera and Terri the Dutch Doll were the featured striptease acts that received marquee status. Ten years earlier it had been Red Skelton, Gypsy Rose Lee and Valerie Parks. Katherine wondered if she would be around long enough to see her own name up in lights. The thought kind of pleased her, but then she hastily reminded herself of secretarial school and the matter at hand. She wondered if secretaries made thirty-five dollars in one day. She made a mental note to ask Marlena next time she saw her.

She headed down the street, eyeing the barkers at the door of each club sideways. The barkers were trying their best to coax passers-by into their respective clubs, but each was basically promising the same tantalizing dancers and the same great drink prices. Even the barker at the Desert Club was not unique. There was a still-open restaurant across the street and Katherine realized she hadn't eaten since breakfast. She darted between the traffic and slipped into Molly's Kitchen. She ordered a ham and egg sandwich, a dill pickle and a carton of milk to go. The woman behind the counter looked at her curiously as she made change.

"You aren't from around here, are you?"

Katherine shook her head.

"Thought so. You got that new-in-town look on your face. How do you like The Block?"

"I think it's the ticket to a better life," Katherine said slowly. "I just got a job up at the Desert Club."

"Congratulations, hon. You got the looks, that's for sure." She handed Katherine her bag and smiled. "See you around."

"Yeah, thanks." Katherine smiled and turned to head home.

Six

Harry Tennyson

Harry Tennyson had learned to be a man of refinement. His life was orderly, efficient, and complete. As he stood in his library among books he would never read, martini glass in hand (he never really *liked* martinis, but Society had deemed it the gentleman's drink), he realized he had everything a man of Station would want. His wife Dolores, the daughter of a city councilman, had been brought up in strictest Catholic tradition and catered to his every whim. She was there at his side on every occasion to present the perfect Ozzie and Harriet facade. His children, well-mannered and perfectly groomed, attended very expensive private schools. He had an upstairs maid, a downstairs maid, cook, and chauffeur. Yeah . . . *everything,* including beautiful showgirls who were always very eager to please.

His concentration was broken when Eugenia announced dinner. Harry checked his watch—six o'clock. Right on schedule.

The family dressed for dinner.

As he walked towards the dining room, his daughter

cascaded down the staircase, arms extended towards her daddy for a kiss. At fifteen, she already knew how to get anything she wanted from him. As a matter of fact, she was the only woman in Harry's life who could get him to jump through hoops.

"Daddy, you look absolutely divine!" Shirley squealed with delight.

He kissed her on the forehead, then pulled her away from him.

"Princess," his voice gentle and tender, "you look so beautiful and grown-up. Is that a new dress?"

"Daddy, you *noticed!*" Shirley beamed as she twirled around the hallway showing off her new dress. "Mother and I went to Hutzler's Palace yesterday, and when we saw it, we just simply *could not* resist! Mother said it looked so exquisite on me, and the *color*, Daddy look how it . . . "

"Shirley, I thought I told you not to wear that dress until I had a chance to tell Daddy we bought it." Dolores emerged from the darkness. She was a thin woman with a big, jet-black bouffant hairdo that made her look like a beekeeper's wet dream. Her seventeen-year-old son, John, stood silently by her side at the entrance to the dining room.

"Oh, Mother, I *told* you there was nothing to worry about. Daddy absolutely *loves* it, don't you, Daddy?"

The ringing of the telephone interrupted his answer.

"Eugenia!" he called out to the maid. "Get that! And remember, the family is not to be disturbed during dinner."

"Yes, sir."

Eugenia had been with the family for fifteen years and knew the routine, but she knew it gratified Harry to play "Lord and Master," and Harry knew she let him act the way he wanted. As he watched her walk away from him, he remembered the first day he hired her. She was a beautiful black woman. Tight ass, firm tits, big round mouth. And more than willing to pull a little overtime with him.

The nights they spent together were ones he would never forget. He would enter her room quietly late at night, slide into her bed, and slowly undress her. While his hands explored every inch of her body, she never said a word. *He* never said a word. And that somehow made it even more sexy. Eugenia would simply turn around, spread her legs, and thrust her hips to receive him in a sort of musical rhythm. And the best part was that neither one of them ever discussed their liaisons . . . *ever.*

"Harry, please join us, dear." The sound of Dolores' voice brought that memory to a screeching halt.

It annoyed Harry that he had no time for himself. Each time he would be deep in thought, some asshole would interrupt him. But if that was the price he had to pay for being Harry The Lord Tennyson, well then, it was worth it.

As he was about to take his seat at the head of the table, Eugenia walked in.

"Excuse me, sir. I *know* you said you was not to be disturbed . . . " Her expression communicated a dread sense of urgency that was not lost on Harry.

"Then don't do it!" interjected his wife, Dolores, who held Harry in her steely glare as she spoke. "Mr. Tennyson has given you an order and I would appreciate it if you, for once, would do as you've been told!"

"Madam, I understand, but—"

"Don't you but me, Eugenia. One more word out of you, and you are fired! Serve the dinner and take a message." Dolores flushed. Her lips almost completely disappeared when she was angry. Harry tried not to look at her when she was happy, much less when she was mad. Although she was the "perfect" wife, he hated her.

"Dolores, calm down." Harry's manner was terse and annoyed. He hated scenes—especially one caused by his wife in front of his staff and children. "I'll take the call in the study. Thank you, Eugenia."

"Harry . . . " His wife looked like she'd been slapped in the face.

"Please start dinner without me," he said.

"Hurry back, Daddy." Shirley's concerned plea was the last thing he heard as he walked out.

To get to the study, Harry had to walk down a long hall

flanked by tapestries. The interior of his home looked more like a castle than a house in Greenspring Valley. Although Harry thought his decor was tastefully done, the fixtures and accoutrements screamed *new money*.

He took a seat behind his oak desk, picked up the receiver and bellowed: "Talk to me, and it better be good! I'm eatin'!"

"Sorry to disturb your dinner hour, boss." It was Syd. "But we got some complications down here."

"Whatever it is, *handle* it, Syd. That's what I pay you for."

"Boss, Little Marvin, he's in jail."

"So what's that to me?"

"He's asking for *you*, boss. He said you okayed it."

"Okayed *what?!!?*"

"Him and his coons got picked up today at Patterson Park, and he's raising a stink down the precinct saying you said it was cool for him to be there. . ."

"*What . . . ???*" Harry couldn't believe his ears.

"Little Marvin caused such a stink that the chief called Delvecchio."

"He called my father-in-law!?" Harry could imagine the old man's shock at hearing that Harry had thrown in with the niggers.

"Well, I guess he figured that was the best way to track you down . . ." said Syd.

"That little, no-good, fucking sonofabitch!" Harry yelled into the phone. "Listen, you dumb fuck! Can't you handle anything without me? Ain't you got no fucking brains?" When Harry got this steamed, the East Baltimore in him always slipped out. That was one of the chinks in his armor no amount of money had been able to hammer out of him.

"Syd, when you hang up the phone, you get your fat ass to Benny the Book, and the two of you go down to wherever the fuck they're holding that little black runt. Have Benny pay the bail, and you get Marvin to my Desert Club office, you hear me?"

"Yeah, I got it, boss . . ."

Harry suddenly composed himself, and in a hushed tone said, "I expect you guys to be there waiting for me. I'm leaving now."

64

He hung up the phone and stormed out of the house.

Johnson was outside polishing the right fender of the big, black Chrysler. When he saw Harry, he straightened up, awaiting his orders, and opened the car door to allow Harry access to the big back seat.

"Take me to the office!" Harry commanded. He was halfway down the driveway before he thought about everybody eating without him. Yeah, like any of them really cared . . .

The trip to the Desert Club would take exactly 45 minutes, and Harry had to calm down. Men under pressure took unnecessary risks. He lit a cigarette, inhaled deeply, and started to relax himself. With each drag of his Lucky Strike he felt more at ease.

"What was that little motherfucker *thinking*?" he muttered.

"Sorry, Mr. Tennyson, I didn't hear the question," Johnson the driver said.

"Nothing, Johnson, just thinking out loud."

"Yes, sir, Mr. Tennyson."

"On second thought, Johnson," Harry said, "what do you know about a guy called Little Marvin?"

"Well, sir, he's got a rep for being one tough little dude."

"Yeah, yeah, you live in his neighborhood, right?"

"Sir?" Johnson was puzzled by this question. He had lived in the Tennyson house for over ten years.

"Have you ever seen him?"

"Sure, I've seen him. Once in awhile me and some of my friends sees him in the clubs down on the Avenue. He's a little guy what talks big and walks around with two of the biggest, darkest men I ever seen."

"I know all that, Johnson. I wanted to know if you *knew* him, you know, personally. Is he your friend? You're all friends, aren't you?"

"Mr. Tennyson, jcs cause we's Negroes don't mean we all knows each other. I jes does my job, and the one day a week I got off, I spends with my family is all."

"Thank you, Johnson." You poor fuck, thought Harry.

He ended the conversation and watched the houses roll past his window as his big car glided down Park Heights

Avenue. It was called the longest street in the world—stretching all the way from Israel to Africa—because it originated in the heart of the city's wealthy Jewish district and terminated at the frontiers of the Black neighborhoods. He spent the rest of the ride smoking and watching the architecture change . . .

Johnson turned the corner of Baltimore Street, stopped in front of the Desert Club, then walked around to open the car door.

At the entrance to the club stood Joey. A little, skinny, good-for-nothing wop who waited for him like a doorman at the Emerson, thought Harry. All he needed was a jacket like Napoleon to complete the picture. A cousin of Dolores', Harry had given him the job of a barker just to keep her quiet.

"Hey, Harry! How you doing?" Joey asked.

"Just open the door, Joey," Harry said in disgust.

Harry walked through the club amidst a lot of "Hi, Harrys" from the girls in pasties, and then he went up the stairs to his office.

Syd greeted him.

"Hey, boss, we did just as you asked. He's in there waiting. Ain't saying a word. He says he's waiting for you."

"Who's in there with him?"

"Jerry, Benny, Jack, and Bruce."

Before Harry reached the door, Syd already had it open.

Little Marvin sat with his back towards the door. Harry walked in behind him and slapped him on the head.

"Hey man, what you be . . ."

Harry cut him off.

"Listen, you little cocksucker!" Harry leaned in so close to Little Marvin he could smell him. He grabbed Marvin by the lapels of his suit jacket and said, "What the fuck do you think you're doing?"

Little Marvin kicked back his chair and shook himself loose from The Lord's grasp. He pointed his jeweled index finger at Harry's chest and whispered, "You listen to me, Mr. Lord."

Jerry stood up and pointed his piece at Little Marvin.

"Get your goons to sit down." He kept tapping his finger into The Lord's chest. "Nobody fucks with me, man."

Harry raised his arm and the quartet hesitantly relaxed their stance.

"Sit down, Marvin."

Harry walked around the side of his desk and sat down. He rested his forehead on the palms of his hands and didn't say a word for what seemed an endless amount of time. Nobody spoke.

When Harry finally looked up, Marvin was the first to speak.

"Man, you dicked me," he said in amazement. "I trusted a white man and what did I get? I got pushed around by the cracker patrol. What the fuck?" Little Marvin sat there with his mouth hanging open in utter amazement.

"You, sir," Harry said, "are an asshole. Not even two days after I gave you that territory you got yourself in trouble. You are probably asking yourself, 'What the fuck?' Precisely, my sentiments: *What the fuck.* This was a test Marvin. I wanted you to prove yourself. You failed."

"Again with that bullshit talk? I ain't biting now."

Harry leaned closer to Marvin keeping the distance of the desk between them.

"Marvin, you showed no brains at all going down the park in the middle of the day. There's only so much I can do to protect you in that neighborhood. My promise to you is that no other parties will be involved in dealing. That area, it's completely yours. But I won't be there to save your little black ass from going to jail. If you're such a smart little man, Marvin, you'd better start proving it to me."

"Yeah . . . ? Or *what?*"

Harry stepped on the question forcefully. "Or else I stop this bullshit!"

"Like how?!"

Marvin Harper was a tough little nut. Harry would never admit it to anybody, but the drug dealer plainly scared him. Harry had thrown his own ass into this crack and there was no way out other than the supreme bluff, the old "scam-skie."

"Like, very simple," said Harry in a voice that was a full register lower than his normal voice. "I take back my territory, give you the lousy half-mil', and get *you* the fuck outta my life."

The reaction was instantaneous. Jerry cleared his throat, and big Syd pushed back in his chair like he might pass out. Marvin's eyes widened and his jaw fell slack. "You gonna *what?*" he said.

In that instant, Harry knew he was still in the game. The advantage had swung to him, and he went after it like a junk yard dog on an intruder's leg. "One more fuck-up like this one and it's over. You take your money and don't ever bug me again."

"Man, I was only—"

"I don't care *what* you were doing!" Harry's voice boomed so loud he even scared himself. He was really getting into the part he was playing. It was *good* to be The Lord. He stood up, moved quickly to Marvin's chair, and towered over him. "You don't get it, do you, Harper?"

"Huh?" Marvin for a moment looked like a young kid.

"They call it the 'underworld'," said Harry. "That means you are down below the horizon, below the line of fire. It means keeping a low profile. It means not parading up and down Eastern Avenue like it was Pennsylvania or Fremont! If you want to be part of the *under*world, Marvin, you've got to play by the rules."

Marvin didn't say a word for a couple of minutes. The silence started gnawing everybody like rats at your pant-legs. "Yeah, I get the picture," Marvin said finally. "So how you want this one played out? What do I do?"

Harry kept the steely expression in place, but inside he was smiling like a kid locked in a candy store overnight. "You stay outta the East Side, you hear me? I'll set you up with the management of the Surf Club—every hophead musician that plays this town hangs at the Surf, and it's in the heart of East Baltimore on Monument Street. From there, I'll pipeline you to all the junked-up hookers from The Block, and I'll plug you in with Chief Cloudwalker."

"Chief *who?*"

"He's the head of the Lumbee Indian bunch that lives down on Wolfe Street near Johns Hopkins. That's a good neigborhood for you to start in because it's half white, half black. The chief loves his smack and so do most of his people. They'll work for you if I tell them to. They can pass for white in East Baltimore, and they'll get your shit out on the streets."

"Man, I don't need no Indians to—"

"You need what I tell you you need," said Harry. "Or you can take the half-mil' and fly like a good little crow."

Marvin leaned forward, but let the insult pass. It was working. Harry knew he had him where he wanted him.

"All right, Mr. Tennyson," said the drug dealer. "Let's do it your way."

After they'd escorted Marvin Harper out the back door (Harry didn't want any of the customers at the show-bar to think he'd started letting Negroes in), he walked downstairs to go home. The Chuckie Whitestone Trio lazied their way through their first set of the evening and Harry was plain tired, as well as hungry. He was distracted, too, still thinking about what a stupid grandstand act he'd pulled off. If Little Marvin had wanted his money, Harry would have had to shoot him, and Harry never wanted to shoot anybody. But that's the way it would have to happen because if Harry didn't button Marvin, he would be a dead man himself.

That final notion kept replaying across the front of his mind like the moving sign they had in Times Square. He was so distracted he almost didn't notice the new girl on the front bar.

Almost.

Almost is not *didn't.* Harry smiled as he turned to assay the new girl's act. It wasn't much of an act, really. She looked totally natural up there. Smooth skin, pretty hair, a gorgeous face, and a pair of jugs like the taillights on a new Caddy. She had it all.

He handed off his coat to Luther, the Negro busboy, and made his way to the bar. "Evening, Mr. Tennyson," said Louis, the bartender.

"Gimme a scotch straight up, Louis."

"Yes, sir, Mr. Tennyson."

Harry surveyed his kingdom. The club was packed for a

Wednesday. This was good. Cash flow had to be up from last week. He needed to take in some extra dough. The fucking liquor supplier was raising his rates. He scanned the room, checking for the regulars, new guys, the cops. Everything looked good. He spotted Judge William "Wild Bill" Long from the Municipal Court over at table two, talking it up with Marlena. The guy's hands were all over her, but Marlena, the slut, wasn't complaining.

"Where's Artie?" Harry barked over the bar.

"I think he's in the back, doin' the books," Louis said.

Harry spotted a pretty blonde setting beers at table six and signaled to Louis again. "Who's the new chick on stage?"

"Her name's Katherine Louise."

"Never seen her before." Fucking Artie wasn't supposed to go hiring new talent without running it past him first. Harry wanted his thumb print on every piece of ass on stage. If he liked her, it was a go. Artie was just supposed to weed out the trash, that's all. The asshole needed to be reminded whose name was on the bottom of his paycheck every week. But Harry had to admit the new girl was sweet to look at. She had a certain air of innocence about her which Harry really liked. But, he was also willing to bet she'd been around the block a time or two. Something in the way she moved her ass. Like it had been handled. What he especially liked was her mouth. It was big and full. Lips like that could probably work magic.

He made his way to the side door and pushed it open. Down the short hallway he could see the light on under the manager's office door. He shoved it open.

"Artie, what's the deal with the new girl? You know I like to check 'em out first."

"Yeah, yeah, Harry, I know. But Angie cancelled on me for tonight and this girl Katherine was in here yesterday looking for a job. The timing was right. I thought she had the look, you know?"

He eyed Harry sideways from his desk, waiting for approval. Harry decided not to let him off easy.

"Look, asshole. You do your job the way I tell you. If that means fucking calling me up in the middle of the night to say

'Harry, can you get down here first thing in the morning to check out a potential new dancer?', you do it. See, my name's on the line here. I want to know personally that each girl that strips on my stage is grade A material. I like classy chicks, no trash. But I decide who's classy. Got it?"

Artie nodded wearily and sighed. "I hear you, Harry, I hear you. But I must say, you can rest easy tonight. This girl Katherine is a major hit. She ain't never danced before, or so she says. And she gets up there and it's like she's fucking making love to the fat guy at table one. She had him coming in his pants. It was amazing. You could hear a pin drop when she finished. Then there was applause like I ain't heard in awhile, except maybe for Marlena. Harry, we got a winner here, trust me."

"Okay, okay, Artie. I believe you. When's she go on again?"

"Tomorrow, and then I'm gonna offer her weekends. So look for her Friday night. Oh, and Harry, get this. She's a farm girl from West Virginia! It's perfect!"

Harry nodded and ducked out of the office and headed back into the club. He spotted Katherine at the bar and made his way over to her. Up close she was quite stunning. Her hair was a very pretty, soft blond. Not the fake kind.

"Good evening, Katherine," he said.

She spun around and looked at him with the deepest blue eyes he'd ever seen. He felt a stirring somewhere in the pit of his stomach.

"Good evening, sir," she responded. "May I get you a drink?"

He smiled at her polite banter and shook his head.

"No. I'm Harry Tennyson, the owner. I just wanted to welcome you aboard. I understand tonight was your first show. I'm sorry to say I missed the entire performance, but I hear you are quite talented."

She blushed slightly and fumbled for her words.

"Oh, I'm pleased to meet you, Mr. Tennyson. And thank you for the job."

"From what I can see, I should be thanking you, Katherine. I look forward to catching your next show."

He turned and strolled away, signaling Luther to fetch his coat. The stirring in the pit of his stomach had not subsided, and he felt irritated now that he was heading home to Dolores. He made his way to the front door and out to his Chrysler parked at the curb.

SEVEN

SENATOR Edward Higgins

Edward Higgins was an ambitious man.

He had risen to the office of state senator because he was a powerful lawyer with money who made some very wise investments just after World War II. He made lots of friends in political office, and when he followed their path into the world of influence and corruption, Ed discovered a very important fact—he liked it.

He had his eye on one of Maryland's senatorial posts in Washington, and the grapevine said he had a good chance in the 1958 elections because one of the incumbents had been planning to retire.

Having grown up in one of the state's westernmost counties, Ed Higgins lived a sheltered childhood. His father had worked as a forest ranger until he retired to run a boat rental shop on Deep Creek Lake. Life was simple and very straightforward. It wasn't until young Edward went off to college at the University of Maryland in College Park, which is just a cab ride from Capitol Hill, that he realized he had a yen for a life in politics. By the time he'd graduated from the

University's law school located in Baltimore, Ed Higgins had thoroughly disassociated himself from his humble, woodsy-folksy beginnings in Western Maryland.

Also while attending law school, he discovered he possessed an insatiable desire for beautiful women. And one of the best places to see them was The Block, which at that time was just a nickel trolley ride across town on Baltimore Street. Ed liked the loud music and the slick patter of the barkers and the bartenders. He liked the bright lights and the glittering costumes of the strippers.

On the night he was made a full partner at the law firm where he worked, he was out celebrating with his friends, and they'd made their way to The Block, ultimately to the Desert Club. As they sat at the huge mahogany bar and watched gorgeous Pam Gail drop one piece of sequined finery after another, Ed struck up a conversation with the club's owner, Harry Tennyson.

He'd heard of Tennyson because he was rumored to be a kingpin in many of the city's biggest rackets. But nobody had ever been able to nail him for anything, so either the guy was slicker than Brylcreem or he was an Honest Abe type. And the longer Ed Higgins stayed in the legal and political arenas, the more fully he realized that the phrase "honest man" was one of those oxymorons they taught you about in English class. Right up there with "jumbo shrimp" and "military intelligence."

Regardless of Tennyson's true nature, Ed found that he liked the man because he was a no-bullshit guy. You always knew where you stood with the guy because he didn't pull any punches. After years of learning the art of subterfuge and legal legerdemain, Higgins appreciated Harry Tennyson's straight-from-the-shoulder approach to everything. If you wanted to have fun, Harry was the man. If you wanted to play a number, get jerked off or laid, bet the Lions against the Bears or the Red Sox over the Yankees, Harry was the man.

Ed and Harry hit it off very well that night and gradually became friends. Ed liked The Lord because he had connections to the underbelly of society. Harry liked Higgins because the young lawyer and soon-to-be state senator had connections with the decision-makers and power-brokers.

Everything cuts both ways, Tennyson always said, and Ed knew it was true.

By the mid-fifties, Harry and some of his rackets-buddies had come up with a grand scheme to run "pleasure boats" up and down the Potomac River within the confines of Charles County in Southern Maryland. That county had legalized slot machines and "charitable" casino gambling. Serving and buying liquor by the drink was also legal throughout the state, but across the river in Virginia and the highly popular resort town of Colonial Beach, *none* of the above pastimes was legal.

Tennyson's idea was brilliant and yet simple—build piers off the Virginia side of the Potomac that were long enough to reach the Maryland territorial divide, pull his pleasure boats up to the docks, and let the puritanicalized Virginians stream aboard where they could be treated to dance bands, slot machines, wide open bars, and even crap tables and blackjack.

The plan reached both the Maryland and the Virginia legislators with all the grace and aplomb of a burning stick in the eye. Everybody had an opinion and everybody had something to gain or lose by backing or renouncing the plan. Charles County liked it because they would gain revenue from slot machine licenses and a cut of the charitable funds raised by the "casino nights."

Naturally, Harry Tennyson courted the favor and approval of whatever legislators and movers and shakers he could find, and Ed Higgins was on the top of The Lord's list. This, especially after one lawmaker tried to push a bill that would only allow someone to board a boat from the Virginia side of the river if they could reach the conveyance by walking, but without the aid of a pier.

As silly as it sounded, the bill picked up support and Harry decided to do some research. Enlisting Ed Higgins, Harry and his right-hand man, Syd Daniloski, drove down to Colonial Beach, Virginia. It was early October.

"This is the biggest bunch of crap I've heard yet," said Harry as he and Ed departed his big sedan at the foot of an old fishing pier that Harry's boat company was planning to purchase and renovate.

Ed Higgins chuckled. "What do they want these people to do—*wade* out to the boats in their bathing suits?"

"Of course not," said Harry. "What they *want* is for people to not have any fun."

Ed nodded and looked out at the old pier. "Let's have a look at this thing, Harry."

Tennyson looked back at Syd seated behind the wheel. "Stay here and keep an eye out for any trouble."

"You got it, boss."

Ed started walking out along the pier and Harry followed close behind. The wood was gray and split in many places. The weather had beaten it up, and years of neglect had left it like the rotting skeleton of a beached whale.

"How far out does this one go?" asked Ed as he neared the end of the pier.

"Not far enough. Gonna cost about ten grand to fix it up and extend it," said Harry.

"The water looks deep. Even in a bathing suit it'd be over folks' heads," said Ed. "This pier is the only—"

He never finished the sentence as he suddenly vanished right in front of Harry.

Not exactly vanished. More like plummeted.

The boards beneath Ed suddenly collapsed and sent him downward as though he'd stepped on a trap door. So quickly did he knife into the brackish, silt-filled river that Harry had no chance to even attempt to catch him or keep him from going all the way through.

"Christ on a crutch!" yelled Ed as he bobbed back up. "This water's *cold*!"

"Hang on!" yelled Harry as he swung himself off one of the pilings, grabbed Ed's hand, and pulled him up.

"And it's real fucking deep!" said Ed as he scrambled back to the pier. His double-breasted, Glen plaid suit clung to him like cheap gauze wrapping. His shoes were encased in blocks of river mud from his trip to the murky bottom.

"Jesus, I'm sorry, Ed . . . " said Harry. "Don't worry, I'll take care of that suit."

Ed looked at himself and laughed. "I think we *definitely* have to fight that legislation!"

They both laughed as they walked back to the car, carefully.

When they reached the sedan, Harry looked at Syd with a perfectly serious expression.

"Take your clothes off, Syd. The senator's got a little problem."

Ed watched as Syd slipped out from behind the wheel and began to disrobe without a word. The big guy stripped down to a pair of white boxers and asked if the senator would like those, too.

"Uh, Harry, this is okay, really . . . " said Ed.

"I insist," said The Lord.

"All right, but please, Syd, keep your shorts on, okay?"

They drove back to Baltimore in the back seat while Syd wheeled up U. S. Route 1 practically naked. Just minutes before, the state senator had been swimming in the Potomac River. He was now swimming in 300-pound Syd's suit. Ed Higgins wondered about what would make a man so loyal, and hoped that someday he would have people equally loyal to him.

Eight

The Block

The mood of the Baltimore public changed toward The Block in the mid-fifties. There were increasing public complaints about nudity and alleged prostitution. At the time, nineteen strip clubs (all owned by men) and one "neighborhood" bar, the Midway, dotted The Block.

About once a month, a group of men would meet at their usual table in the Sequin Club. They would have their drinks on the house and the "sitters" (the girls who sat at the bar and hustled overpriced cocktails for the promise of a hand-job) would be available on an "as needed" basis. The group consisted of the chief of police, a representative from the district attorney's office, plus several city councilmen. They would meet with Bo Sandler, the club owner, The Lord, and several of the "bosses" from the Bel Air Market crowd (the Italian mob in Baltimore).

Each month, they would discuss the amount of crime occurring on The Block—from the victimless stuff like prostitution, gambling, and bar-sitting, all the way up to the serious felonies like muggings and drug-trafficking. If something was out of hand, it would be curtailed and controlled at these meetings. There was an agreement among all these men that as long as crime was kept in its harness and allowed to cavort within the show-bar district, there wouldn't be much trouble from the outside world.

This arrangement existed for generations. It was not a good system, but it was a system that worked.

Whenever the public outcry did arise and the reporters would descend on The Block, Harry could always be counted on for a good quote. His usual went something like this: "The Block contributes something to the city. We provide a place for people to come and enjoy themselves. This is one of the best-policed areas in the city. Everything in one place—it's easy to police and keep it orderly. We haven't done anything wrong. We're legitimate businessmen down here."

This was a time when people started moving to suburbia and building big houses. However, the majority of families still lived in row houses in the city.

The men ruled over their spouses. There was no feminism.

All of the major gamblers and mobsters were married and had families. They lived a good family life and would take their wives to dinner one night per week. But they also went out with their girlfriends, maybe to the same dinner club, before or after they took their wives. Although the mobsters and gamblers were very strict, they treated their families right. The families basically never knew what business they were in, and if they did, they never argued about or discussed business.

At around 11:30 a.m., the main bookies and numbers guys would have lunch at the Carousel on Charles Street. Then they might go out and catch a few races at the track. (Horse racing in Maryland was year-round and was held at Pimlico, Laurel, Bel Air, Hagerstown, Bowie, etc.) If they had good information, they would go out in force. If they thought there was a fixed race, they would either flock to the track or, while at the track, bet with some other gambler who didn't know that the "fix" was in. They discussed cars, horses, other bets, girls, and different scams.

80

After the track, they would usually go home for dinner and then head back out. They would say that they had to make collections or whatever, since they all had "fronts," or other jobs. Some drove cabs, sold insurance, or worked for installment companies and other legitimate businesses. After they took care of whatever business they had to do (and maybe they didn't have any business to take care of), they would go to The Block.

Nine

Katherine Louise

Katherine Louise was a hit on The Block. Just one short year after her arrival in Baltimore, she was one of the favorite featured acts at the Desert Club and a favorite of Harry The Lord Tennyson as well. People came from all over the city and surrounding counties to see her act on Friday and Saturday nights. She was pulling in close to three hundred a week and some weeks, with tips, she even surpassed Marlena. Katherine was billed as one of the classiest acts around, and her moves were fast becoming legendary. She took pleasure in her new-found status, as well as her vastly improved standard of living. She now rented a large, spacious apartment on North Charles Street, complete with its own private balcony and lots of twelve-foot-high windows. And she was keeping good company these days.

She sat at her dressing table, dabbed at her lipstick with a tissue, and started to let down her hair. There was a loud knock at the door.

"Come on in," she called out over the strains of Buddy Holly playing on the little radio in the corner.

Syd poked his head in shyly. "You decent Katherine?" She smiled. He'd seen her act dozens of times and still he was the perfect gentleman when it came to chitchat.

"Come in, Syd. I'm just fixing my hair." She ran a brush through the strands, and allowed the soft curls to fall over her shoulders. "Where are we going tonight?"

"Over to the Harvey House. Dinner and drinks. Is that all right?"

"It's wonderful. I'm starved." He held out her coat as she slid into it and picked up her purse. She tucked the night's tips into the side compartment and they turned to go.

Outside, the limousine waited in the rain, sleek and black. Syd whipped out an umbrella and escorted Katherine to the car. They rode together in silence, the partition between them and the driver firmly closed. Katherine watched the people scurrying along the streets in the rain and was thankful for the warm, comfortable car. She turned to look at Syd.

"How long do we have tonight?"

"I'm not sure. A couple of hours at least."

She turned back to the window and watched as several fat drops of water wobbled their way across the window of the speeding limo. She hoped her dress was all right. She'd gotten it at the Palace yesterday on sale. It was a midnight blue with a sweetheart neckline and it fit snuggly across her hips. The shoes matched, as did her handbag. She felt good. He should be pleased.

The car pulled up under the awning of the Harvey House and Syd ducked out and swung around to her side. She held his arm as she stepped out and they went inside. The maitre d' smiled with recognition and took Katherine's coat. As they were escorted toward the back of the restaurant, Syd walked a measured distance behind. Katherine smiled warmly when she saw Harry. He was seated facing the door, able to survey the entire restaurant from his table. He never took his eyes from her as she slid gracefully into the plush cushions of the booth. They looked at each other for a long time, then he glanced over to their right. Syd was seated three tables away, busily scanning the wine list.

"You're breathtaking, Katherine. I can't stop looking at you."

"Thank you, darling. I was delighted when Syd told me you were free tonight. I thought you had a dinner party to attend."

"I begged out. Dolores wasn't feeling well so we cancelled. Then some very urgent business came up that I had to take care of, so I apologized profusely to my wife and rushed right over here." He smiled his warm, sexy smile and Katherine felt a tingling somewhere deep inside.

"I'm so glad. I really wanted to see you." She stole a glance over at Syd. "I hope poor Syd isn't getting tired of this running around in secret all the time. He's such a dear man."

"Sweetheart, I don't pay him a small fortune to be nice. He's here to protect me and you for that matter. Believe me, he's well-compensated."

The waiter appeared and Harry ordered an expensive bottle of champagne and some hors d'oeuvres.

"What are we celebrating?"

"You mean you don't know?" Katherine shook her head.

"One year ago today, you debuted. Remember? I missed most of your opening act, but everyone was raving about you?" Katherine smiled at the memory and thought briefly about how far she'd come since then. Her technique had greatly improved.

"So, I got a special evening planned for us."

"Whatever are we going to do?" she asked playfully, as if she couldn't guess.

"You'll have to wait and see." He picked up her hand and touched the brilliant aquamarine ring on her finger. He'd given it to her for her birthday two months ago and she adored it. She loved the feel of his hand around hers. It felt so secure.

Dinner was delicious. Rack of lamb, baby carrots sprinkled with cashews, wild rice, baked Alaska for dessert, and lots of good wine. The waiter had just brought Katherine's Brandy Alexander and the Grand Marnier for Harry, when Harry dropped her hand abruptly and motioned to her to move. As rehearsed, she slid quickly out of the booth and headed straight back toward the ladies' lounge. She went inside, applied some lipstick, and ran a comb through her hair. Then she re-emerged, and slowly made her way back to the dining room and slipped into the chair Syd had pulled out for her. She smiled at him and picked up her brandy. A subtle laugh escaped her lips as she and Syd pretended to share a lovers' joke. Out of the corner of her eye, she could see Harry offering a drink to his unexpected guest, his father-in-law. All traces of her had been wiped from the table.

They sat for half an hour, she and Syd, drinking slowly, chatting absently, waiting for Delvecchio to get up and leave. Finally he did. They all watched as the squat little man made his way out the front door, then Harry got up and followed. Katherine forgot how the rest was supposed to go. Did Harry take his own car, or did he wait for her in the limo? It was all so confusing. Sometimes Syd would drive Harry's car home. She decided to just wait for her cue to leave. The wine had gone to her head and she wasn't thinking very clearly. Syd nodded to her and they both got up. The maitre d' rushed over to hold her chair and handed her coat to Syd. They made a quiet exit.

Harry was in the limo, champagne glasses in hand. He rolled down the window a crack and told Syd to take the car to the club.

Then he turned to her. "Sorry about that, honey. I got this little in-law problem sometimes. The man keeps poppin' up in the damndest places." He laughed softly and handed a glass to Katherine. "You did great, Katherine. Just like I told you. Nobody was the wiser."

"I hate sneaking around, Harry."

"I know, baby. But we got no other choice right now. You're the classiest, most gorgeous thing around, and God knows I would love to be able to show you off right, but I got this thing called Dolores over here. She's like the eternal thorn in my side, that woman. But it's all about connections. Her old man, you know, he's an important guy in this town. I can't be screwin' around on the man's precious daughter right in front of his face. You understand, don't you honey?"

"Yes, Harry, of course. It's just a shame, that's all. Dolores should let you go. She doesn't really love you." She wanted to say, "Not like I love you," but she caught herself. "That's a whole issue in itself. We got better things to talk about. Like you and me and getting on with this little celebration I got planned." He leaned forward and pressed the button on the sliding partition. "We're ready. Press on."

The car nosed forward and they were off to some secret destination. Katherine sipped her champagne and snuggled up closer to Harry. She was glad when he kissed her. She needed to feel him near her. She needed to make the best of the little time they would have together tonight. Sometimes a whole week would go by and the only time she would have alone with him would be a stolen minute or two back behind the club, or in her dressing room before a show. His lips were full and warm and she needily opened her mouth to him and sought out his tongue. She wondered why Dolores Tennyson had allowed this man to escape her clutches. She had to know a good thing when she saw it. Harry's hand was at the back of her neck, massaging, tickling underneath her hair, all the while sucking on her tongue and driving her crazy. When she pulled back and looked into his eyes, she could see the desire there, dancing in the irises. She wanted him inside of her like never before. She could feel the wetness between her legs already.

"I'm going to make you feel exquisitely good tonight," he whispered, and bent to kiss her again.

The car came to a stop outside the Meridian, a small hotel with an elegant purple and gold awning. Harry told her to go inside and wait in the bar for ten minutes. He handed her a pack of cigarettes, a fancy European brand, and instructed her to smoke one, and when that was gone, light another. "When it's halfway gone, get up and go to the fourth floor. Room 412." She nodded excitedly and got out of the car. They had only spent one other evening in a fancy hotel. Harry was afraid of getting caught in most of the big places downtown. Usually they were driven to out-of-the-way motels on the interstate. This was indeed a treat.

Katherine made her way to the handsomely decorated bar and took a seat at a small table. She ordered a soda water and lit her cigarette with delicate precision. It tasted good. She blew dainty streams of smoke upward and smiled at the two men eyeing her from the bar. But even as she smiled, all she could think about was lying naked with Harry. He really had a magnificent physique. Very muscular for a forty-year-old. And no bulging stomach. Harry was proud of his taut, firm stomach. She finished her cigarette, lit up the second, and glanced down at her watch. Four minutes to go.

When the time was up, she rose and slowly strolled to the elevator. The numbers fell from 6 as the car came to rest at the lobby and the door opened. A Negro man stood at the controls and greeted her with a warm smile. His teeth were as white as fresh fallen snow against his ebony skin.

"What floor this evening, ma'am?"

"The fourth please."

The doors closed and they rose rapidly. Katherine tipped the man as she got off and walked down the long hallway to room 412. Harry opened the door before she could knock. He swept her off her feet and carried her to the bed. There was more champagne chilling by the side of the bed, and candles glowed from the coffee table in the corner. Katherine was thrilled. He had really gone to a lot of trouble, and all to commemorate her debut. He was such a thoughtful man.

"Darling, everything is just beautiful! Thank you so much."

She reached for him and kissed him deeply, once again opening her mouth for him. He slid her shoes off and his own as well, then reached over to pour the champagne.

"A toast to the most beautiful creature on God's green earth," he began. "Katherine, you're the best thing that's ever happened to me and I want you to know how happy you make me." He set the glasses back down and loosened his tie.

"I want you, Harry," Katherine said quietly. "Now."

He turned and lifted her dress to peek at her long legs encased in sheer, black stockings. She grabbed his hand and helped him to slip the straps of her dress off her shoulders. Then he reached behind to unzip her. She wore a lacy, black bra beneath, one he had bought. A minute later, the dress lay in a heap on the floor and Katherine was busy unbuttoning Harry's shirt. She tossed it to the floor and pulled him down beside her. She relished these moments of lovemaking. Harry always surprised her, and this was no exception. He had reached for his glass and she watched as he took a sip and swirled the liquid around in his mouth. Then he dipped his finger into the glass and proceeded to place droplets of champagne down her neck and between her breasts. When he bent to kiss the droplets away, she felt an electricity jump through her and arched her back to him. He ran his tongue through each drop and she allowed a moan to escape her lips. His hand slipped under the bra and massaged her breasts. She was really enjoying this.

He kissed his way down, running his hands in wonderful fluttering movements up and down her sides. She could feel his warm breath through the sheer silk of her panties and began to tremble slightly. He sensed her excitement and smiled up at her. Then her body tensed as he tugged the elastic upward and darted his tongue inside in short, quick movements. The feeling was incredible and she was eager for more. As if he'd heard her, Harry removed the panties in frustrated haste and began to taste her. She felt the warmth spread throughout her body as his touch and the effects of all the champagne combined to work their magic. When he moved back above her he was ready. She felt him, rock hard beneath his expensive trousers, and quickly helped him out of them.

Harry had a way of making her feel like the only woman in the world when he entered her. He always moved in slow, tantalizing movements that frustrated and excited her at the same time. As he slowly moved into her, she found herself slithering down against the cool cotton sheets to meet him faster. He reached beneath her to grasp her bottom and she moaned as he suddenly thrust hard into her with a deep, satisfied sound of gratification. They were without question, made for each other sexually. Katherine believed that no one could do for her what Harry did. And she knew for a fact that Dolores didn't have the foggiest notion of how to satisfy Harry. The woman favored the immobile, stare-up-at-the-ceiling approach. It used to happen once or twice a month. But now they slept in separate rooms, so, thankfully, it didn't happen at all anymore. The thought of Harry making love to Dolores sickened Katherine.

She opened her eyes to watch Harry's face. She enjoyed looking at the pleasured expression it wore. His eyes were glassy and his lips appeared swollen and flushed. She placed her hands on either side of his face and drew him to her mouth in a long kiss. He continued to push deeply into her and she matched his every move with precision, bringing them together each time with intense force. They both smiled. Katherine could sense every part of him that touched her. The pressure of his strong thighs as they pressed her legs apart. The weight of his hips as they rose and fell against her, and the heat of his mouth upon her as it sought out and found her nipples. They moved together for a long time, working to so many crescendos, then backing away, intensifying their need for release. Then suddenly they couldn't wait any longer. Katherine could feel it rising deep inside her like a wave. She ran her hands along the crevice of his ass the way he liked her to do as he was coming. He arched his back and groaned loudly. She rubbed against him, feeling his spasms inside her and then slowly started to come. It was a delicious feeling. A white-hot flash went through her and she closed her eyes for a moment to ride it out. When it subsided, she opened her eyes to find Harry watching her with pleasure.

"That's what good little girls are made of," he said jokingly.

She laughed a throaty laugh and nudged him.

"Are you making fun of me?"

"No, sweetheart. I'm paying you the highest compliment. Only you could be so enchanting in bed. But even when you're naughty, you're still a good little girl at heart."

"I think I hear a compliment in there somewhere," Katherine said as she pulled the sheet up over them and turned over to pick up her glass. "What a wonderful night this has been Harry. Thanks for remembering my anniversary."

"It's been my pleasure. You inspire me. You're the reason I get up every morning. You're the reason I don't sleep with Dolores anymore."

Katherine was glad he'd brought up the subject of Dolores. She really wanted to get the scoop on the situation. If they weren't sleeping together, what was the point of staying together? Their kids were old enough to survive a divorce.

"Harry, about Dolores . . . "

"Forget her. She's an old hag. She's a sorry decoration I gotta carry on my arm to make people happy. She's nothing, Katherine."

"She's your wife."

"Yeah, honey, and I explained to you, I can't leave her now. Not with Delvecchio watching my every move. He's got me covered with some old business that wasn't quite kosher and he keeps things on The Block running smoothly as long as he and I get along, see? I can't be divorcing Dolores and pissing him off."

Katherine sighed. "I know Harry, I know." But she couldn't help feeling like partially used goods. She wanted to be Mrs. Harry Tennyson. Then she could really hold her head up in this town. People respected Harry and, consequently, respected his wife. Only Dolores was undeserving of that respect. She never loved Harry. She only loved what he represented. Why else would she have let her marriage fall apart? But Harry clearly was not going to discuss things further tonight. And he really had gone to a lot of trouble to make things nice for her. She was grateful.

"I understand what you're saying, Harry. I won't bring it up again." Not tonight anyway.

They lay there together in the warm, comfortable bed and talked about the next time they would get together. Harry had a scheduled trip to Washington and wanted Katherine to join him. She perked up at the idea and kissed his cheek.

"I'd love it! We could do some sightseeing together."

"Well, I have work to do, but we could dine together and maybe see a show or something. Would you like that?"

"You know I would, Harry."

"Great. Syd will let you know the plan." He swung his legs out of bed and stood up. He stretched his arms above his head and Katherine reached out to touch him.

"Do you have to go now?"

He nodded sadly and leaned over to plant a kiss on her forehead. "I hate to, but I can't be out all night."

Katherine gave him a sad smile. "Go take your shower, Harry. I'm a little sleepy. I think I'll stay the night if it's okay."

"Whatever you want, sweetheart. I'll call you soon."

Katherine watched him disappear into the bathroom and sighed. She ran her hands over her body beneath the sheet, remembering the things they had just done. That would have to hold in her thoughts until the next time. Whenever that might be. She reached for the cigarettes on the table and lit one. As the candles danced, creating spooky shadows on the fabric-covered walls, she smoked and listened to the sound of the shower washing away Harry's sins.

TEN

CHARLES WHITTIER

Around eight o'clock Charles decided to call it a night. The second shift of dancers was about to kick in and the Desert Club had started to fill up. It was his second night back on The Block and he was beat. Research told him that the club had been different in its heyday. He pictured the place with cabaret-style tables and cigarette girls. The dancers on The Block used to leave a lot more to the imagination back in the fifties and early sixties. They took the time to apply stage makeup and sequins and feathers to liven up their act. Back then, there was a little more art involved in the game of striptease. Burlesque to him had always conjured up something kind of glamorous and this place just wasn't cutting it. He took a last look over his shoulder as Yolanda sauntered out onto the bar and flashed a toothy smile. She looked pretty sad. Overweight and butt-ugly, she really needed to leave her clothes on. As he turned back toward the door, he caught a glimpse of a surgical scar below her rolled stomach. Nice. Probably a Cesarean.

Outside, the April air had turned cold and a damp mist was

falling. Shit. His trench coat was back at the hotel. He searched up and down for a cab. Traffic was chugging along East Baltimore Street. Several cars were filled with horny-looking teenage boys scoping the hookers. Look, but don't touch, Charles thought to himself. In this day and age you'd have to be a pretty desperate motherfucker to hook up with street trash. Ever since he'd done the piece on AIDS in American colleges, Charles took note of how many assholes out there were willing to risk their lives for a fuck. No sign of a cab. He'd have to hoof it. Twenty minutes and he'd be in bed. He stepped up the pace.

He was leaving a section of the street that had been cordoned off, commandeered by machinery and laborers. The three buildings closest to the corner were going to be leveled within the next two or three weeks, and one of them was the fabled Desert Club, one-time jewel of The Block. Charles reminded himself to get back there during daylight to get some good pictures before it was too late. He might come up with something that would make a nice current-day coda to the article.

He rounded a corner and the Stouffer came into sight. He needed a good night's sleep, then tomorrow he'd hit The Block again in the daytime and take a good hard look at it, warts and all. A couple of man-on-the-street interviews and maybe he could start to nail down this dude, Tennyson. There had to be somebody around who knew him well. Charles had been in town three days and Mosley wanted an outline by the end of the week. Goddamn editor.

The sheets felt great. Smooth, cool, just like home. Charles picked up the stack of news clippings on the night stand and started to read. Harry Tennyson, alias The Lord, was big time in Baltimore back in 1957. The article heralded the Desert Club as the place to be. Tennyson owned pieces of several spots on The Block, but the Desert Club was his baby. The club was one of the most "happening" joints on The Block, and The Lord primarily catered to the upper-crust set----politicians, Hollywood types, and out-of-town big spenders.

He married a city councilman's daughter and had two kids. Charles studied the picture above the article. It revealed a

94

softer-looking Harry Tennyson. Not like the guy in the publicity photo he'd seen that first night at the club. The man in this photograph was standing with his arm draped around the shoulder of City Councilman Delvecchio, his father-in-law. It was election night, November 4th, 1956. Delvecchio had just won re-election and was all smiles. In the background was Dolores Tennyson, Harry's wife. She wasn't smiling quite as big. In fact she had sort of a tightlipped grimace on her face. Charles' gaze shifted back to Harry. The guy bore kind of a funny resemblance to Bogie—same long face, large nose, and soft, doughy-looking complexion. But at the same time he looked like he was, without question, a mean sonofabitch. Charles would bet his next paycheck that Dolores Delvecchio Tennyson could attest to that. He made a note to check his files for an address for Harry The Lord Tennyson's widow.

As he sifted through the mountain of articles, Charles began to understand some of The Lord's connections in Baltimore back in the fifties. The guy was into everything. There was a small piece on gambling boats that was intriguing. Apparently Tennyson had entered into a partnership with some questionable people with possible Mafia connections. There was some sort of investigation, but nothing had come of it. The gambling boats were a big success, attracting an especially large following in the political arena. Maybe that's why the city councilman's wife, Dolores, was so tightlipped. Then for some reason, the boats just fizzled out. The article didn't give a reason. The Lord apparently acted as a liaison between The Block club owners and the lawmakers in Annapolis. Charles was willing to bet that Harry had a couple of them in his hip pocket. And then there was something about some black dude called Little Marvin of all things. A drug dealer. You don't say.

Over an eggs-and-bacon breakfast the next morning, Charles scanned through a stack of old newspapers in search of more photographs of The Lord. In several of the photos there was a huge, expressionless guy hanging tight in the background, eyes always on Harry, looking every inch the bodyguard. The paper didn't identify him. Boys from the 'hood, Charles thought with a smile. They probably grew up together.

The big, dumb dude protecting the smart, little dude from cradle to grave. If this guy was still alive and still in Baltimore, he would find him. Time to hit the pavement.

Once again Charles made his way from the hub of tourist activity over to The Block. He needed to find some old-timers. Old-timers always got a story to tell. Where did geezers hang when they had no place else to go? Eat joints. Probably a diner of some sort. As he looked up and down the street, Charles didn't spot too many diners. A couple of pizza places and a restaurant/bar. One block up he spied Hartley's Dinette. A filthy-looking dive with streaky windows and a dog-eared menu posted on the door. Liver and onions was the special of the day, and a sign promised low prices and all you could eat. The eggs in his stomach did a somersault. He strolled in and scanned the seats at the counter. Not surprisingly, there were a couple of old guys perched on stools, heads bent to their plates, heavy shoulders stooped. Charles pulled up a chair next to an older man and signaled the waitress for a cup of coffee. She came his way, pouring the last drops out of the pot into a white ceramic mug. Charles eyeballed the grains dripping into the cup and changed his mind.

"Make that an orange juice, miss." She rolled her eyes slightly and turned away.

Charles glanced at the two men to his left. One looked like he might keel over and croak on the spot. Had to be pushing ninety. His fingers were so crippled they practically bent in half as he struggled to grip his fork. He was chewing at a record slow pace, the corners of his mouth drooling. The man next to him was a little more with it. About seventy or so. He was reading the *Baltimore Sun* and shoveling in hash browns. The waitress set a tall glass of OJ in front of Charles, and pushed the ticket across the counter.

"That'll be a dollar twenty-five," she snapped. Charles reached into his coat pocket and fished around for some change.

"Prices keep goin' up and up don't they?" the geezer next to him remarked. Charles nodded.

"Damn rip-off if you ask me. No wonder we got so many

homeless," added the geezer.

The guy swiped at his mouth with a napkin and folded his paper.

"You eat here often?" Charles asked.

"Every other morning. My wife goes for treatment over at Mercy Medical Center. I been comin' here for years, though. I eat over at Molly's Kitchen, too. They got great meatloaf on Thursdays."

"Did you ever hang out here back in the forties and fifties when The Block was a big deal?" Charles eased his notebook out of his back pocket and flipped it open.

"Oh, yeah. It was real nice back then. Real fancy, too, believe it or not. The whole area was a nice place to come on a Saturday night. You could catch a show, have a couple of drinks and a late night snack for next to nothing. I used to get breakfast here on Sundays. The whole meal would cost me a buck seventy-five. Now you can barely get a cup of coffee." The guy gave Charles a once-over.

"You a newspaper reporter?"

"I'm writing a story for a magazine, actually."

"Oh, yeah? What about?"

"The Block back in the glory days. You know, kind of an *exposé.*" Charles took a swig of his orange juice and jumped in. "You ever hear of a guy named Harry Tennyson?" The man thought for a minute and nodded slowly.

"Yeah . . . I seem to remember that guy. Big-time club owner around here, right? Used to drive through sometimes on Saturday nights. You know, fancy car and whatnot."

"Any idea what happened to him?"

"Nah. My wife and I just used to come down here with friends. I remember the guy because he was always in the papers. Married some politician's daughter, I think. What was that guy's name?"

Charles made a couple of notes in his book. "Any idea of where I might find someone who knew Tennyson?"

The man cast a nosey look at Charles' notebook and shook his head. "Like I said, I just come down here for the hospital." He thought for a minute. "But you might want to go by Molly's.

A lot of older guys frequent the place. Maybe somebody there could help you."

Charles thanked him and ducked out of Hartley's and into the sunshine. Just a block down on the left was Molly's Kitchen, a cozy joint alive with the smell of frying bacon. He slipped into a booth. When the waitress came around he ordered another orange juice and asked her who the regulars were. She gave him a curious look and nodded over at a table toward the back. "Those three back there are in here all the time. Why you askin'? You a cop?" Charles shook his head as he got up and moved toward the table.

"Excuse me, gentlemen," he said clearing his throat, "my name is Charles Whittier. I'm a writer for *Esquire* magazine." Blank stares. "It's a national magazine. I'm doing a little research on this part of town for an upcoming article and was wondering if you would share some of your experiences." A couple of deep sighs around the table as the oldest of the three slid his plate over and cleared a space.

"Have a seat, young man," he said gruffly. "I think we could tell you a story or two. Hell, eighty years . . . I could tell you a lifetime of stories."

Charles sat down next to him and shook his extended hand. "The name's Barney," the old guy said.

"Well, what I'm specifically interested in Barney, is life around The Block back in the fifties. My magazine is doing a big story on old-time burlesque. Seems there's a lot of interesting stuff that happened right here on The Block." He surveyed the group.

"Any of you ever hear of Harry The Lord Tennyson?" He looked around the table, searching their clouded eyes for signs of recognition. This could take awhile.

"*Hear* of him?" Barney mocked at last, with a grin. "Hell, Syd over here was his shield." He nodded his head at his buddy as a slow chuckle emerged from old guy number three in the corner.

Charles looked at the man named Syd across the table. He studied him for a minute. The guy was close to eighty, but the face was still fairly recognizable. Same angular features, expressionless eyes. Standing, the man was probably still over six feet. And still very heavy. The bodyguard. A steady smile spread across the man's wrinkled lips and revealed a perfect set of very white dentures.

"You worked for Harry Tennyson?" Charles asked, unable to believe his luck.

"Yes, I did."

"What was he like?"

"Well, now, that's a loaded question," Syd replied. His monotone voice was no surprise. He paused for an eternity and toyed with the spoon in front of him. "Harry and I were schoolmates," he offered, as if he were reading Charles' mind. "We came from the same neighborhood. Our mothers were in the women's auxiliary together. Harry was my closest friend . . . kinda like a brother."

"So what happened to him?"

"Well, now, I don't exactly know. It's a bit of a mystery." The other men at the table fell strangely silent. Barney was busy dumping sugar into his cup, while the other one, an Italian with deep-set gray eyes, started to fold and refold his napkin. "Harry got into some trouble and disappeared," Syd continued. "They never found his body, but the police called it homicide. They gave up looking for him a couple of weeks later."

"You never heard from him?" Charles asked. Syd shook his head. "Did you stay in touch with any of his family . . . his wife?" Charles was scribbling fast in his notebook.

"Well, Dolores never took to me too well. She's his wife. Used to say I scared the shit out of her 'cause I'm so damn big." The slow, steady smile again. "I took that as a compliment. But Katherine . . . now she and I still talk to this day."

"Katherine? You mean *Louise*?"

"The same. Harry's lady. You probably heard of her. Katherine Louise." Charles thought back to his brief interview with the stripper. She hadn't mentioned Harry Tennyson.

"They were having an affair?"

"Oh, yeah. But it was a lot more than that. Those two were joined at the hip. Harry got her started in this town."

"Boy, she was a hot one, wasn't she Syd?" Barney piped up.

All three men nodded in agreement.

"Yeah, Barney. Katherine was a looker, no question."

"So you were Tennyson's bodyguard?" Charles asked eagerly.

"I guess you could call it that. I handled business for him, too. He had a lot goin' on, you know."

"Anything illegal you know about?"

The old guy smiled, then started to rise, and the others slowly followed suit. Irritated, Charles jumped up. Where the hell did these guys have to rush off to?

"Hey, Syd. Can I call you Syd?"

"Okay."

"Any chance we could get together sometime soon so I can ask you a few more questions? I think you could be the key to this story." The guy appeared to ponder the idea, then finally let out a long breath and cocked his head.

"You planning on using my name?"

"I don't have to."

"Well, all right, then. You can give me a call tomorrow if you want. I'm in the book under Daniloski."

The old men shuffled toward the door of Molly's Kitchen, waving at the fat woman behind the counter. Charles followed. Once outside, Syd reached into his breast pocket, pulled out a pair of thick sunglasses and slipped them onto his long nose. Eyes shielded, he suddenly appeared younger and more sinister.

Charles reached out to shake his hand. Barney slapped Syd on the arm and grinned. "Hey, Syd, what was it Katherine used to say about old Harry? You remember. She'd be comin' out of his office late at night, all smiles."

"*Praise The Lord*," Syd replied. "She used to bat those big baby blues and say, *Praise The Lord*." He extended a hand to Charles. "Talk to you later, Mr. Whittier. Don't call me before nine."

The three guys shuffled off down the street as Charles watched, mouth open, wheels inside his head spinning.

Two hours later Charles was on the phone to Syd's Elm Avenue home in Hampden. The old man answered on the

second ring and spoke gruffly without preliminaries. "Yeah?"
"Syd, it's Charles Whittier." A pause. "The writer?"
"Yeah?" Dead air.
"Well, I'd like to get together again. Today, if you can spare the time." Practice golden silence, Charles thought. He bit his tongue to hold back the urge to further state his case. The old Jewish professor reared his wise old head yet again. Maybe college hadn't been such a fucking waste of time after all.
"Where?"
"Excuse me?"
"Where? Where do you wanna meet?" Charles put a check on his excitement and mentally panned the harbor area near his hotel. He wouldn't mind talking to the guy somewhere away from The Block. Maybe he'd be more willing to let his guard down.
"How about the Rusty Scupper Restaurant?"
"Never been there. Let's meet at Sabatino's."
"Never been there," Charles countered.
"Little Italy. It's my favorite place. See you around five."
"No problem. I'll be there."
"Oh, and Charles? Dinner's on you, right? I figure your fancy magazine can afford to spring for a meal."
"I'd be happy to treat you." The guy wanted to talk after all.
Located just east of the downtown harbor area, Little Italy resembled much of residential Baltimore with the exception of the awnings that dotted the streets, boasting typically Italian names and promising delicious cuisine.
Sabatino's was on the corner of High Street and Fawn, a rather inviting looking place. He half expected the fat chick from behind the counter at Molly's to greet him at the hostess desk, but when he ducked inside, he was pleased to find the decor more in keeping with what he was used to. The maitre d', a friendly guy named Vince, directed him to the back of the restaurant where he found Syd, sipping a glass of red wine and studying the menu intently.
"What looks good?" Charles asked as he slipped into the chair across from the old guy.

"Well, now, I was about to give up on you, Mr. Whittier," Syd commented without looking up. Charles glanced at his watch. It was five-oh-five. Not big on patience this guy. Syd called for the waitress, Angie, to bring him another glass of house red.

"Sorry I'm a little late," said Charles. "I know your time is precious, so why don't we get started."

"Hold it. I'd like to order something to eat first." He scanned the menu's list of appetizers and decided on fried calamari and the house salad. Passing on the appetizer, Charles ordered the same pasta dish as Syd. Syd's refill arrived and he took the glass in hand and leaned back in the booth. He breathed in deeply and finally settled his eyes on Charles. Clearly, he was now ready.

"All right, so you wanna know about my old buddy, Harry. What a piece of work he was. I was with Harry for, oh, a good twenty years. As I told you, he was my childhood pal. But see, he was always the smart one. And he always had the girls, lined up around the block they were. Pretty ones, ugly ones, fat ones, skin and bones. All types were attracted to old Harry. But of course he never looked past the beautiful ones. That's why it kinda threw me when he took up with Dolores." Another gulp from the wine glass.

"Don't get me wrong. There ain't nothing wrong with Dolores in the looks department. She was just a little wholesome compared to Harry's other women. I guess he liked that about her." Charles figured Syd was being kind. It was tough to compare any woman to the beautiful strippers of the fifties.

"But Harry and I grew up good boys. We didn't get in no trouble. Once we were out in the world, Harry started to realize he had a real talent for winning people over. That was the salesman in him. He was running a good numbers thing by the time he was twenty."

"Why did Harry need a bodyguard?"

"Well, I wasn't a bodyguard, exactly. It was more like his personal assistant. There were people who wanted to get close to Harry, but he didn't have time for none of them. And as things started happening for Harry, he suddenly was worth a good deal of money. People worth money need looking after. You know how that goes."

The salad and calamari arrived and Syd leaned forward to shovel in a couple of bites of salad. Charles checked to see that the tape in his pocket recorder was running and waited for Syd to continue.

"Harry enjoyed success. He was always on the lookout for the next sweet deal. Like with Katherine. She arrived a young nothing and he turned her around in no time. She became big stuff. But she only had eyes for Harry. Never did nothing with nobody else. She was a first-class act, no question."

"So Harry was a club owner, he ran around with a classy girl on the side, and ran a numbers racket. What else?"

"Well, he set up the gambling boat casinos with Dolores' old man riding his coattails. The boats were exclusive at first. Just high rollers and politicians. But pretty soon the word got out and people were coming from all over."

"How did Harry die, Syd?"

"I don't know that he did die."

"What do you mean?"

"Exactly what I said. They never found his body. Harry vanished off the face of this earth. No card, no phone call, no nothing to nobody." Syd's face clouded for a minute. There was hurt deep in the shadows of his aging gray eyes.

"You think he's still alive?"

"Nah, I guess not. I guess I know deep down somebody did Harry in. God knows there was reasons."

"What kind of reasons?"

"Well, lots of people were jealous of Harry's success. There was this Negro fella called Little Marvin. He swore up and down that he could kick Harry's ass, you know, move in on his territory. Marvin ran the drug traffic in East Baltimore. Harry was the one who handed it to him on a platter, but you know there wasn't no real traffic there to speak of. But Little Marvin thought he'd fucking died and gone to heaven." Charles watched as Syd reflected for a minute. Their meals were placed in front of them. The pasta smelled fantastic.

"Yeah, Little Marvin had reason to see Harry gone. So did a couple of politicians, including his father-in-law, Delvecchio. Remember, you said you ain't gonna use any names."

"But what exactly would the murderer have been after?"

"Well, the police claim this was unfounded, but I believe old Harry had some big money stashed. That's why somebody did him in."

"What kind of money are we talking about?" Charles asked, leaning forward in his chair.

Syd swallowed a mouthful of linguini with white clam sauce and took another swig of wine.

"From maybe a half to a couple of million dollars for starters. That big enough for you?"

"So what happened to the money?"

"Beats me. I never pushed it. The police were tightlipped about the whole case, ruled it 'presumed dead minus a body.' When I tried to force the issue with the money, I got a door slammed in my face. Nobody was talkin', especially Delvecchio. He was busy playing the good father to weepy-faced Dolores. She was real broken up. She ain't been the same since."

"You think I could talk to her?"

"Who's stoppin' you? She lives up in Guilford. Fancy place."

The waitress slipped the check under a glass and Charles reached for his wallet. "I want to thank you for your time today, Syd. I may need to contact you again if that's okay."

"Sure, you keep feeding my face like this and we can meet everyday if you want." He chuckled and wiped his mouth with his napkin. Charles got up and waited for him to follow. "You go on ahead. I'm gonna sit and enjoy this fine ambience they got here. I only get over here every once in awhile. It's nice to sit and relax." Charles nodded and reached across the small table to shake the old man's meaty hand.

"I'll be in touch."

"I'm sure you will, Mr. Whittier. I'm sure you will."

ELEVEN

THE ARTICLE

Strolling through today, it's difficult to imagine The Block and the word "class" ever being used in the same sentence. The bars and strip joints that pepper East Baltimore Street now are your average, run-of-the-mill flesh houses reeking of stale beer and seedy thoughts. Drug raids and prostitution arrests are common occurrences in and around The Block.

Perhaps even more surprising, to those unfamiliar with Baltimore's Block and its colorful history, is that it represented a major link in the national entertainment circle. Big acts were common. Regulars included Ukulele Ike, Ruth Etting, Jack Smith and Morton Downey. But stars we all know well, such as Gypsy Rose Lee, Valerie Parks, Blaze Starr, Jackie Gleason, Red Skelton, Milton Berle, Eddie Cantor, and Abbott and Costello, were headliners.

In those days, it was okay to be associated with striptease acts because the business was a true art form. The lurid connotations that embrace the profession today didn't exist. That's partly because striptease was exactly that. A tease. The girls left a little to the imagination. They wore elaborate costumes with feathers and sequins. They were beautiful, elegant young women who were respected and admired. They took great pride in their work.

As the Prohibition era came into play, life on The Block changed little. Club owners were eager to maintain the spirited nature of The Block as best they could, so BYOL hot spots were common. And quietly amidst the ruckus created by Prohibition an icon emerged on The Block.

It was housed in a basement warehouse at East Baltimore and Frederick Streets; a subterranean hideaway known as The Music Box. The proprietor, an infamous character named Maurice Cohen, supplied the ice. You had to bring your own liquor. There were no big-name acts or feather boas in the basement, so the nightly entertainment consisted of how fast you could consume your bottle's contents so as to beat the heat of The Music Box as it went to work on your bowl of ice. Maurice Cohen might have felt the power of inspiration during those sweaty, intoxicating days because not long after, he renamed his club the Oasis.

Cohen was a bulldozer of an entrepreneur. He enjoyed the art of bravado, and he's actually credited as the inventor of the striptease. His ladies were always a class act. Akin to "dressing for dinner," they were dressed to perform, sheathed in elegant evening gowns and accessories. They would sit and chat with patrons, waiting for their cue, and when the music started, they'd rise and stroll among the customers, shedding their peau de soie like rose petals to reveal barely-there costumes.

The Oasis was a big draw for Hollywood types, too. Even John Barrymore performed there one night. But central to the club's success and longevity was Maurice Cohen. Dubbed "the Mayor of The Block," he even came before the city planning board when part of Baltimore Street was scheduled for demolition and renovation, and dazzled the politicians with a public relations spiel that forced even the most dubious planners to reassess the economic vitality of The Block.

Unfortunately, Cohen lacked the art of finesse when it came to personal finances. He was later convicted of tax evasion on the basis of a clandestine surveillance by the police, centering around the delivery and pickup of linens at the Oasis (allegedly for bordello supplies). The IRS labeled it "unreported income" and, eventually, Cohen's brother took over all operations.

TWELVE

DOLORES TENNYSON

Dolores stepped behind the wheel of her Buick Roadmaster on her way to Hutzler's Palace to get her hair done. It was going to be a big night and everything had to be perfect.

She started to review the day's events: the caterers had the evening menu taken care of, the valet knew what to do, and, with the help of a decorator, Dolores had ensured her home had the perfect feeling of Christmas. Everything was planned and under control. The Tennyson's annual Christmas party was sure to be a success.

Still, Dolores felt uneasy.

It was far too quiet in the car and her thoughts overwhelmed the feeling of the season.

"I want to feel the joy in my heart!" she yelled.

Tears were welling up in her eyes as she tried to steer the wheel of her brand new car. She knew she had to stop acting so childishly. Harry hated to see her this way. He got so angry to see her behave so silly, he always said, 'Dolores, you've got everything, but you act like you've got nothing.' He was right. She had to tune out the silence so she switched her radio to

WITH-AM and was greeted by Rockin' Robin asking for everyone to be a little thoughtful of his neighbor at this time of year.

"What a laugh," Dolores whispered to herself. "That's all I ever think about. What can I get you, Harry? How can I help the church this week? Shirley, do you need anything?" The only person who was considerate of her was her son, John, and he didn't have much time for her anymore. He was growing up.

A blaring car horn brought her back to reality. She hit her brakes suddenly and her car skidded forward and came to a stop inches away from a dump truck. Her heart was pounding so hard it felt like it was going to explode, and her hands—she couldn't release her grip from the steering wheel.

"Lady. . . ? Are you okay, Lady?"

Dolores blinked and looked through the windshield to see a crowd gathering around her car.

"Wha-what?"

"Are you okay, ma'am?" A policeman had opened her car door and was standing there looking very impatient.

"Yes," she said, forcing herself to be coherent.

"You almost hit that truck, ma'am. I'm going to need to see your operator's permit."

Dolores fished around in her purse for her patent leather wallet. Where was the damned thing? When she handed the officer her license, he looked at it for what seemed like far too long.

"Is there something wrong?" she asked finally.

"Uh, no, ma'am," said the burly old cop. His face looked like a road map that had been folded too many times. His name plate said *Donovan*. "Do you mind if I ask you a personal question?"

Dolores looked at him with surprise, trying to imagine what he wanted to ask. "What is it?" she asked with as much dignity as possible.

"Well, I was wondering if you were any relation to Mr. Harry Tennyson . . . "

Dolores was stunned, even though she knew she shouldn't

be. "He's my husband."

The cop tilted back his hat, exhaled slowly. "Listen, ma'am, where are you headed? Maybe I can help."

"I was just going down to the Palace . . . " Dolores felt strange talking to a stranger who was suddenly acting like he knew her.

"That's still part of my beat," said Officer Donovan. "Let me drive you the rest of the way so you can relax."

Before she could respond, he was sliding in behind the wheel.

A few minutes later, they pulled up in front of a majestic-looking building on Howard Street. Hutzler's Palace, as it was known, had a beautifully ornate entrance designed to make customers feel like royalty as they approached it. It appealed to the image of what the *nouveau riche* craved. And Dolores was exactly that.

Officer Donovan parked the big Buick right in front of the main entrance and promised her there would be no citations on her windshield when she returned.

Dolores had regained her composure and walked in with an air of refinement. There was no denying it was Christmas. Every inch of the store was decorated with wreaths and holly. The Salvation Army was there in full regalia with a Santa ringing the bell for donations. Salespeople greeted her at every turn, wishing her and others a Merry Christmas. There was even a robed choir walking throughout singing *Silver Bells*.

It was enough to make Dolores sick. She feigned a smile to all who greeted her and made her way to the stairs.

At the entrance of the beauty shop stood a giant Christmas tree and as Dolores walked into the beauty shop, Trudy caught her arm.

"What in the world happened to you?"

"What do you mean?"

"Dolores, I've known you for years and I can read you like a book. It's Christmas, and you don't look very joyous. What's happened to you?"

"I almost got into an accident."

"Oh, my God! Did anyone get hurt?"

"No, but I met a policeman that knows Harry. I think they all know Harry."

Trudy had been doing Dolores' hair for years, and her coming in once a week was one of few pleasures she had.

"Come sit down right here and tell me what look you want."

"Has my mother come in yet?" Dolores asked.

"No, so let's get to the juicy stuff before she gets here," Trudy said as she wrapped a smock around her customer. "Who's going to be at your party tonight?"

"The usual crowd. A lot of stuffed shirts that I have to pretend to be honored by having them attend my party."

"You do this every year and every year you complain about it. Why do you keep it up?"

"Come on, Trudy, you know it's what I have to do. It's what's expected of Mrs. Dolores Tennyson. Although lately, I haven't been too happy with that title. It's starting again."

"You're kidding. With who?"

"I don't know, but all the signs are there."

"Don't you have any idea?" Trudy asked as she started to comb out the bird's nest that was Dolores' hair.

"Not a one," Dolores shrugged.

"Oh, come on, you've got to have some idea."

"No, really, I don't. He's quieter than usual. Disappears for hours on end. You know, the usual."

"Dolores, he *is* a busy man."

Trudy finished combing out the hairspray and led Dolores to the shampoo chair. Although there was a person for every job in the place, Trudy was the only one to work on Mrs. Tennyson. She was beautician, shampoo girl, and psychiatrist rolled into one. Dolores confided every deepest, darkest secret to this woman. She trusted her.

"Why does he do this to me, Trudy?" Tears surfaced once again. "I do *everything* for him."

"Dolores, I gotta tell ya, maybe it was a mistake to get separate bedrooms."

"What other choice did I have? I can't have him laying next to me when I know he's been with heaven only knows what kind of trash . . ."

"Men need certain things. You cut your nose off to spite your face when you did that. I told you not to . . ."

"Trudy, just wash my hair."

"All right, but don't say I didn't warn you."

Dolores knew that on some level Trudy was right. But the thought of . . . she couldn't even think about it. The warm water and Trudy's magic fingers gave Dolores a momentary break from her troubles. She let her mind drift. Funny, having her hair washed always made Dolores want to take a nap.

"Hellooo, little girl." That singsong voice could only be one person—Mary, her mother.

"Hello, Mother." Dolores opened one eye to find her mother's big blond hair and red lipsticked face staring down at her. She always wore too much makeup.

"Everything ready for the big night?" Mary asked her daughter as she took a long drag from her Pall Mall.

"Yes . . ."

"Daddy and I will be there with bells on. Isn't it grand having parties? You get all gussied up and get paraded around by your hubby. And to hobnob with the *crème de la crème*. . ."

"Mother, what did you have for lunch today?"

"What?"

"What did you have for lunch today?"

"Dear, whatever do you mean?"

Dolores wanted to ask her if she'd had tongue sandwich, the way she babbled on and on, but thought better of it. She wasn't mad at her mother. She was mad at herself for being such a pushover and not leaving Harry. But how would that look? And besides, she loved him. Didn't she?

"I was just wondering if you'd had lunch yet and what you had. Just small talk."

"Oh! Well, I met with all the girls and we had the most lovely . . . "

Dolores tuned her out and went back to her thoughts. Maybe she was being unfair to Harry. What if he was busier than usual? He *could,* after all, be working.

"All finished," Trudy said. "Let's go back to the chair."

"See you later, Mother."

The shampoo girl was busy lathering Mary's hair, so she waved "bye" at her daughter. Dolores guessed her mother, too, was off to "nappyland."

Trudy guided her to her station and again posed the question.

"It's do or die time. Get it? Doo or dye. Listen to me, will ya? I'm a regular Lucille Ball." Trudy laughed at her own joke.

"Can you suggest something to make me look younger?" Dolores' face was serious and her lips seemed to have vanished.

"Lighten up, will ya? I just made a great joke and you didn't so much as giggle."

"Trudy, I need your help. I have to look younger or more glamorous or something. Harry is surrounded by all those girls and I can't compete. I need something different." There was a sound of desperation in her voice.

"Hey, hey, just relax. I got the perfect thing for you." Trudy leaned closer over Dolores' right shoulder and whispered into her ear. "Do you trust me?"

"Yeah . . . I guess so." The answer was not one of true confidence.

"Listen, you either trust me or you don't. You can attend your party tonight looking like you usually do, or," Trudy spun Dolores around to meet her face to face, "you can be an honest to God knockout! What's it going to be?"

Dolores thought about it for a moment, bit her lower lip and said, "Do it!"

Trudy left Dolores for a few minutes to prepare, and when she came back she told Dolores of her plan.

"Platinum blond?"

"It's the latest style and the lighter color will take years off your face."

"Platinum blond? Don't you think that's a bit drastic?"

"Listen, Dolores," Trudy said as she put on her rubber gloves, "what color hair do most of the showgirls have?" Trudy didn't wait for an answer. "If Harry is getting a little on the side, what do you think this woman looks like? You want him to notice you, change your look." Trudy was speaking

114

matter-of-factly. "What are you wearing tonight?"

"I'm thinking of my black . . ."

"Forget it, Dolores. Take your wallet downstairs and buy a red dress with shoes to match. I'll put a little green bow in your hair and you'll be the belle of the ball. All eyes will be on you tonight. Harry will have no choice but to notice you. To make yourself desirable to Harry, you'll have to make yourself desirable to other men. Trust me, sweety, it's the only thing that'll work."

At that moment Mary was being led to the station next to her daughter.

Dolores stared at her mother and wondered why she was always so . . . so happy. How did a person become that way? All the other women she knew had more than their share of complaints, but not Mary Delvecchio. She could always come up with some reason to stay cheerful. Inside, Dolores screamed, Wake up! Instead she asked, "Mother, should I dye my hair?"

"Perfect! I've been wanting you to change your look for years. After all, a woman is like a car. You have to update the model every year to keep your man happy."

"Yeah, but every year cars get sleeker and sleeker," Trudy injected, laughing at her own joke.

"Dolores, you just never mind her. It's good to have a change," Mary said as she thumbed through a copy of *Life* magazine.

"You're just gonna love it, hon." Trudy turned Dolores away from the mirror and started to work her magic.

Three hours later a new Dolores emerged. Platinum blond and with much less hair. It was upswept and tied into a French knot in the back. The bow Trudy promised was small and placed discreetly in the twist of the knot.

"Trudy," Dolores was mesmerized, "is that me?"

"Yeah, hon, it's you and you're a knockout. Whadda tell ya?"

"I love it! Thank you. Mother?" Dolores' turn was much like a little girl nervously showing off her first grown-up hairdo.

"Little girl, you look absolutely divine. Let me go with you to get a new dress."

Trudy walked the two ladies to the door.

"You'll just send this bill to Harry's bookkeeper, Benny, as usual. All right, Trudy?"

"Sure, Dolores. Hey, you can hold your head up proud tonight. You look fabulous."

"Thanks, I mean it. You're a wonderful friend." Dolores pulled Trudy towards her, gave her a hug and slipped an envelope with an extremely generous Christmas tip into her hand.

Trudy reached for the door, but someone else was pulling it open and she stumbled trying to reach it, but caught herself. As the door opened, Dolores found herself eye to eye with a woman sporting her exact hairdo, color and all. It was almost like looking in the mirror, except her reflection was much younger.

"Katherine, it's you!" Trudy seemed a bit surprised. The four women stood there staring at each other for what seemed to Dolores an eternity. Finally, Trudy spoke.

"Dolores Tennyson, meet Katherine Louise. She's the one that inspired me to give you this new hairdo. She works down the Desert Club."

"They say imitation is the sincerest form of flattery." Katherine's manner was confident as she addressed Trudy and walked past without so much as glancing in Dolores' direction, then said, "Very nice to make your acquaintance, Mrs. Tennyson."

Dolores slowly turned to Trudy and whispered, "Why did you say that in front of her?"

Trudy stood there shaking her head and said, "Hey, I didn't mean nothing by it. Honest."

Dolores hadn't heard a word. She had already walked out of the shop.

THIRTEEN

THe Block

There were a number of powerful, influential, and wealthy people who came into the Desert Club. Not wanting to be seen by the crowd watching the stripper out front, they hung in the bar at the back. They liked the action back there where bookies and other characters hung out. There were bankers, politicians, Westinghouse executives, judges, etc. The entertainment was cabaret style where the strippers danced around and sat on your lap if you were seated at a table. They were not to be confused with "sitters" who solicited drinks and sex but did not dance at the club.

Kenny Hadel had what they called the "picture concession" at a nightclub uptown called the Club Charles. It was a decent racket where he would go around the tables and find tourists and couples who wanted a memento of their big night out. He'd flash them with his big 8x10 press camera, run downstairs to a hurry-up darkroom in the basement, and give them their print that same night.

When he decided to expand, as all good businessmen do, he just walked into the Florida Club on The Block and started taking pictures. He had a buddy parked in an old Jewel Tea Company van on Holliday Street where he was developing the prints. Things were okay until he thought he could get pictures of the best-paying customers at Harry's Desert Club.

Big mistake.

Harry walked up behind Kenny Hadel and grabbed him by the collar as Big Syd grabbed his Grafflex camera.

"You keep your business up on Charles Street," Harry told him, "or you got no business at all."

And that was the last time Kenny thought about expansion.

Harry got his nickname, The Lord, because of his lofty position as the unofficial top man around The Block. It's obvious, though, that whoever nicknamed Harry Tennyson The Lord still remembered the British writer Alfred, Lord Tennyson from twelfth-grade English class. However, this reference to the author of the "Charge of the Light Brigade" was lost on most of Harry's friends and associates who had trouble with the days of the week and using a fork.

Originally, Harry was a cab driver who used to be a "beard"—that is, he made bets for bookmakers who thought they had a sure thing on a fixed horse race or ball game. What happened was that Tennyson once "booked" the bets himself, he didn't pass the money on to another bookie. He took a risk, made thousands of dollars, and became a major racketeer.

FOURTEEN

DOLORES TENNYSON

Dolores took a step back and surveyed her table. Eugenia had polished the silver to perfection and the Baccarat crystal shimmered beneath the soft glow of the chandelier. Her mother's antique linen tablecloth fell exquisitely to the floor and the new holiday china with miniature holly berries adorned each place setting. She reached over to rearrange a stray flower on the centerpiece and smiled. Elaine Stevenson will be impressed. A lot of thought and preparation had gone into planning the perfect Christmas dinner party. The goal was to create an elegant and intimate setting for ten that would allow Dolores to be at the helm at all times. Harry may be the man of the house, but she was the hostess of this little get-together.

The guests had been carefully selected. Mother and Daddy were a must. Then there would be the chief of police, Bob Kilpatrick and his wife, Irene, and State Senator Ed Higgins and his new lady-friend, Judy. He'd been seeing her for about a year now, his first serious relationship since his wife's death two years ago. And, of course, George and Elaine Stevenson were invited. George's company sold formstone, an economical housing facade that was fast becoming the rage in many city neighborhoods. He had made a killing last year, and he and Elaine had spent the summer traveling throughout the Riviera. Dolores would give anything to go to France. She had all sorts of coffee-table books from Paris and the Riviera, but so far Harry had only managed a train ticket to New York.

As she made her way to the kitchen, she paused to admire herself in the hallway mirror. She brushed a loose strand away from her cheek and turned to adjust the gold comb at the back of her head. Trudy was right—the new color did suit her. Yes, Harry will definitely notice me now, she thought.

The off-the-shoulder red dress was sleek and formfitting with a slit to the knee and tiny, silk-covered buttons that ran down the back. The red peau de soie pumps were a perfect match and quarter-carat diamond earrings sparkled in her ears.

"Eugenia," she called out as she entered the kitchen, "don't forget, soup first, then salad, and be sure you offer the senator oil and vinegar. He's allergic to dairy products. Also, serve from the left and don't speak unless spoken to."

"Yes, ma'am."

"I hope you've explained to your niece how important this evening is. If she wants the opportunity to work for me again she'd better do a good job tonight."

"Don't worry, Mrs. Tennyson. I've made it perfectly clear to Ruby what you expect of us. She's a good worker and she'll do as I say."

"Fine. I'm sure you realize that her performance is a direct reflection upon you. I don't want any mishaps."

Dolores made a mental checklist: the oysters Rockefeller first, followed by lobster bisque and Caesar salad, then linguine smothered in onions, and the main course of rolled tenderloin with ham and artichoke hearts. For dessert, a simple flan would be served. She stood poised at the counter, her red lacquered nails tapping impatiently, and wondered where the hell Harry was. Just then she heard the door open and she caught his reflection in the chrome of the Waring blender. She stood motionless, waiting for his reaction.

"Eugenia, where's Dolores?"

She raised an eyebrow and slowly turned to face him.

"Harry, I never realized you were so familiar with the help."

"What the . . .?"

This was a rare moment. Harry was speechless, which made Dolores a tad uncomfortable. She didn't know what to make of his reaction.

"What did you do?"

"Do you like it, Harry?" she asked quietly, sounding a little more pathetic than she intended.

"Do you think this look is suitable for a woman your age? What with the children and church and the PTA, what will people think? You trying to look cheap or something?"

His words cut through her but she fought back the urge to cry. She wasn't going to let him see how he hurt her.

"Well, Harry, I did it for you, but besides that I thought it was time for a change. Trudy at the beauty shop kind of talked me into it. She got the idea from another one of her customers, Katherine something or other . . . "

Harry seemed to straighten at the mention of the name. Dolores couldn't help but notice his discomfort as his eyes darted around the room in search of more comfortable ground. Dolores wasn't about to let him off easy.

"Katherine Louise, yes, that's it," she paused for emphasis. "You must know her Harry, she works at the club. One of the better dancers from what I hear. Do you know her Harry?" She moved casually across the floor to him and reached out her hand.

"Here, darling, let me take your coat."

He handed it to her silently. His loss for words was all she needed to know that Katherine was indeed his latest.

"You have twenty minutes to shower and change," she said as she walked out of the room.

Dolores handed the senator his drink and returned to her perch on the ottoman near Elaine Stevenson. They were discussing the latest line of hats on display at Hutzler's and admiring each other's shoes. The party was in full swing and everyone appeared to be enjoying themselves. Judy Sweeny extricated herself from the senator's clutches and made her way towards Dolores and Elaine. The neckline of her dress scooped dangerously low and Dolores feared the worst as the woman leaned over to rest her drink on the coffee table. Elaine rolled her eyes in distaste as Dolores forced herself to feign interest.

"So, tell me, Judy, how did you and the senator meet?"

The woman sauntered over to the love seat and sat down.

"I used to work for Patuxent Cruises, and last summer we sponsored a floating casino night for some of the big companies in town. Harry was having a big night at the craps table where I was helping out. All the senators were there, and Harry introduced me to Edward."

As Judy droned on about her fabulous luck at landing a state senator, Dolores wondered who had been Harry's companion that night because it certainly hadn't been his wife. She spied him out of the corner of her eye making small talk with the police chief and her father. We've got them all fooled, she thought. They think we have the perfect marriage.

She checked her watch. It was five 'til eight, time to usher everyone in to dinner.

The ladies complimented her on her table as Harry directed the seating.

"You've done it again, Dolores," George, the formstone king, spoke. "Everything looks and tastes wonderful. It must feel good to have a husband taking care of you so you have the time to make these get-togethers perfect."

"I guess so, but I do a little more . . ."

"My little girl does throw a swell party. My little woman here taught her well," Delvecchio wheezed out.

Dolores' mother puffed out like a peacock on display.

"Like I always told Dolores, the secret to a good marriage and happy home is to keep your man proud of you at all times. Right, dear?"

"Yes, Mother. Well, Harry, are you proud of me?" She didn't know what had come over her to ask such a thing in public, but it felt good.

"You know how I feel about you, Dolores." Harry's answer was noncommittal as usual. He steered the conversation in another direction.

The sonofabitch did it again, she thought. Although on the exterior everything was peachy to her guests, Dolores realized her attempts to draw Harry back to her were not working. She'd have to come up with a new strategy.

The dinner continued without a hitch. Small talk ensued back and forth with Judy making a complete and utter fool of herself. What could the senator have been thinking of? Dolores hoped she wouldn't be accompanying him on his future campaign trail.

After coffee and dessert were served, Harry suggested the men follow him to the library for cigars and cordials. The ladies retired to the living room.

Elaine Stevenson was telling the group about her trip abroad when Eugenia entered the room, excused herself to the guests and whispered to Dolores, "Excuse me, Mrs. Tennyson, there is a Deputy Chief Applegate at the door wishing to speak with the chief."

Dolores took it in stride. Having officials at her party lent itself to such occasions. She stood up and excused herself from the rest of the group.

As she walked towards the deputy chief, she checked her reflection in the mirror. I don't care what Harry says, I look good, she thought to herself.

She approached the high-ranking police officer. "Good evening, Deputy Chief Applegate. I see that there is no such thing as a night off when one works in public office."

"I'm awfully sorry to disturb you, Mrs. Tennyson, but it's my understanding that I can reach Chief Kilpatrick here tonight. His orders specified emergencies only, and I'm afraid we've got one."

"Oh, my, I hope it's nothing too serious," she said, thinking immediately how silly she must sound to him.

"Please come with me," she said, escorting him to the library.

Fifteen

Harry Tennyson

"An old joke goes this way: My father told me never to go to a burlesque show 'cause I'd see something I shouldn't see. Finally, I went to a burlesque show. He was right. I did see something I shouldn't see. I saw my father sitting in the second row."

The men in Harry's library laughed and nodded their heads in agreement at what he had just said. They had taken time out of Tennyson's annual Christmas party to discuss a little business. The wives hated that part of the evening, but it gave Harry the opportunity he needed to bring him a little closer to the politicos in attendance, and it gave them a nice break away from their wives' trivial chatter.

After the room quieted, Harry continued, "Gentlemen, I don't understand what all the commotion is about. Business is as good if not better than it's been. Look at what's happening uptown. Those fine supper clubs and night clubs are *dying*. Money isn't what it used be, what with the shipyards and aircraft plants closing up. The fabulous forties are over! We need to keep doing what we're doing."

Harry surveyed the room. He could see he had their attention. He glanced at his father-in-law, sloppy as always, he thought, but still very powerful.

"We just got to keep the do-gooders quiet." Robert Kilpatrick, the chief of police, sounded like a broken record. No matter what problems arose, he always chanted the same song, his mantra, so to speak.

"There's been a lot of talk about prostitution running rampant down The Block . . . . "

"And there's another thing," Harry interrupted the chief mid-sentence. "Maybe it's time we changed the name of our little corner of the world."

"Yeah, right. To what?" The gruff voice could only belong to one person, Vincenzo Delvecchio, his father-in-law.

"I've been doing some research into that and what I've decided on is 'The Great White Way.' It seems to me that it's the perfect solution. We get some public relations men to do the job. They'll build up a whole new image for us and that should keep everyone at bay. We as club owners can't deny our ladies the opportunity to make a little money on the side, can we? After all, this is America, land of the free, right, Senator Higgins?"

"Hey, isn't that what they call Times Square?" asked the chief, but nobody answered him.

"That's true, Harry, but when my constituents start yelling morality, I have to do as they request. After all, I am a public servant and have taken an oath . . ."

"Yeah, yeah, yeah, get off your soap box." Delvecchio stopped Senator Edward T. Higgins from continuing with his campaign speech. He turned to Harry, chomped down on his cigar a few times and asked, "What is it you want, my boy? You want us to turn the other way? You want us to allow you to continue to corrupt the citizenry of this great state?" He chuckled at his own remark, then suddenly got serious. "Just stay out of trouble, Harry. Be careful of your associates and stay out of our way. Don't mess with anyone that can bring you down or will give us cause to have to intervene in your goings-on. We all like to visit your establishment. We like the girlies up on stage. Shit, just take one look at your mother-in-law, son. I love her and all, but I need to look at some fresh new pussy *once* in awhile. We can't have the likes of—Bobby, what was the name of that little nigger?"

"Little Marvin."

"Yeah, that little 'coon, Marvin, calling for you from jail ain't good news, Harry. I won't bother with why he did. I don't care, just don't let us get wind of that kinda stuff, because—"

Dolores tapped lightly and slipped past the library door to face the assembled group. "Excuse me, gentlemen . . . "

They stared up at her from beneath a thick layer of cigar smoke—except for Harry, who sprang from his chair and advanced upon her. Leaning close, he whispered harshly in her ear, "I thought I told you *never* to interrupt me when I'm doing business in this room."

She seemed to enjoy ignoring him, continuing to look at the group of men as she said, "I have a Deputy Chief Applegate here to see the chief. He says it's an emergency."

As if on cue, a youngish-looking, blond-haired man wearing a trench coat slipped in behind Dolores. He looked embarrassed but resigned to his duty.

Genuinely surprised, the chief stood up and looked at his officer. "What is it, Applegate?"

"May I speak to you in private, sir?"

"Nonsense, Applegate, don't you know who these men are?" The chief gestured at the men sitting in the library. "We have no secrets in this room."

"Sir, I have sensitive information." Applegate stood there shifting his hat from one hand to the other. The fact that he was nervous to be there was lost on no one.

"I'll tell you what," said Delvecchio. "Stevenson, would you mind leaving the room for a few moments while we discuss this matter with the deputy chief?"

"No, not at all. Politics was never my bailiwick anyway." George started out of the room.

"Your what?" said the councilman.

Everyone chuckled nervously and the formstone king used

that opportunity to exit gracefully.

"Sir." The deputy chief stared at Harry. "Maybe it would be a good idea if you left the room also."

"Nonsense! Harry, you stay put." The chief was getting flustered. "Listen, Applegate, it's one thing for us to send out that one fella, but you can't kick a man out of his own library. Whatever is so important, just say it."

"Perhaps we should leave the two of you alone." It was the senator's turn to speak. "Applegate made a good point. Let the two of you hash this out, and if you should need our input then we can discuss it. But until that time, why don't we do things the way they should be done."

"Why, you spineless wimp," said Delvecchio.

It was apparent to Harry that his district councilman's tank was, as usual, more than half full while the evening was still young. No bourbon bottle was safe when Vinny Delvecchio was in the room.

"What about all that bullshit about caring for your constituents? Aren't you the least bit interested in the day-to-day of your hometown?"

"That's not the point, Vinny. And get your finger outta my face."

"Gentlemen, can we *please* get to the bottom of this?" Harry knew the routine, they'd go at it for hours if someone didn't stop them.

"I'm not so sure—"

"Applegate, I am ordering you to tell me what has brought you all the way here to Greenspring Valley and given you reason to disturb me at this lovely party."

"Sir, there's been a murder."

"Murder?" the chief looked to be in utter disbelief. "You came down here to tell me about a *murder?*"

"This one's different, Chief. It happened at the Surf Club."

"On Monument Street?" Delvecchio's face was flushed. "Hey, that's my district!"

"The facts as we know them are as follows . . . " Deputy Chief Applegate reached for his notebook out of his coat pocket. He flipped a few pages and began to read.

Sixteen

Marvin Harper

A big, shiny Cadillac pulled up to the front of 3204 Dukeland Street at precisely 11 p.m., and Leroy Johnson was already waiting by the porch steps.

"Okay, Leroy, you ready?" Little Marvin Harper rolled down the car window and asked his newest associate.

"Yep, I got it down cold. I even got a busboy uniform, see?" He opened his coat and grinned as he walked towards the car.

"Leroy!" It was a woman's voice that echoed in the darkness. "You get your bony, little ass back in this house NOW!"

"Forget it, Mama." Leroy jogged the few feet remaining and got in the car.

"Sweet Jesus, that woman can drive you insane if you let her. Bitch thinks she can run my life," Leroy said somewhat apologetically to Marvin.

"Leroy, are you sure you're ready?"

"I go in, collect, get out. I got it."

The car's next stop was the Surf Club on Monument Street. Little Marvin watched Leroy disappear through the kitchen door. He smiled inwardly and could hardly believe what had happened to him in the last few months. And all this thanks to a white dude that called himself The Lord. Jeeez!

Harry The Lord Tennyson had promised Little Marvin the world and had amazingly delivered. Even gotten him out of jail with no charges placed against him. Marvin marveled at the fact that that had been the only real stumbling block in his quest for the gold. Taking hold of the East Side, with Harry Tennyson backing him, had been like taking candy from a baby. The Lord had taken care of everything, even set up the runners. Three nice, innocent-looking white chicks. If their mamas and daddies had any idea what their little princesses were up to—

The door to the alley swung outward, banging into the nearest trash can. Looking up just in time, Marvin saw Leroy and a big, beefy white guy come staggering across the threshold like two awkward partners in a marathon dance contest. They were holding on to each other's clothes and both yelling at once. The white guy broke loose, flinging Leroy across the opposite wall of the alley.

"I never bought my smack from no kitchen-help nigger, and I ain't about to start now."

Leroy kept his distance but stood tall.

"Well, in case you haven't noticed, the times have changed," he said. "You been ridin' a pretty tall Horse my man, and nobody rides for free!"

This seemed to only infuriate Sonny Wycheck even more. "Listen buddy, if your boss wants his money, tell him to come down here and get it himself." He turned his wide shoulders as if to re-enter the club, dismissing Leroy Johnson without waiting for a reply.

The reply he got was one he could have never expected.

Marvin had to smile as he watched Leroy launch himself after Wycheck like a chicken hawk after a fat old hen. He was on the white jazz drummer before he'd taken his first step into the kitchen. The two men went down in a flurry of quickly thrown punches, and trash barrels started rolling around making a hell of a noise. Little Marvin was proud of Leroy but he knew he couldn't let it go on. Business was too good to get this kind of bad publicity.

As he reached for the door handle to his Coupe de Ville, he took his eyes off the alley fight only for an instant.

But, in that short amount of time, something happened between Sonny Wycheck and Leroy Johnson. Things changed from ugly to deadly. Turning to face the two men, Marvin saw something flash in the solitary street lamp and he knew it was Leroy's blade.

Don't cut him! Lord Jesus, don't cut the white man!

But Leroy couldn't hear him, and it probably wouldn't have stopped him anyway. Johnson's eyes widened, glaring at the red-faced man looming over him. In a wide swinging arc, the knife slashed into the loose, flabby skin of Wycheck's neck. The drummer gurgled out a wet scream that Marvin knew would be the last sound he would ever make. Leroy was up and running like he was getting timed in the hundred-yard dash, as Sonny Wycheck slid down the side of the alley trying to put himself back together.

Jumping back into the car, Marvin keyed the ignition. The Caddy's big V-8 rumbled to life and the back wheels started spinning against the loose gravel by the curb. As Marvin wheeled the land yacht away from the alley, Leroy was hanging on to the "shotgun" door.

SEVENTEEN

HARRY TENNYSON

" . . . and I've got three eyewitnesses who made Little Marvin's powder blue Coupe de Ville leaving the scene." Applegate closed his notebook.

An awkward silence surrounded them like a bad odor. The men were clearly uncomfortable with the implications of Applegate's report. One by one, they all turned to look at the same man—Harry The Lord Tennyson.

Harry sat there like a statue, afraid to move. He was trapped. Glad he'd been there to hear it all and, at the same time, wishing he had left the room. He *knew* what they were thinking. They had spoken volumes with their silence. He felt the blood racing through his veins, and the loud thumping of his heart overshadowed any chance he had to make a clear decision.

All he could think of was Mutiny on the Bounty. A few short minutes ago he had them in the palm of his hand. Now their stares bore holes into him, draining him of energy and resolve.

"Shit!" Delvecchio pounded his fist into his hand. "We

shouldn't have let him go."

"Even if we'd kept him, he'd 'a been out by now. But that ain't the problem." The chief turned to face Applegate. "Where's Marvin now?"

"We haven't been able to locate him. We've issued an APB, and we've posted sketched composites of Marvin in the area surrounding the club. So far, we've turned up nothing." The deputy chief's voice was emotionless.

"Sonny Wycheck. Why does that name sound familiar to me?" the senator said to no one in particular.

"Sir, we need to notify a next of kin, but we wanted to check with you first. Sonny Wycheck was pretty well-known. Wouldn't be surprised if his murder made the papers." The deputy chief looked stiff and uptight. He needed a blowjob in the worst way. Harry could have set him up, but it didn't look like he was in any position to make an offer.

"We can't have that!" The senator began to pace the length of the floor. "Let's not have those nosey reporters involved. They live for this kind of stuff. Can you imagine what they'd do?" He turned to face Harry. "Why would Marvin be there again?"

This was the first time Harry had been addressed and it caught him off guard. He stumbled over his words. "I don't know. As a matter of fact, I don't know why he was there in the first place." Beads of sweat appeared on Harry's forehead.

Easy now, Harry, get a grip on yourself, remain calm, remain calm, he repeated over and over to himself. He clenched his fist so tight his knuckles were turning white. He had nothing to worry about. He hadn't made contact with Marvin for a long period of time. These were politicians, after all, and they were doing what they did best—pinning the blame on someone. Boy, they sure did work fast. Not two seconds after they got their information and already they're setting up a political scapegoat. Well it ain't gonna be me! Harry thought.

"Come off it, Harry!" Delvecchio's drinking was faster now. "It's always bugged me that Marvin asked for you. You put my butt in a sling back then, but I managed to smooth things out for you. But now, now you have to—"

"Now hold on one minute. Surely you're not suggesting I put Marvin up to this, are you?" Harry stood up and walked towards the councilman.

"Why'd he call for you, Harry?" Delvecchio's upper lip curved into a sneer.

"Jesus Christ, you crazy old bastard! That was over a year ago!" Harry couldn't believe what the councilman was implying. "Look, it's simple. Little Marvin hit big on a number. He called me, wanted to make a deal. Said if I could get him out of a jackpot with the cops, he'd trade it for his winnings."

"You can't be serious. You can't expect us to believe that little black muskrat had the sense to do something like that, can you?" Delvecchio's rage combined with the booze was beginning to make him sound like a madman.

Suddenly Harry balled his hand into a tight fist and without thinking about it, without even winding up, struck Vinnie Delvecchio square in the jaw.

The old guy's face lit up like a pinball machine when you hit the "extra ball" socket. The blow actually forced the breath out of his jowly cheeks, and the air rattled with the sound of collapsing bellows.

"Good God, Harry!" screamed the senator.

"Stop him!" said somebody else, but there was no need.

Harry's rage was spent, and Delvecchio was already sliding down the side of a Regency-style chair to become one with the Persian rug. His eyes had rolled back and his lids struggled to cover up the whites. His mouth bled from the corner.

Harry just stood there, feeling everybody watching him, and he suddenly realized what it must feel like to be nailed into a coffin. The air all around him was disappearing. He felt the walls closing in. He couldn't believe that what his own father-in-law had said had goaded him into sucker-punching the old guy. He started to walk out the door, but the police chief grabbed hold of Harry's arm and said, "You'd better tell us all you know."

Harry stormed towards the door, but the senator stopped him.

"You're sweating, Harry. It's not pleasant to see anybody

sweat. It gives others the feeling you're trying to hide something. You're not hiding anything, are you, Harry?"

"Let go of me, Senator." Harry yanked out of the senator's grasp, leaned close and whispered, "I will be most willing to discuss this matter with the police. I have absolutely nothing to hide. I don't know why this murder happened. I have, I repeat, nothing to hide. You, Senator, should not be so quick to judge." Harry turned to see his guests staring at him. They painted an interesting picture. The formstone king returned, glass in hand, his mouth gaping.

Then the the women appeared at the entrance to the room, just in time to see Councilman Delvecchio fumbling to his feet, looking like he'd been dragged through a bar fight. The women looked appropriately shocked. Harry's three so-called closest friends were plotting against him. Harry, having composed himself a little, spoke evenly in a soft whisper.

"I think it'd be best if the party came to a close. There's not much to celebrate, considering the unfortunate circumstances surrounding this evening." He turned to face the police chief. "I would be very happy to lend my assistance in this investigation, Bobby. Is nine a.m. a good time for us to meet tomorrow?"

"Yeah, nine's good." The police chief looked down at his shoes.

Harry turned and walked up the stairs.

He closed the door behind him and loosened his tie. His room had everthing a man could want, right down to his own private telephone line. Imagine that, two lines in one house. It was times like these when he missed Katherine the most. He walked over to the bed, sat down and picked up the phone. It seemed forever before she picked up.

"Hello." The voice was soft and sexy.

"Hey, babe, I miss you."

"Harry!" She squealed at the sound of his voice. "Did you leave your party just to call me?"

"The party was a disaster. It's over."

"Oh."

He heard the disappointment in her voice. He should have

lied.

"Katherine, I wish I could be with you right now."

"Come over, make some excuse, or tell the truth, Harry. Just tell the witch, 'I'm sorry to hurt you but I have to go be with the woman I love.' Tell her you don't love her, Harry."

"Katherine, relax. I called you to hear your sweet voice and to tell you that I'll see you tomorrow. I have something I need to talk to you about. "

"Good, because I need to talk to you, too. There's something I need to tell you . . ." Her voice changed. It had an edge to it.

"Look, if you're gonna harp on me about Dolores again—"

"Harry, I'll see you tomorrow, okay?" She cut him off. "I need to get off the line now, I'm expecting a call from my mother." She softened again, but he knew the "mother" thing was a lie. Katherine hadn't spoken to her for a long time. Since he wasn't in the mood for any more confrontations, he decided to play along.

"All right, see you tomorrow." He heard the click of the phone before she had the chance to hear him say, "I love you."

Harry had been so wrapped up in the conversation with Katherine he hadn't heard the door open. He turned to face Dolores. She was standing with her hand on the door knob, glaring at him.

"Who was that on the phone, Harry? Was it Syd?"

"What do you want, Dolores?" he said as he continued to undress.

"I want to know what's happening. What was that scene downstairs all about?! I want to know who was on the phone. I want to know—"

"Dolores," Harry took a deep breath, "what happened downstairs was a mistake. A guy got killed. Tempers flared. Your father and I will take care of things. I'll be working with Bobby to clear it up."

There were tears in her eyes. "And on the phone, Harry?"

"That was nothing that concerns you. I was just taking care of a few things, cleaning up some loose ends."

"Do you always clean up loose ends with 'I love you'?"

He was tired and she was bugging him. Little Marvin, Katherine, and now, Dolores. If this was a test, it was too much for one man to take. All he wanted was some rest. He'd be able to take care of everything if everyone would just leave him alone for a little while.

"Tell me, Harry! Tell me who was on the phone." She walked into the room and stood in front of him, legs apart and fists clenched. Damn she had nice legs. Too bad they led to a glacier. He looked at her face and saw her father. Right now he hated her father more than he'd ever hated anyone before. He lost it. He walked over to Dolores and pushed her.

"What the fuck do you want from me, Dolores? I have enough to think about without you harping on me about every little thing. It was business."

Dolores was visibly shaken—he'd never touched her like that before and she looked like a deer caught in headlights. And what she did next he never expected out of his mousy little wife. She straightened up, got a steely expression and said, "Don't you ever touch me like that again. I have put up with much too much from you. I've looked the other way when you've cheated on me. I've looked the other way when you've lied to me and my father. But I won't look away anymore. Hear this, Harry The Lord Tennyson," her words full of contempt, "you *will* be a husband to me. You *will* treat me with respect and courtesy. Because if you don't, I *will* tell my father, and I *will* bring down Harry The Lord Tennyson." Her tone was deliberate and slow.

"Are you threatening me?" Harry felt a vein pulsing at his temple.

"Think of it what you will." She was calm, too calm—it unnerved Harry to see her this way. He was the one who had the upper hand. This wasn't the way it was supposed to be. "Oh, and Harry, tomorrow that telephone comes out! Syd will just have to rest easy without your nightly 'I love you'." She walked past him without a glance, her head held up high. "I'll expect you in my bedroom. A husband sleeps with his wife."

138

EIGHTEEN

The Article

Baltimore's Block in those early days of the twenties and thirties was awash in contradictions. Congressmen and society debs, black-tied gentlemen and fur-clad ladies paraded the streets alongside the prostitutes and the fun-seekers. Alcohol was cheap. A bit of the bubbly sold for 10 cents a glass and the entertainment was often the crème-de-la-crème of the East Coast nightclub circuit.

And The Block was even a popular hangout for kids. The obvious reasons aside, during the day it was a Saturday afternoon treat. One older gentleman, David Stein, remembers his youth.

". . . in 1933, I could get a quarter, and it would last all day. The number 15 streetcar cost a nickel, a hot dog and soda or two hot dogs were a nickel, and it cost 10 cents to see a movie."

What more could you ask for? "They even had a side show, over near the 408 Club at Playland. You could see snakes and raccoons in cages, a bearded lady and a sword swallower, and a lady doing the shimmy." All the women wore costumes that stayed on.

There was another club back in the thirties and forties that was big business. The Two O'Clock Club featured a glamorous chorus of girls who reflected what America wanted to see at that time. Beautiful, naive women, often blond, who simply entertained.

One afternoon, one such damsel appeared for a three p.m. chorus rehearsal, looked up at the clock on the sign over the club with its hands fixed at two o'clock, decided she was early for work and returned to the Lord Baltimore Hotel to get another hour's rest. Perhaps one such blond beauty inspired H.L. Mencken's companion, Anita Loos, in her most famous character, Lorelei Lee, of "Gentlemen Prefer Blondes." These performers were American beauties whose naivete was most often genuine and whose optimism was reflective of the audiences to which they catered.

In addition, the club was home to tango teams, and "Astaire-Rogers" dancers, and one favorite juicy tale. The Two O'Clock Club featured a solo artistic dancer named Roberta Jonay, who just happened to be a protégée of First Lady, Eleanor Roosevelt. Ms. Jonay, a close friend of the first family, was a guest at FDR's White House and at Hyde Park. However, when she debuted on stage in Baltimore, and Two O'Clock Club owner Sam Lampe delivered a kind invitation to the First Lady, the White House issued a terse, but refined decline. Ms. Jonay went on to become a Baltimore favorite, and for years her words of wisdom on beauty and exercise were copiously detailed by the local papers for all women to admire and emulate. Is it any wonder that the revered Mrs. Roosevelt elected to disassociate herself?

Each club on The Block had a host. Not a barker, which is what you'll find today, but a well-dressed doorman who stayed inside and greeted people as they entered. A doorman made $15 a week, a fortune considering a beer was only 25 cents and drinks for the girls would run you 35 cents. Former doorman, Joe Finazzo, remembers the days he hosted at clubs like Lucky Eleven and the Gayety Theatre.

"Everyone came for the shows at the Gayety," he recalls. "Then they'd go visit the bars on The Block. The Gayety sold bottled beer for 50 cents, even through the fifties. There was a gym above the club, and this guy Benny used to promote fights back then. A lot *of champions came by to work out or just socialize . . . guys like Max Baer, Rocky Marciano, Joe DiMaggio and Mickey Mantle."* Imagine that. Joe DiMaggio and Mickey Mantle hanging out in a small gym on The Block in Baltimore!

"Yeah, so the Gayety used to have a burlesque and boxing show on Friday nights. It only cost a dollar and ran from nine 'til two a.m. It was even cheaper if you wanted to sit in the "peanut gallery" . . . you know, you go up the fire escape to the upper balcony on the third floor. Nobody even asked for your age card— if you looked eighteen, you got in. If you didn't, back down the fire escape you went."

World War II brought a flock of servicemen to the doors of The Block. They would visit Frenchy the tattoo artist, who also ran a 25-cents-a-day boarding house. Frenchy had studied the art of tattoo with the great De Saule, but perfected the pigmentation technique with his 110-volt vibrator to create quick, painless tattoos which could be implanted in eight colors and in designs of the servicemen's choosing.

There was a great story which took place in the forties. A gorgeous woman named Hilde used to frequent the old Oasis club and talk to the sailors. She was really a spy for the German government, and a lot of military and supply ships blew up because of the information she got from the sailors. Jack Mallot, the political boss, found out about it and advised the FBI. They set Hilde up one night and caught her. She was arrested and convicted of espionage. Years later, Jack was given a medal by J. Edgar Hoover.

As the war years progressed, support industries in Baltimore were booming. Bethlehem Steel Corporation, Maryland Dry Dock and Westinghouse were all busy. The city was going full speed ahead, and The Block thrived as the place where everyone headed for fun. Celebrities such as Martha Raye and Jackie Cooper came to town.

After World War II, many clubs on The Block emerged with a new and decidedly more obvious format. The country was a different place. Television was taking hold and competition for an audience to entertain was fierce. Clubs popped up on The Block boasting more provocative names like Club Pussycat and Club Inferno. The names connoted the shift in appeal from the *pearly to the prurient. The "bump and grind" of girlie shows and go-go was born.*

Nineteen

Harry Tennyson

"Harry! What a surprise!" Katherine's eyes glowed with excitement.

"Yeah? Let me tell ya about surprises." Harry stumbled and fell into her apartment. His hair was messed up and his breath smelled like he had just gargled with Jack Daniel's. He was high and he loved it, anything to numb his senses. But it wasn't enough. What he had learned today would need a lot more than a bottle of sour mash to cure. He would need a good fuck, too. "You wanna know about a surprise?"

"Oh, Harry, you've been drinking." Katherine rushed to his aid. She tried to help him up but he kept falling down. They did this little dance four more times until she let him go.

"You, my love, need coffee. I'll go make a fresh pot."

As she turned to walk away, Harry grabbed hold of her ankle which made her stumble backwards and fall dramatically into his arms.

"Harry, playing a little rough, are you? Well, Daddy, your little kitten just loves that," she purred.

Harry grasped the bun in her hair and pulled it backwards. Katherine smiled a very sexy, turned-on smile. Her eyes were half closed and her lips turned into a pout.

"What is it you want, Daddy?" She asked in a whiskey voice. "Do you want what Mommy has?" She placed her hand to Harry's crotch and squeezed.

"What's in there, Daddy? Is it a present for me?"

All Katherine had to do was talk and Harry would be able to "come" right there on the spot.

"Yeah, baby, it's for you." He let go of her hair and she kneeled between his legs.

"Can I open it, Daddy? Can I open my present?" She didn't wait for an answer. His pants were unzipped and she gently pulled out his dick.

"Oh, Daddy, it's so big! I wonder if I can put it all in my mouth? Can I try?"

She licked up and down the sides of his dick, stopping at the top to suck. She took the entire thing in her mouth and made noises of ecstasy as though this was the best thing she'd ever tasted. Not one part of him was ignored. While she sucked and licked, his balls felt the gentle touch of her hands. Just as he was ready to explode, she stopped and asked, "Can you put it in me now? I need it now, baby!" She stood up, slipped out of her skirt, and straddled his body. Once the panties were off, she positioned her pussy right in front of Harry's face.

"Eat me," she said as she grabbed Harry's head and forced it between her legs.

"Eat me, Daddy."

He grabbed her firm ass and held on as she rode his face. Somehow they managed to get Katherine flat on her back. Harry stood up and quickly slid his pants off. She laid there playing with her pussy lips.

"Daddy, please hurry, I need you in me now!"

"You want this? Is this what you want, you little slut?" Harry's face was turning red as he pushed his body into hers.

"Do me, Daddy, yeah, just like that." He looked at her face and wondered for a brief moment if she was faking any of this.

"This pussy belongs to you, take it whenever you want," she whispered breathlessly into his ear.

Who cares if she's faking it, he thought. She was the roller coaster at Coney Island, she was Citation going down the stretch, she was like an engine ready to break its seals. He could feel her squeezing him, kneading him, *working* him. And the whole time she never took her eyes off him. Face to face, Harry stared into her eyes and felt like he was leaning beyond the edge of a cliff. There was a pressure building that was going to push him over. And he had this feeling that if he fell to the bottom of her blue eyes he'd never reach the surface again.

"Now you have to fuck me, Daddy."

"Jesus Christ! What do you *think* I'm doing!" Harry felt himself pistoning in and out of her without effort, without thought even. She brought out every natural reaction a man could have and left him wanting for more.

"I want all of it, Harry. Give me every inch of you. Give me everything you've got. I need everything! Give it to me, Harry."

There was something about the way she spoke those lines that seemed almost too much in control, too much more meaning than he wanted to admit. If he wasn't on the ride of his life, if the alarm bells weren't sounding to abandon ship, he might have given this last notion more attention. But there was more direct and dirty business to take care of. Katherine grabbed him with muscles no woman should have without a permit and yanked the biggest load out of him since he was sixteen years old.

Rolling off and staring up at the ceiling, he fought the feelings of total exhaustion. He pulled himself onto her sofa and caught a glimpse of her hand still between her legs. She was massaging it, playing with it as if she could extend the moment in a kind of afterglow. He tried not to watch, but couldn't help himself as she licked herself off her fingers. She did this with a flourish that was not graceful. And it was certainly not sexy to him. The word *slut* crossed his mind. Suddenly he realized how sick-drunk he was. His equilibrium was barely good enough to keep him from wobbling off the couch. He had rug burns on his elbows and knees, and whose crazy goddamn idea was it to do it on the floor anyway?

He watched her stand and approach him. The closer she drew to the couch the more pungent the odor of their sex assaulted him.

"Wanna lick, Harry?"

"Please, don't be disgusting."

She laughed cynically. "Disgusting? If I'm so disgusting maybe you should forget about the coffee and leave." Stalking off to the bathroom, she pulled a robe off the back of the door and covered herself in a quick reversal of form. She was back in an instant leaning over him like a harridan.

"I'm not kidding, Harry. Get out of here right now!"

Realizing she meant business, he struggled to get some coherency in his thoughts and keep the slur out of his voice.

"It's not you, baby. I'm sorry, but I have a lot on my mind, and not much of it's very good."

He told her about the murder, the fight with Dolores' father, and his possible indictment.

"They don't really have anything on you, Harry. I think you're letting this get out of control."

"It's already out of control, don't you see that? Or are you too stupid?"

She slapped him. It came out of some nether world beyond her hip. He never saw it coming and was actually too drunk to feel the pain of its sting. That didn't mean it pissed him off any less. He tried to stand up, lost his balance and fell to his knees. What an asshole, he thought.

"I'm sorry, you didn't deserve that," he said. "I didn't mean it."

"I'm not stupid and you did," said Katherine. "I understand you're upset, but I'm not going to let you take it out on me."

"This is no bullshit rackets thing! They didn't haul me in to slap my hand for running numbers or even a couple of 'after-hours' joints. This is drugs, Katherine! The Lord doesn't fuck with drugs. The cops don't really care about that 'cracker drummer' buying the farm! What they really care about is Harry Tennyson unloading a boxcar of heroin on the streets of East Baltimore. What they really care about is Harry Tennyson turning the white trash into junkies!"

"Harry, calm down. You're not a drug dealer. They can never prove you are." Katherine turned and glided into the kitchen to turn on a new General Electric percolator pot.

"Katherine, these guys don't have to prove a motherfuckin' thing. We're talking about a city councilman, the chief of police and a state senator. And you can bet your pretty little ass they've got the mayor hooked into this, too. My ass is grass, honey."

Katherine rushed to his side and placed her fingers gently against his cheeks. "It's all so simple, don't you see?"

"Simple? What are you talking about?"

"This is the chance we've been waiting for! It's fate, Harry. This was meant to happen."

"*What*!?"

"You have enough money to last us a lifetime. We can go to Europe or London or even some island where nobody knows us. We can leave all this mess behind us and never look back."

"Katherine—"

"Oh, Harry, it's so romantic. Let's do it."

He staggered to his feet, moved to the window and looked away from her as he began laughing. The dumb broad didn't understand a thing. She was just like all the rest of them. What did she think this was, a Bogart and Bacall movie?

"What's so funny?!" There was an edge of anger and surprise to her words.

He felt her draw close to him, her long fingernails digging into his shoulder like a hawk's talon. It hurt and it made him mad. Wheeling quickly, he caught her with the back of his hand squarely along the leading edge of her delicate jaw.

"You crazy dame!" he roared as she was driven to the carpet under the fury of his attack.

"Harry!" she screamed as he reached down to grab her hair.

Lifting her up towards him, he saw her cowering away, saw the fear in her eyes.

"Please, don't, please don't hurt me . . . ."

There was a weakness and a frailty in her voice that he did

not recognize. Oddly, it had the unexpected effect of enraging him even more. He didn't like to see her like this, yet he reveled in the opportunity to let the anger froth out of the seething cauldron his life had become.

Still clutching the hair on the back of her head, he delivered a punishing right hook to her face. The momentum of his swing and follow-through spun him around so that he not only lost his grip on her, but his balance as well.

Turning, actually spinning, the lights in the room and from the window began to carousel before his eyes. A darkness deeper than he had ever known threatened to fall on him like the final curtain on the final act of a very bad play.

TWENTY

KATHERINE LOUISE

"Harry, I'm leaving The Block for awhile."

The words danced across the room as if she'd announced she was throwing a party. She was looking at him when his eyes popped open. He'd been sprawled across the carpet like a club fighter who went down in Round One. She turned away in disgust and walked to the bathroom.

"What are you talking about?" he called out.

She heard him struggle to his feet and follow her down the hall.

"I'm going to leave The Block for awhile, out of town . . . on tour."

Standing before the mirror, she saw his reflection as he came up behind her. Katherine made no effort to hide her badly bruised face. She actually made a dramatic moment of applying some pancake makeup to her bruise.

The expression on Harry's face was a sour mixture of shock and shame.

"George Winslow hired me. He's taking me and a couple

of other girls on tour. We start at the Silver Slipper in D.C. next week, then the Purple Moon in Philly and the Metropole in New York. If everything works out, we might get to Chicago and down to New Orleans. I might be gone a couple of months."

"Like hell! Katherine, what the fuck are you talking about? Have you gone fucking crazy? You can't just up and go work for some schmuck whenever you feel like it. You work for me." The anger in his voice was cutting. The desperation was almost too much to bear.

"Look, you can't just announce that you're leaving. Forget the damn club. What about me, Katherine? What about us?"

Spinning to face him, she pointed to her blackened eye. "This is about us, Harry."

"I was drunk and crazy! You know I didn't mean it."

"You know I can't ever let you do that again."

"I'm sorry."

"You know, I wasn't gonna go on this tour. I was going to tell you about it tonight and tell you that I turned Winslow down. But while you were lying there on my rug and I was trying to pick myself up and find some shred of dignity, I decided that I have to go. At least for a little while . . . "

"Katherine, you can't—"

"We need a break, to think things over, to sort things out. Besides, Harry, you've got a lot of fires to put out. You don't need a 'crazy dame' around to make things more difficult."

"But I need you."

"Maybe you do, but not right now."

She watched him slump against the wall of the hallway, watched the resignation and defeat seep into him.

"This is a one-in-a-million opportunity. I'm going to make a lot of money. Plus I get to travel." She turned away from him and back to the mirror. "I can't let you stand in my way."

"Katherine, we've got a great thing going here. Don't mess it up."

"Harry, we had great sex. Now we've had great violence and I don't like the looks of things. I can't figure you out anymore. I offer you a chance to be with me the rest of our lives in some fantasy getaway where nobody even knows our names, and instead of you appreciating what I meant by that, you choose to smack me down and humiliate me. What's happened to you, Harry?"

"What's happened is my whole fucking world is falling apart! All of a sudden everybody's out to get me—even you."

"I'm sorry you see it that way. You forced me into this last decision."

"I don't want you to go."

"I know."

"But you're going."

"Yes."

"Are we over?" There was a heavy pause.

"It's up to you, Harry. I want more. You know that. If you can't commit to me, I have to move on."

"But you'll be back in two months..." he sounded so puny, so unlike The Lord that all the low-lifes looked upon like some cheap Caesar.

"The tour is six weeks, but I might spend a couple weeks down in the French Quarter, whether I'm working or not." It was nice being the noncommittal one for a change.

"Fuck it. I'm getting out of here," he said, trying to work up some honest anger. "Call me if you need anything, Katherine. I'll worry about you."

Katherine nodded as he turned to look at her.

"Be careful," he said.

"I will."

"Will you call me?" he asked.

"I'll try."

"I want to love you, but maybe I don't know how to do it," he offered.

Katherine looked away as he walked to the foyer. She watched his back as he turned the knob and slammed the door behind him. She rushed over to listen to his fading footsteps.

"I want to love you, too, Harry," she said softly as she twisted the deadbolt into place and touched the turbulent, bruised flesh under her eye.

TWENTY ONE

THE Block

The two "card rooms" on The Block were located above
the Villa Nova Club and The Jewel Box. The frequenters of the
card rooms were part of a loosely-knit club of older men who
were either retired or semi-retired. Women were not allowed
into the rooms, but smoking of cigars was. There were no hard
and fast rules on anything else, and it never occurred to any of
the players that they were all white, mostly Jewish or Italian,
and that no blacks were ever seen there. But a *de facto*
segregation existed all the same.

The card rooms were exceptionally spare, with blank
walls, bad lighting and several sets of tables and chairs. The
games of choice were gin rummy and a less familiar pastime
called "millions" (a form of pinochle), which was very popular
among the older players.

Both rooms were serviced by an Igor-like fellow who went
by the name of Abe. No one knew his last name and he'd never
offered it in 35 years of go-fering for the players. Abe had made
a comfortable living running up and down the stairs of the card
rooms picking up and delivering soft drinks and deli

sandwiches, cigarettes and candy.

One of the players, an old bowlegged man named Shappy, who had been a bartender on The Block for almost 40 years, always brought his own food, a bag of hamburgers from The Little Tavern. He wouldn't eat anything else, saying, "It was them Tavern 'death balls' that kept me alive so long!"

You never saw Shappy on The Block without a bag of burgers in his hand.

Shappy had a habit of sweeping all of his table money—bills and loose change—into a paper bag when he was finished playing and ready to leave the card room. He never counted his money at the table.

Everyone in the card room knew about Shappy and his little brown bag full of money, as did people on the street where the clubs were. Naturally there was always speculation about how much money Shappy was taking home that way, and how easy it would be to grab it from him. Shappy, however, was a clever old gent.

One night, in fact, someone on The Block came up fast behind Shappy after he left the card room with his little paper bag. The guy knocked Shappy down as he grabbed the bag and ran off into the night. Everyone crowded around Shappy as he pulled himself back on his feet and, seeing that he was not hurt, asked how much money he had in the bag that was now gone forever.

"Not much," said Shappy, who calmly reached deep into his side pants pocket and pulled out another brown paper bag that he shook so the coins inside would jingle.

"Well, then, what was in the other bag?" someone asked.

"Hamburgers," said Shappy. "I was takin' 'em home for the dog."

TWENTY TWO

CHARLES WHITTIER

Charles Whittier took old Syd's advice about Dolores Delvecchio Tennyson. There she was, plain as day, in the white pages, just waiting for him. Guilford address. Charles knew it was a ritzy area. Probably a lot like where he grew up back in Virginia. She lived on Poplar Street. Nice neighborhoods always have street names like that. Grove Lane. Maple Drive. Some rich fart somewhere decided those kind of names evoke an aura of refinement.

Charles swung the Corsica onto Poplar and scanned the homes with a trained eye. Old, elegant, tastefully landscaped with azaleas and forsythia and such. Dolores lived in the middle of the block. Hers was a large Tudor-style home. The immaculate velvet lawn was lined with pink tulips.

He parked at the curb and pulled the rearview mirror over to study his face. He was clean-shaven and smelled good. A *nice* black man. He wore a sport coat over a crisp striped shirt and navy slacks. His loafers wore the requisite tassles that said Ivy League. Dolores Delvecchio Tennyson would let him in.

He rang the bell, which chimed a classy range of chords.

The black woman who answered wore a starched maid's uniform. She was about sixty and quite attractive. Charles flashed her his best Hollywood grin and the questioning eyes flickered for a moment.

"Hello, ma'am. My name is Charles Whittier. I'm a writer with *Esquire* magazine, and I was wondering if I might speak with the lady of the house?"

"What about?"

"I'm researching an article on The Block and was referred to her by a gentleman named Syd Daniloski. Said he was a close friend of her husband's. I just have a couple of questions . . . " His voice trailed.

"One moment, please." The black woman shut the door firmly and he listened to her retreating footsteps.

Minutes later, the door opened again.

"Please come in, Mr. Whittier. Follow me."

The place was exquisitely furnished. Lots of expensive crystal and Louis XIV furniture. A curving staircase wound its way up to the second floor and around again up to a third. Charles admired the art work as they passed the living room.

Dolores Delvecchio sat primly on a navy blue chintz sofa in a glassed-in sun room. She looked exactly as he had imagined. Well-preserved, either through exercise and a healthy diet, or by an expensive plastic surgeon. Most likely the latter. She was a pleasantly plain woman with swept-up, blondish-gray hair, tired eyes, and lips painted a pale pink. But most remarkable was the sallow complexion. She had attempted to camouflage it with heavy foundation, without much success. The explanation lay on the tiny glass table beside her. It was three-thirty in the afternoon and her martini glass was half empty. A pitcher of refills sat on the rolling tray behind her.

"Mrs. Tennyson," said Charles, extending his hand, "thank you so much for agreeing to see me. I apologize for arriving unannounced, but I've got a deadline." He crossed the room to shake her hand and stood waiting for a reply.

"Sit down, Mr. Whittier." The voice was commanding. Charles took a seat at the opposite end of the sofa.

"Eugenia," she said evenly. "Bring in that tray of cookies, please. Mr. Whittier, can I offer you a martini?"

"No, thank you. Perhaps a glass of water, though," he smiled up at Eugenia again, and this time she smiled back.

"Mineral water okay?" she asked politely. Charles nodded.

"What is this article all about?" Dolores asked.

"It's about The Block in its heyday—the original Block . . . and the people who ran it."

"You mean Harry," she said matter-of-factly and took a swig from her crystal glass.

"Well, yes, among others. But I'm finding it was your husband who had the most clout down on The Block in the fifties."

"That's true. Harry was The Lord of The Block." There was some sadness in the powder-blue eyes. Charles thought of his interview with Katherine Louise. The sadness had been there, too. A real heartbreaker, this guy.

"How well do you know Syd?" he asked.

"He was Harry's right-hand man for years. He was like part of the family for awhile, right up until Harry died."

"What did you think of your husband's power? Wasn't he a big-time 'mover and shaker'?"

"Harry was in a sinful business, Mr. Whittier. God strikes down those who dabble in the devil's game. Harry profited from the business of naked women and paid fornication. His money was dirty. His women were dirty. I may have loved him when I married him, but he changed right before my eyes. He got caught up in the glory of Satan's power."

Charles did a reality check and paused to regroup.

"The Desert Club was a legitimate club, wasn't it, Mrs. Tennyson? They were licensed to feature burlesque."

"My last name is Delvecchio. I don't go by Tennyson anymore. And there was no license that said Harry could sleep with those girls. That's what he did, you know. Slept with the lot of them. Harry and I had separate bedrooms, you can bet."

Eugenia came back with the Evian and cookies. Charles was grateful for the interruption. Dolores Delvecchio Tennyson was not only slightly looped, but slightly off balance.

The water eased its way down his throat and Charles tried again.

"Well, I find his disappearance strange. Do you mind talking about the police findings and your husband's last days?"

"The Lord shall judge the people. Judge me, O Lord, according to my righteousness and according to mine integrity that is in me."

Dolores reached for the martini again. "Mr. Whittier, my husband was a sick man. He believed in the powers of the flesh. That was the extent of his so-called power. 'Thou shalt destroy them that speak leasing: the Lord will abhor the bloody and deceitful man.' That's Psalms 5," she said with a sigh.

Charles caught a glimpse of Eugenia lurking in the doorway. She wore a smirk on her face. She seemed to take pleasure in the older woman's gibberish.

"I would like to include a passage in my article that addresses your husband's mysterious disappearance. I understand he had secreted away a lot of money . . ."

"Who told you that?"

"I don't remember. I believe I read it somewhere."

"Well, if Harry left any money, I never saw a penny. He had a $100,000 life insurance policy, all of which I put into a trust for the children. I refuse to spend his ill-gotten gain. Besides, my father left me enough to live comfortably."

"Could the million have been a possible payoff for information Harry had on someone? A politician maybe? Or someone in the police department?"

"Mr. Whittier, I'm feeling rather tired, and I really don't think I can be of much help. My husband doesn't deserve to be in your article. The Block is full of trash, haven't you heard? Poor, white, disease-ridden trash."

Eugenia eased out of the shadows and smiled apologetically at Charles.

"I'll see you to the door, sir," she said.

Charles rose and thanked Dolores Delvecchio Tennyson. A slip of a woman who couldn't hold her liquor any better than she held on to her man. What a fucking waste of time!

He drove back to the hotel downtown and valet parked. He

158

was feeling frustrated. Somehow he needed to get to the bottom of Harry and whatever it was that was his undoing. A woman in neon blue bicycle pants jogged by and Charles realized he was horny as hell. How long had it been anyway? Too long. He needed to get Julia in town and quick. Maybe she could catch the five o'clock train.

Upstairs, he dialed Julia's office and waited.

"Julia Collins."

"Charles Whittier." He could hear her smile.

"It's about time. Where the hell have you been? I've left a million messages."

"I want you."

"You should."

"I want you now. Come to Baltimore for the night."

"Charles, I can't. I've got a proposal to get out tonight and appointments all day tomorrow."

"Cancel them."

"I can't."

"I need you, babe, like never before. It's inhuman to go this long."

"Is that all I'm good for? Seriously, Charles, how's it going? Are you coming home soon?"

"I hope so. I just came from a nothing interview with this guy Tennyson's widow. What a sorry-assed bitch. Drunk in the middle of the afternoon, talking a bunch of Jesus crap."

"Sounds like fun. Any big breaks?"

"Nah. She was basically useless. The thing is there's more to this story than just a rich strip-club owner who lived the good life and checked out. The guy was into some bad stuff I think. He was about to come into big-time money and suddenly he up and disappears. I think maybe the money was a payoff, either from a political angle, or maybe the mob. Or maybe my source is smoking crack."

"Hang in there. Maybe I can make it down this weekend."

"Sounds fantastic. I've got a treat for us you won't want to miss. There's this great crab house called Obrycki's. It's a Baltimore landmark. We'll OD on crab soup, crab cakes, and steamed crabs. See you Friday?

She caved in. "All right. Seven o'clock flight."

"Make it the five."

"How 'bout the six? I'll take a cab to your hotel."

"Jul?"

"Yes, sweetheart?"

"You're my best friend."

"I know."

An hour later, Charles stepped out of the elevator and made his way toward the glass doors that exited on to Pratt Street. Across the way, Harborplace gleamed in the night, but Charles had his eye on Pizzaria Unos. A little sausage and pepperoni, extra cheese and mushroom . . .

He heard the footsteps quicken behind him and his New Yorker instinct shifted into high gear. His wallet was in his right breast pocket. The watch was a Seiko, but worth a couple hundred. He only had two credit cards—both were maxed out. Go wild fella. He was almost to the end of the block. Maybe if he stepped it up, he could catch up with that foursome up ahead. No such luck. A blow struck him across the back of the shoulders and he felt his knees buckle. The lights across the street blurred into a fuzzy glow. The guy had hit him with something hard. Very hard. He turned to get a look at the thug just as the second swing came down across his left arm. He instinctively reached up to cradle it and felt a strong blow to his face. At that moment, he saw his attacker's dark eyes and brilliant white teeth in the street light.

Hispanic. And strong as hell. His arm was broken. No question. His last thought was of Julia. Ridiculously, he pondered making love with his arm in a cast . . .

Charles awoke later in a hospital bed. He took in the stained ceiling boards and pungent odor of disinfectant in an instant, then looked down at his body. There was indeed a thick cast on his left arm, shoulder to wrist. Shit. He felt tightly bandaged across his shoulders as well, and his face was alive with pain. He raised his good arm and touched the bandages there. The right side seemed okay. The left was where it hurt like hell. A nurse breezed in.

"Good, you're awake. How are we feeling?"

"Bad. What the hell happened?"

"You were attacked. Hit with a blunt object in front of your hotel. I'll bring you some more painkillers." She looked down at him with a smile. "That's all I know. There's a policeman in the hall. Should I send him in?"

"Please."

Detective Deming was a beefy, red-haired man with a heavy gait. Charles felt his bed vibrate as the man crossed the room.

"I'm Detective Dwight Deming, Baltimore City Police Department. How are you doing, Mr. Whittier?"

"Great, just great. Any idea who nailed me, Detective?"

"That's what I'm here to find out. Do you remember much about the attack?"

"Just that I heard him coming. I knew I was about to get robbed or something. Just as I was about to take off, he hit me across the shoulders. I don't remember much else, except he was Hispanic, or maybe Italian."

"Ordinarily I'd chalk it up to a regular street assault and robbery, only this guy didn't take nothing. You still got your leather jacket, your wallet, your watch. Why do you suppose some guy would attack you in the middle of a busy block for no reason?"

"I'm not sure, Detective."

"What are you doing here in Baltimore? I see from your records that you're a New Yorker. On business?"

"Yeah. I'm researching an article for *Esquire*. My editor sent me down here two weeks ago."

"What's the subject of the article?"

"The Block. You know, burlesque in its heyday."

"You dig up anything juicy?"

"I'm not sure what you mean." Charles' face was killing him. Where the fuck was the nurse with the Tylenol 3?

"Well, I was just wondering if you'd come across any questionable characters is all."

161

"I'm currently focusing on a guy named Harry Tennyson. He was Lord of The Block in the fifties, then disappeared without a trace in 1958. He's been presumed dead, even though no one ever found a body. That's the only questionable character so far. I don't think that's worth pummeling someone on the street."

"Yeah, well, you never know, Mr. Whittier. I'd like you to stay in touch," he handed over a card. "You see or hear anything that gets under your skin, give me a call. I'm familiar with the Tennyson case. I know the guy was presumed dead. I also know he might possibly have been involved in something not quite kosher. And I'm not talking about the gambling and prostitution. That's off the record, okay?"

"Sure. What else do you know?" Charles forgot his pain.

"Not much. I think you should watch your back though. And stay in touch."

Charles watched the cop leave and wondered why the hell someone was suddenly trying to do him in. The attack was surely a warning. The guy could have killed him if he wanted. Someone out there wanted him to stop snooping. Here he'd stumbled on a great story researching a fairly routine skin piece. Then he finds his main character may have died shortly before coming into some serious coin. Now, just after interviewing the dead guy's wife, he gets jumped on the street and nothing is stolen. He was on to something. He was on to something big. The nurse came in with the pills. He popped them and reached for the phone. Julia's visit needed to be postponed. There was no need to jeopardize her safety, too.

Twenty Three

Marvin Harper

"Why'dja do it, Marvin?" Deputy Chief Applegate's long, pale face was only several inches away from his. He had seen some pretty ugly white dudes, but this guy looked like he should be hosting the late night horror movies on Channel 13.

"Do what?" said Marvin, trying to act disinterested and control his temper at the same time. "I ain't done a thing. And your people picks me up in front of my girl and drags my butt to this stinkin' place. I. Ain't. Done. A. *Thing.*"

"I got witnesses that made you at the scene of a crime, son. And that means that maybe you did a very serious thing."

"Like what? Why don't you say it, Applegate? What's the goddamn charge?"

Applegate leaned back, shook a Chesterfield out of his pack, stuck it in the corner of his mouth, but didn't light it. It bobbed and jittered as he spoke, and Marvin wondered if the cop played this little routine just to distract and piss off the guys he grilled.

"What's the charge? Second Degree if the judge is feeling

good, but you can bet your blue-black hide I'll push for Murder One," mocked Applegate.

Marvin almost laughed. "Yeah, right. You'd never get anybody to believe I premeditated to kill a cracker drummer."

The deputy chief looked across the interrogation room where Sergeant Ham O'Leary sat stoop-shouldered and looking like a tired old frog in the shadows. "What do you think, Sarge? Think we can get the big one to stick?"

O'Leary was a big man with a big mustache that extended away from his face. He stood up, walked across the room, and took a seat opposite Applegate and next to Marvin. "Boy," he said, "it seems to me that you don't know who you're addressing." He leaned closer, making his speech more deliberate. "You see, we could beat the truth out of ya and no one would be the wiser. Seeings as how you are so dark, Marvin, nobody'd see the bruises."

Little Marvin sat as still as a statue in a park. He didn't move. Instead he concentrated on the steady beat of the falling rain against the window. The room had been painted a dingy green that the years of tobacco smoke had turned into an ugly brown. The light bulbs in all the lamps seemed dim because there was so much grime on them. The room, he thought, looked like it had seen and heard way too much, and the scene he was playing out tonight wasn't going to be anything special. He synced up his breathing to the rhythm of the rain and it soothed him. They had nothing on him and they knew it. He didn't kill that beefy white guy. No way he was going down for that one.

"Marvin, what's the matter with you, boy?" Applegate again pulled up close to Marvin and, this time, grabbed his jacket to shake him. "Boy, I'm talking to you. If you'd rather not say anything, that's just fine with me 'cause you're not leaving here until we get some answers."

"I've got nothing to say, so why don't you just forget it."

"Well, the way I figure it, the longer you stay in here, the better it is for our citizenry."

Applegate walked to the door, stopped, and with a backward glance said, "Oh, yeah, and, ah, the longer you stay in here, the less money you make." He chuckled and walked out.

Marvin watched the two other detectives in the room follow Applegate out. He was alone in the room now. This was when you were supposed to sit and sweat awhile.

Marvin slumped in his seat. What the fuck kinda shit was he going to have to face this time? What the fuck was that Leroy thinking when he hauled off and sliced his customer? The cops told him he had been seen, so giving up the little brother was of no use. Marvin knew Leroy Johnson would start singing like a canary.

He had to think of some way to get out of this mess fast. He never thought he looked good in stripes, and he'd sooner cut off his balls than go to jail. Especially for someone else's crime.

The door opened once again and Applegate walked in. The Chesterfield was finally lit, and the deputy chief was trying to look mean. On the street, Marvin wouldn't have been scared of this man, but the badge—the badge gave him power and this was something out of Marvin's control. Right now, the cops would be able to do anything they wanted. Marvin knew they could get away with it. He looked at the white man. It was his move.

"Look, Marvin, I don't want to play games anymore," said Applegate. He inhaled and blew out a thin stream of smoke towards Marvin's face. "I've been thinking about what you said and you not really knowing why you were picked up. Maybe you just forgot. It wouldn't surprise me 'cause I hear tell niggers ain't as smart as us white folks."

Marvin smiled in spite of himself. He turned away from the window and faced his interrogator. He held a steely gaze on the deputy chief. "You trying to get me mad? So mad that I'd try somethin' stupid? How long do you white boys think we gonna fall for a tired old bit like that?"

"You have any better ideas?"

"Well, it just occured to me that I didn't get my one phone call. You mind if I make my one phone call?"

"Who would you like to call?"

"My lawyer."

"Your lawyer? Now that's interesting, Marvin. The last time you were here, the log book says you didn't call a lawyer. You called Harry Tennyson."

"Yeah, well, I want my lawyer tonight!"

Applegate chuckled. "Besides, Marvin, you made that call the moment you walked in here. The desk sergeant has it logged in the book."

Marvin felt like he was trapped in a cage. These cops had it all figured out. Everytime he thought of taking a step in any direction, they were already there ready to block him.

"You're dealing Horse out of the Surf Club," said Applegate. It was not a question.

"Man, I ain't never been down there. Colored ain't allowed in there. Why would I waste my time trying to get in that joint?"

"Marvin, you trying to get one over on us? Your Caddy ain't the kinda car that lets you vanish into the night. If you're gonna lead a life of crime, Marvin, the first rule is don't get noticed."

"Who saw my car by the Surf Club?"

"That doesn't matter, Marvin. Suffice it to say that I have eyewitnesses there. We know what you're doing whether you want to admit it or not. You're in a lot of trouble, unless maybe we can work out a deal."

"Deal?" Marvin was dumbfounded. "Deal?" he repeated. "I ain't about to set up no deal with no white guys no more. You cain't be trusted, none of y'all. Forget it, no way, no how."

"*What* other white guys, Marvin?"

"I ain't talking no more. I want the NAACP down here now."

"Other white guys like Harry Tennyson?" asked Applegate.

"Harry just owed me a favor, that's all."

"Let me explain something to you, Marvin." Applegate pulled a chair up close to Marvin and straddled it. He lit another cigarette and offered one to him. "I believe you when you tell me you didn't kill Wycheck. But the plain facts are we will push you for this one unless you can help us."

"What the hell are you talking about?" Marvin asked.

Applegate chuckled once again. "You know, I would have never believed it if somebody had told me The Lord would be selling junk with a two-bit-zoot-suit 'coon from the Avenue."

Marvin looked at the deputy chief, unable to hide his confusion. Something about the way he made that last remark didn't exactly fit.

"Well, like I said, Harry owed me one."

Applegate shook his head. "Nah, that doesn't wash. I want to know how you talked Tennyson into becoming a drug dealer."

Marvin could feel his own jaw slowly falling open. "You mean, Harry doesn't deal?"

"He hates the shit. As corrupt and slimy as Tennyson might be, I never figured him to push junk."

What the hell was Applegate really saying!? That Harry never dealt? That Harry wasn't dealing right now? That Harry had . . . yeah, that's exactly what Harry had done! Marvin felt the muscles in his hands tighten as he white-knuckled the arms of the chair. Harry Tennyson had fucked him out of a half million dollars by giving him a drug territory he never owned in the first place. Marvin had to smile. The Lord, he was one slick motherfucker.

But now he was going to pay for being so slick. Marvin regarded Applegate and spoke in a low voice.

"Supposin' I could help you. How's I know I could trust you?"

"I guess until it's over you'll never really know for sure if you can trust me. But the way I see it, you got two choices. Either you trust me with the hopes of walking away a free man, or you go to jail. 'Cause I *can* make sure you do that."

"Okay," said Marvin. "Tell me what you need, tell me what I get. For real."

"Marvin this is the deal. Help me bring The Lord down and I'll make sure you walk away scot-free. Tell me all you know, and you can go back to the Avenue to sell your shit and gamble and fuck those pretty little black girls."

Marvin considered this, wondering what the real motivation was here. From what he knew of Applegate, this cop was not all that interested in cultivating what you might call high moral fiber. Marvin was not ignorant of the internal politics and the lust for power that drove small men like

Applegate. It was no secret that Chief Kilpatrick had been riding in Harry's green pocket for a long time. You didn't have to be a genius to figure that down-goes-Harry would also mean down-goes-Chief Kilpatrick. And who better to step into the empty seat than Deputy Chief Warren Applegate? Okay, he thought, and what about me? I get to do my biz and hang Harry out to dry at the same time. Not bad for starters, but he was going to need to hear more. He looked at the deputy chief and tried a small smile.

"All right," he said. "Let me get this straight. You're going to let me do as I been doing if I turn Harry?"

Applegate nodded and took a final drag on his Chesterfield.

"What's the catch?"

"Simple, I'm not really interested in frying little fish like Negro drug dealers. I want to fry a big one. As long as I don't see you or hear of you dealing your shit or talking your trash in any of the upstanding, working-class, white neighborhoods of this city, I don't care what you do, Marvin. That's my bone I'll throw to the newspaper writers and the two-faced politicos who will want to have their own explanation for why I'm going to bring down my chief. I look good and you go back to the flat rock you tried to crawl out from under."

Marvin didn't speak for a moment. He let the words sink in. Words. They had so many meanings if only you took the time to really listen to them. If you weren't paying attention, what Applegate was saying was pretty cut and dried. But there was also that shit between the lines, that notion that sometimes Marvin found himself thinking about in the middle of some nights . . . those nights when he couldn't sleep. Those nights when he had to face the fact that he was enslaving his people with a whole new set of chains. And here was this nasty-assed cop telling him too much of the truth. Yeah, it was fine to be a drug dealer, as long as you sold it to the 'coons—they're just a bunch of animals anyway. Marvin had to think about that whole thing, wondering if maybe there was a small part of him that believed that shit might be true.

"Hey," said Applegate, "we haven't got all night here. If you don't want the deal, just say the word, Marvin, and I'll have the

DA measure you up for three hots-and-a-cot at Central. Of course, that will only be a cup of coffee. Your 'hard ride' will be at the pen."

Marvin snapped himself out of the funky thoughts, the serious kind of thinking that always scared him. Scared him a lot more than the law and the "system" could ever do.

"Okay, Applegate, let's make a deal . . . . "

TWENTY FOUR

SENATOR Edward Higgins

Higgins hadn't slept well in days. The buzz in his head was deafening. His headache started the night of the Tennysons' Christmas party. Hadn't let up since. Harry had decked Delvecchio and publicly humiliated him. Not suprisingly, the little man had sworn up and down revenge on his son-in-law. Higgins was worried that revenge was going to spill over onto him. Harry had some serious dirt on him and would use it in a heartbeat if he had reason. Higgins was deeply troubled. The whiskey hadn't helped. The "uppers" only made him worry more intensely. Even a couple of hours in the sack with Judy and her big tits hadn't eased his nerves.

It was ten o'clock and he'd just sent Judy home. He couldn't concentrate along with her incessant dribble any longer. The phone rang. It was Delvecchio.

"Ed, can we meet tonight? I need to talk to someone."

"What about, Vince? I'm kind of tied up right . . . "

"Don't give me that shit, Higgins. This is important," the man bellowed through the phone. "Meet me at The Jewel Box in an hour."

"What's this about, Vince? I don't have time for small talk."

"Look, Higgins, make time. And it ain't small talk. I wanna talk about Harry. He's gettin' just a little too big for his fancy-ass britches if you catch my drift. I need to assess the situation, and I think you can help me shed a little light on things."

There was a lengthy pause, then finally Higgins spoke. "I'll see you in one hour." He put down the phone and headed for the shower.

The Jewel Box was a warm, sweaty place with action on stage, but plenty of out-of-the-way tables in shadowy corners that concealed those occupants in need of privacy. Delvecchio hovered at one of these tables, his meaty palm wrapped around a highball glass, dark eyes panning the room then settling on the girl gyrating on stage. Higgins approached the table and couldn't help noticing the dancer himself as she turned and bent at the waist, offering a beautiful view of her prized possession through a sheer, black scarf. He slid into the chair opposite Delvecchio.

"You're late."

"I told you I was busy. I got here as soon as I could."

The senator allowed his eyes to drift back to the girl on stage. She was doing some pretty incredible things with that scarf. Suddenly he was feeling horny all over again. Maybe it wasn't too late to get Judy on the horn and tell her to catch a cab . . .

"Higgins, I didn't invite you here to eyeball pussy. We got problems with my son-in-law, and I want you to help me figure a way outta this situation."

"Vince, Harry and I are tight. I don't want to get in the middle of your little family squabble. That's your business."

"Cut the crap. I ain't talking family here. Harry fucking layed me out the other night, in front of everybody. He's giving up on us, Ed. We ain't part of the plan no more, see?"

Higgins signaled the waitress for a beer and thought for a minute about what Delvecchio was saying.

"Go on, Vince. What are you getting at?"

"What I'm getting at is that Harry's prepared to send us

both down the river. He seems to have lost his sense of respect. This thing we been working on with the offshore boats . . . you think he's not gonna dump us once it's up and running?"

Higgins was big on the casino boats. He had a bill sitting in the state legislature in Annapolis as they spoke, waiting for the go-ahead. Right now they only had a temporary license. Senator Ed Higgins wanted to see to it that gambling boats became big business in Maryland. Delvecchio was his biggest supporter and both were in it up to their necks with Harry Tennyson. If a little illegal activity came into play, they were willing to look the other way so long as they got their cut. Now it was looking like Harry might cut them loose.

"Harry's not going to dump us, Vince. We're his meal ticket. He needs us to keep him in business. No license, no boats. No boats, no money. Get it?"

"I got it, Higgins. You're the one who's in the fucking dark. Harry's got other supporters. Hell, he don't care about your stupid bill. He doesn't need us. He's making a killing right now with the two boats he's got. If he gets shut down, he'll just take his money and go home. You and I both know they could be running drugs through there. And hookers, too. I spied several of his sluts last time I was out there shootin' craps." He leaned forward, eyes narrowing.

"See, Harry and that goof, Syd, got a couple of buddies in the mob who are ready and willing to kick in some dough. Whatever it takes to keep things up and running and generating cash." He paused as the waitress delivered the senator's beer.

"What if someone were to let on to, say, *The News American*, about the possibility of some things that ain't quite kosher going down aboard the good ship lollipop, eh?" Delvecchio chuckled nervously.

Higgins didn't like where this was headed. He was about to announce his intent to launch a campaign for the U.S. Senate seat. He had big plans. In fact, he was already thinking about how to clean up his act. For starters, he needed to quit hanging with cheap-looking broads, and find himself a wholesome-looking girl. And he needed to avoid meeting the likes of City Councilman Delvecchio in sleazy strip joints.

He scanned the room for familiar faces. Good, no sign of reporters or colleagues from the state capitol. Suddenly he felt like he needed to get the hell out of there.

"Look, Vince, first of all, we can't be meeting in places like this. Next time, make it someplace decent, will you? Like Sherry's Place on Broadway. Let's not be stupid. Secondly, I'm not so sure you and I should be butting our noses in where we don't belong, if you get my point. Hookers on the boat? Okay. Drugs? Not Harry. And what's this about the mob? That's a dirty three-letter word, man, a very dirty word."

"I wanna get this asshole, Ed. I'm serious. Relative or no relative. Besides, he's been fucking around on the side, upsetting the hell out of my Dolores. I won't stand for that. The man has gone too far. He's running around town with Katherine Louise for Christ's sake!"

Higgins conjured up a mental picture of Katherine and for a moment had to admire Harry. She was quite the looker. In fact, too bad she was a stripper because otherwise she had all the makings of a first-class lady. He took a swig of his beer and set it down firmly.

"All right, Vince, what exactly do you plan to do?"

"I'm not sure. What do you make of the situation? I mean we can't just sit back and let Harry bulldoze his way over us. We got a serious stake in this."

"I need to think about this. Harry hasn't given me cause to doubt his intentions yet. All I've got to go on is your word, and we all know what a politician's word is worth." Higgins smiled at his own sick joke.

"Don't get cute," hissed Delvecchio. "Look, you and I have been strong allies in the past. I help you, you help me, everybody in our districts stays happy. Now maybe you got plans for bigger things . . . am I right? See, you can't be running the risk of being exposed if you're serious about becoming a U.S. senator. What would a smart man do in this situation?"

"Watch your step, Vincenzo. I'm not the one getting cute here. And a smart man would get up and walk away from this table right now, which is what I'm thinking about doing. Now,

I think maybe you have a point about Harry. Perhaps he is looking to the mob for assistance. But if that's the case, we don't want to be around when it all hits the fan. I need to hear what Harry has to say. Could be we're getting all worked up over nothing."

Delvecchio shook his head. "I disagree."

"Fine. Time will tell. For now, you concentrate on dealing with your son-in-law and the case of the wayward cock. See if you can distract him by threatening to divulge his nasty little affair. Let me handle the rest. I'll let you know when I need your help."

The music picked up as the next act came on stage. "Lusty Leona" started to strut toward the edge of the runway and the senator allowed himself a healthy peek at the goods. Christ, clean living wasn't going to be much fun. With all the grief he caught from Judy about his roving eye, he could only imagine what a nightmare it was going to be dating a "nice" girl.

Delvecchio was putting on his coat. The man looked worried. Higgins hadn't let on how badly he himself had been feeling. The councilman didn't need to know that, deep down, Senator Ed Higgins was fucking terrified this mess was going to end his career. He had to act fast.

He nodded at Vince as the short, angry man brushed past and made his way to the door. No question, Harry had definitely made a mistake pissing that man off. But Higgins really didn't care about Harry's in-law troubles. He just wanted to be assured that his own political life was secure. He would be willing to forfeit all claims on the casino boats if he had to. Hell, at this rate, he'd be giving up women and giving up money. What was left? Might as well become a monk.

Delvecchio was out to do Harry in. Higgins could either sit back and watch it happen, whatever it might be, or he could take care of things himself. That idea rather sickened him. Or, he could pursue option number three. He could go to Harry Tennyson and spill his guts. Let the guy know what he was in for, and maybe gain a friend.

Funny, in the business of politics, you could have your pick of a whole bus load of girls and a train filled with acquaintances who want to do right by you, but holy shit, try to find yourself one single friend. Kind of like trying to find a stitch of clothing on butt-ass naked "Lusty Leona" up there on stage.

His pounding headache was back, so he paid for his beer and ducked out of The Jewel Box and into the chilly night air. He thought if he hurried, he could make it home before the rain, pop a couple of aspirin and hit the sack. But just then the sky opened up without warning, and it started to rain down on East Baltimore Street and Senator Edward Higgins.

It was a hard rain . . . .

Twenty Five

The Article

The Block began to promote itself as the city grew and gave
way to the counties. Ads ran in the amusement section of the News
American (News Post) announcing "limited engagements" at the
Gayety for circuit strippers like Busty Russell and her Twin
44s, Tempest Storm, and Justa Dream. Irma the Body, a
national headline striptease artist who had a sense of history,
described her trade like this: "There's nothing to get curious
about when you see a stage full of naked women. You gotta
tease a little, with a sexy outfit. A bra, high heels, a garter belt
and stockings. Then peel them off slowly. That's what starts
their hearts pumping. But, I'll tell you," she added knowingly,
"a lot of men I've met promise a helluva lot more than they can
deliver. They come on like Gangbusters and go out like We the
People."

Irma was a regular at the Gayety. She always kept her
audience hot and bothered. Tickling herself all over with a rose,
she'd ask the men, ". . . mostly the ones in the front rows with
binoculars and coats in their laps . . . Hey, lover, wanna smell

my rose? Wanna eat my rose?" The men, appropriately embarassed for a moment, always leaped for the rose and often would stay after the show to request an autograph and offer to buy Irma a drink.

Baltimore was now the largest southern city south of the Mason-Dixon line and had a national population that was sixth in the United States with slightly under a million people. But it wasn't so much home-grown citizens who traveled to The Block since The Block was a place for transients. Within a 30-mile radius of The Block were stationed over 200,000 armed services personnel. Baltimore had also become a major convention city along with Philadelphia and Washington, and the city's 40 miles of waterfront were visited by ships from throughout the world.

It was around this time in post-war Baltimore that the top dog of The Block came on the scene. Harry "The Lord" Tennyson surfaced amidst a history of gambling and bookmaking charges and arrests. Determined to make it as a legitimate and well-respected businessman, he bought out the Collins brothers, a pair of former Irish bootleggers, who owned The Four Leaf Clover. He changed its name to the Desert Club.

Tennyson was a tough, power-wielding sort married to a city councilman's daughter, with two scrubbed young children. He also had a thing going on the side with a gorgeous country girl turned striptease star named Katherine Louise.

The Lord had to watch his back though. Smothered by an entourage of bodyguards and associates, he was under constant surveillance by local, state, and federal types. The Desert Club was his baby, though, and Tennyson took great pride in the quality of his girls and the smiles they threw his way when he entered the club.

TWENTY SIX

DEPUTY CHIEf WARREN AppLEGATE

Mayor Herbert Watson eyed his gold pocket watch, then returned it to its home in his vest. "You've got to make this quick, Warren. I've got an appointment with the School Board in five minutes."

"I realize the importance of keeping confidence up among your constituents. I know what I'm going to say is going to sound like hearsay, but the facts are the facts."

Leaning forward, Mayor Watson asked, "What the hell are you talking about?"

Applegate studied the mayor carefully. This guy didn't like to make waves. He was a career politician, but his time in office was nearing an end with elections in the coming year, and the last thing this guy wanted was to open a can of worms. "I think, no, I know that this truth must be told. You understand, Mr. Mayor, that this thing is too big to be covered up. The truth will leak out, and if the public gets wind of your knowing about this and not doing anything, well ..." Applegate threw his arms up, stood and walked to the window.

"Well, what!?"

"Well, come on, Your Honor, I just don't know how you would fare in the governor's race. In fact, I think it would cook your goose."

Mayor Watson resettled himself in his chair, steepled his hands over a pristine desk blotter, and composed himself by drawing a deep breath. "Okay, Warren, I'm listening . . ."

"I like you very much, sir," said Warren Applegate. "And I especially like what you're doing with running this city. You've done a lot of good here, so I'm —"

"Applegate, I'm gonna stop you right now before you go on and embarrass yourself any further. You were selling me just fine until that last little bit of kiss-ass you were throwing my way."

Warren felt himself blush, but knew there was no turning back now. "You've read the reports, Your Honor. What do you think?"

"It sounds like you've got yourself a pretty good case against Chief Kilpatrick," said the mayor, shaking his head. "Damn shame. I liked Bobby, but he's no different than the rest of us. The day always comes when you have to hang up your guns."

Mayor Watson didn't look particularly bright, still he sat in the commander's seat and was someone worth reckoning with. Either way, he must have done something right to get where he was and stay there for so long. However, Applegate found it hard to stare at the man for very long. The three strands of hair that the mayor insisted on combing from ear to ear left the deputy chief uneasy. Anyone who would go to those lengths to fool other people was in reality only fooling himself. Pity, he thought. "Pity"—that was the word that made Applegate feel strong. Once he was in a position to pity someone, he regained control.

"Forget the bullshit, son." Mayor Watson adjusted his position on the chair and tried to pull his vest down over his belly.

"I don't think the infiltration of heroin into white, working-class neighborhoods is bullshit, Your Honor." Warren hoped such a bold play would not make the mayor assume he was playing one-ups-manship.

"You're right, I really think you've got something here. We need every detail of Chief Kilpatrick's involvement leading up to the drug ring in East Baltimore. That means the secret testimony from Marvin Harper will bring down Harry Tennyson once and for all and anybody dumb enough to stay in his circle."

Applegate nodded. "And don't forget, we think we have enough facts to link him to the murder of the jazz drummer."

The mayor unsteepled his hands, made a fist, and pounded his blotter lightly.

"Oh, yeah, almost forgot about that," said the mayor.

"Sir, it's all right here." Applegate stood up and pushed the manila folder towards Herbert Watson.

The mayor glanced through its contents without really reading anything, then closed it. "This is something for the grand jury. Once the ball is rolling I'll issue a statement to the press, and we'll arrest these guys and let the scales of justice tilt."

Applegate was fighting the urge to run around the desk and hug the mayor. He had finally succeeded in bringing Chief Robert Kilpatrick down! That man was no good from the start and Applegate knew it. Patience and timing was all he needed. The chief had started to hang himself long before Applegate came along and so he decided to give the rope a good healthy yank. The way the deputy chief saw it he was only speeding up the inevitable. Sure, this might be his way of rationalizing what he was doing, but he was smart enough to know that a good rationale let you sleep at night.

"Applegate?" The deputy chief was brought back to reality by the mayor's voice.

"Yes, sir!" Applegate regarded the mayor confidently.

"You know, when Bobby Kilpatrick gets indicted, I'll have to put him on temporary leave, at least until the outcome of any trial. And that means we're going to need an acting chief." The mayor pushed back from his desk, letting his high-back leather chair drift to a stop. He placed his hands behind his head and smiled with the slyness of a seasoned politician.

"Now tell me, Deputy Chief, you wouldn't happen to have anybody that would be a good recommendation, would you?"

Applegate returned the sly grin and said, "Oh, I'll think about it and let you know, but I'm sure you realize I have one very good man in mind."

Twenty Seven

Chief Robert Kilpatrick

Bob Kilpatrick had been pacing back and forth across the length of his darkened living room. His brand new Philco TV filled the room with an eerie, blue-white light while sounds of *The Ed Sullivan Show* permeated the room. Where the hell was Tennyson? It was getting late and Irene would be home from her bridge game within the hour. That would only mean more explaining, and Bob was just about out of explanations for everybody. He sighed and it was a laboring effort. What the hell had happened? How come life had suddenly become such a burden, such a thing to be almost dreaded rather than cherished . . . ?

As he parted the lace curtains that Irene had begged him for, he saw a set of headlights mark the path of a car pulling on to his block. It was a big land yacht, and he recognized The Lord's Chrysler as it drifted up to the curb like a boat just cutting its engine.

Tennyson jumped out and ran up the walk. Bob Kilpatrick moved quickly to the front door, opening it before Harry could knock. "Come on in and hurry up. Nobody saw you, did they?"

Tennyson looked at him oddly. "How should I know? Your call kinda took me by surprise, but if you wanna know the truth, Bob, you sounded so desperate I knew I had to get here right away."

Gesturing the racketeer to follow him into the den, Chief Kilpatrick shook his head ironically. "Yeah, I think desperate is a pretty damn good word for it, Harry. Here, sit down and just listen to what I've got to say." Bob could feel his pulse driving behind his ears like a garden hose with a crinkle in it. The pressure was building, and it was only a question of how long and how much it could take.

Harry sat down and produced one of his hand-rolled, green-leaf Havana's from an inside jacket pocket. "Jesus, Bobby, you look like hell. I know what you're gonna say, and it's not as bad as you think."

"Oh, yes it is. I don't think you know the whole story, Harry."

Tennyson smiled in his usual cocky manner. "Relax, Bobby, we've been in tougher spots before. There's no way I'm going to implicate you. Jesus Christ, so this prick Applegate is trying to look good. What's he got?"

Kilpatrick walked behind his desk and sat down. "He's got plenty, Harry. Enough to get the wheels turning. Something like this: well, it doesn't matter if they get a conviction or not, just getting your name dragged through the mud has ended more than one career. "

"I told you I won't let that happen," said Harry.

The chief covered his face with his hands. He knew he looked pathetic but he couldn't control it any longer. "This is my life, Harry. Ever since I was a little boy, all I ever dreamed of was becoming a policeman. My father was a cop and his father was a cop, and someday I hope Bobby Junior will follow in my footsteps. If I get wrapped up in a scandal at this point in my career, I don't think my son will want to have anything to do with police work."

Harry didn't seem to notice the desperation in his voice. He continued to fiddle with that damn cigar.

"You know what, Bobby?" Harry asked as he leaned

forward in the chair and closed up the space between them. "The way I figure it is that there are only two really good things in life. One is a good woman, and the other is one of these," he said, holding up the deep green Havana cigar.

Bob Kilpatrick just shook his head.

Harry continued. "One of those writer guys, I can't remember who, he said, 'A woman is always a woman, but a good cigar is a *smoke'*."

"I don't get it," said Bob.

"Neither do I, but I always thought it sounded good."

"Harry, this is serious, either light that sonofabitch or put it away. We ain't here to talk about cigars."

The chief suddenly blanched.

Harry hadn't heard a word he said. A sharp pain momentarily raced across Bob's left arm, and he had to steady himself against the desk. Harry stood up and walked over to him.

"Hey, you okay? You look like you've just seen a ghost. What? You want a glass of water or something?"

"Harry, you just don't understand what I've been telling you. This time I can't get us out of it. This time it's for real. They say all great empires have their rise and fall, and, Harry, this is our fall." The chief slumped back in his chair.

"Nah, Bobby, as usual, you're oversensitive to what's going on. So that little shit, Applegate, is investigating Wycheck's death. Didn't you tell me yourself they have Marvin Harper in custody?"

"Had, Harry, *HAD!* That's the point. Applegate had a meeting with the mayor."

"What? You mean to tell me Watson listened to that weasel?"

"Not only listened, Harry, he acted. I have spies throughout the department, Harry. There are good cops, and then there are cops like me—the bottom of the barrel. Us guys keep each other informed and keep you out of trouble. Well, at least we *kept* you out of trouble. What I've been trying to tell you, Harry, is that the grand jury is probably going to have enough crap on both of us to bring everything down."

Finally, the light of realization crossed Harry's face. "You mean to tell me you're taking this all seriously . . . ?"

"Harry," Bobby Kilpatrick was barely audible, "I know that for as long as you've known me you thought I was something of a moron. Someone you could bully or intimidate or get to do your bidding. I did spoil you, so to speak, but you paid me for that privilege. And now it looks like I'm going to pay for my sins. I didn't start out to be a crooked cop. You led me towards the path of temptation and I was weak. I did it for my family. I did it 'cause I just didn't see the harm in bailing you out once in awhile. But now—"

Harry walked over to the chief and lightly slapped him in the face. "Bobby, you're not thinking clearly. We've gotten outta jams before, and we can do it again. We got all sorts of witnesses the night the drummer was killed—"

The chief kicked the chair out from under him as he stood up, took Harry by the lapels of his jacket and pushed him up against the wall. "Goddamnit Harry, this ain't about that night. This is about *all* of it. Drugs in East Baltimore. Conspiracy. Prostitution. Gambling. And anything else they think will make good press!"

The chief let go of Harry and fell to his knees. He cradled his legs and started rocking back and forth on the floor like a mental patient in a padded cell.

The tears started to salt the corners of his eyes and he felt so embarrassed, so weak, so puny. Especially in front of a hard-case, tough-to-crack guy like Harry.

"Chief," said Harry, "acting like this ain't gonna help anybody. Now get your ass up off the floor and tell me what you think we have to do."

"We gotta take the fall this time, Harry. Marvin Harper cut the deal of his life. Don't you understand that he sold you out once and for all?"

"Yeah, I'm getting that impression." Harry walked to the doorway, looking very disdainful, even disgusted. "The only thing I can think of, I don't like. We can take out Applegate and Marvin Harper, but that's murder, and you know how I really feel about that kinda shit."

Bob Kilpatrick nodded weakly.

Harry continued. "It's always been good for everybody to think I had an easy trigger, but I never had much stomach for killing people."

He laughed softly to himself.

"I'm sorry I called you over here tonight. I thought we could work out a plan like we always did, but I can see that there ain't no plan to save us this time. I'm sorry, Harry, it looks like I've been wasting your time."

"Let's wait until tomorrow. Let's sleep on it and maybe things will be a little clearer. It's been a long day, Bob, and somehow I think tomorrow is going to be even longer."

Harry turned without waiting for a response and let himself out the front door. Bob watched him go down the walk, climb into his big car, and drive off into the darkness.

The darkness seemed to have an oddly attractive comfort to him. *Let's sleep on it.* Yeah, that sure sounded good to him. Time for a real long sleep.

There was only one possible way to fix all his problems. And make sure his family name stayed out of the mud.

Reaching into the center drawer of his desk, he found the solution. It came in the form of a blue-black piece of machine steel from the Smith & Wesson factory.

Yeah, the answer was in his hands now. As he raised the weapon to his mouth, he wondered if he would hear the sound of the shell discharging . . . .

TWENTY EIGHT

The Block

It was an unspoken law on The Block back in the fifties that blacks were not allowed in any of the clubs. The shills and barkers who sat out front didn't make any big deal about it either. If you ever saw any blacks even walking up or down the sidewalks, hoping to get a peek inside one of the show bars, it was a rare sight, but you would never see any of them actually attempt to go inside. That just never happened.

The one exception to this was a doctor by the name of Chesterton. He was an old neighborhood buddy of The Lord's, and he was what the blacks used to call a "high-yellow," which meant the subject's skin was practically white. Doc Chesterton looked whiter than many of the Greeks and Spaniards that frequented The Block, and Harry let him come to the clubs for two reasons: he was a friend, and nobody knew he was black.

He also performed abortions for the showgirls.

The most revealing thing about this unwritten racial code was that almost all the clubs had live bands and most of the bands would be primarily comprised of Negro musicians. The show bar district was no different than the rest of the country in the mid-twentieth century.

Rudy Nepper owned a place on The Block next to the Desert Club. It was a small strip joint called the Blue Room. However, from time to time he would change the name of the place if business was bad. For example, he changed it from the Blue Room to the Red Room to the Pirates Den to the Girlie Club. The club name's life depended on how business was.

The world-famous Two O'Clock Club was owned by Solly Goodman who made stars out of strippers. He allegedly made Blaze Starr (formerly Fanny Belle Fleming) a star. He taught strippers all the right dance moves. When the hottest strippers, like a Tempest Storm or an Irma the Body, were in town to play the Gayety, Goodman would have the trainees go to the show and study the dance moves.

Seventy-five percent or more of the strippers on The Block were from out of town. Mainly rural women, they were from the Carolinas and the Virginias, the Midwest, and upstate New York. On the other hand, the waitresses were either Jewish or Italian and from Baltimore, a very conservative and very Catholic town. Therefore, if you were born and raised in Baltimore, you might work on The Block, but only as a laborer, waitress, waiter, or bartender. There was no way you were going to strip.

TWENTY NINE

SENATOR Edward HiGGINS

Higgins ducked out of the committee meeting unnoticed and hurried down the hallway toward the elevators. It was almost lunch time and soon the hallway would be alive with power-hungry lawmakers en route to their fancy lunches around Annapolis, the state capitol.

Rounding the corner into the central corridor, he spied perky Nan Kligerman up ahead. She worked on the first floor as secretary to Delegate Sam Clark of the Third District, and was blessed with the most incredible ass this side of the Chesapeake. He watched as she jiggled quite purposefully towards him, her tits moving to their own incredible beat. He really didn't have time to waste chasing skirts, but damn, they were everywhere. How the hell was he supposed to get any work done?

"Afternoon, Senator," she chimed. Her fuck-me expression pinned him like a butterfly on corkboard.

"Nan," was all he could manage, but he threw her a knowing smile and feigned dignity. That required her to look away nervously. He was reminded of Judy. "Get your mind out of your shorts, Higgins"—her comment to him this morning when he'd jumped her in the bathroom. Women.

He'd made arrangements to meet Harry at a small, out-of-the-way restaurant in Severna Park. Far enough away from any prying eyes. Higgins was prepared to spill his guts. He'd learned long ago that the only way to get where he was going was by covering his ass and steering clear of complications. There was definitely some bad shit to contend with right now. And covering his ass was priority number one. The choice was simple. If he stuck with Delvecchio, it would be political suicide. He could kiss the U.S. Senate seat goodbye. "Smiling Ed" Higgins was no dummy. That sonofabitch Delvecchio was going to have to fly solo on this one.

Higgins pulled his government issue Ford into the parking lot of Belle's Diner and scanned the four cars out front. Harry hadn't arrived yet. The guy always had to arrive last. So concerned with making a grand entrance, even in the face of his own demise. A trait that really irritated Higgins.

Inside Belle's, he slid into an empty booth near the front window and lit up a Camel. His mind was racing. Okay, Harry's about to go down. No question. Somebody had been "singing" down at City Hall. The palms he'd greased along the way had either closed up or had exceeded their grasp. Somebody like Deputy Chief Applegate or even Hizzoner himself was sharpening their knives for Harry Tennyson. Gambling. Prostitution. Numbers. Even drugs. Higgins was prepared to be the white knight and offer Harry a helping hand.

The front door squeaked open and Syd Daniloski, the big oaf, appeared in the doorway. He nodded toward the waitress behind the counter and took a seat across the room. Higgins glanced at his watch and continued to drag on his "coffin nail." Exactly four minutes later Harry shambled in looking like he hadn't slept in days. He lowered himself into the booth, panned the room in an instant and settled his eyes on Higgins.

"So?"

"What? No 'hello, how's it going?'"

"Cut the crap, Ed. I'm not in the mood. You called me here for a reason. Let's have it."

The waitress, identified by a little name tag as Jonelle, appeared with a smile, but Harry threw her an annoyed glare. Higgins ameliorated politely. Always the politician.

"Just coffee for us, miss. Thank you." She vanished.

When the cups were settled in front of them, Higgins fished out another Camel and eyed Harry for a minute. Careful now, he thought.

"When'd you start smoking?"

"Today."

"What's going on, Senator?"

"It's more like what's going down." He saw the alarm flicker in the man's eyes, then disappear so fast he wondered if he'd imagined it. The Lord was always the cool cat.

"Okay," Harry said evenly. "What's going down?"

"Look, I'm going to have to abandon all unspoken arrangements for awhile and try to finesse things a bit. Press a few palms, kiss some babies. You know I've had my sights on the U.S. Senate, and it's imperative for me to fine tune my public image. I can't afford to be associated too closely with you anymore . . . . "

"What the fuck are you babbling about? Imperative for you to fine tune your image? Drop the political bullshit and just spell it out, Ed. What, you're not gonna be my friend no more?" Harry faked a pout.

"This is serious, Harry. Don't be an asshole. I'm here to help you. The shit's about to hit the old whirling blades. Is that clear enough for you? City Hall is about to unleash the dogs on you, man. They've got a file on you six inches thick and word is they're ready to move."

Harry was looking out the window. He didn't look happy.

Higgins was feeling badly, too, but not as bad as he would if he sided with Delvecchio and risked getting whacked by Harry's goons. There were two schools of thought on just how dangerous The Lord really was, Ed knew. There were those who figured Harry for a very ruthless man, while others said he was a pussycat and had never killed a man in his life. Ed didn't want to know.

"What are you suggesting?" Harry's tone was neutral. "We

don't socialize together anymore? Dolores and I don't have you
to dinner for a month or two? We don't talk on the phone much
until things blow over?"

"No, Harry. It's not blowing over this time. I'm saying we
avoid any contact whatsoever from now on. Indefinitely.
Delvecchio is behind this."

There. He'd said it. Now there was no turning back.

Harry's eyes flickered again. Anger this time.

"All because I decked him? What the fuck is he up to?"

"It's no secret Applegate wants the chief's job. He's
spearheading the investigation, and your father-in-law, Vinnie,
is not running interference for you anymore. You used to have
a very big friend in the City Council, Harry. But since you put
him on the rug in your library, Dolores' old man is looking for
a grand jury indictment. He's out to get you, and I think he's
willing to do just about *anything*." Higgins let the emphasis on
that last word sink in. It didn't take long.

A soft chuckle erupted from Harry.

Higgins shifted on the hard bench. He was getting that
pounding headache again.

"Vincenzo Delvecchio might despise me," said Harry, "but
he would never do anything to hurt his precious Dolores. She's
his pride and joy. The man gets a bigger hard-on over Dolores
than he does for his own goddamn wife." Harry took a sip of
his coffee.

"That's not going to stop him this time," said Ed.

"I think you might be mistaken, Senator. Vinnie might be
wishing for my demise. Hell, he probably has wet dreams about
it every night, but no way is he gonna do me in. He doesn't have
the balls."

"You're fucking Katherine Louise, Harry. That really pisses
him off. You embarrassed the guy at his daughter's Christmas
party in front of everyone. He's mad, Harry. Crazy-mad. And
when a man starts thinking irrationally, it doesn't matter
anymore what the consequences are. He's willing to take the
risks because he doesn't care what they might be."

They sat in silence for a moment and Higgins sneaked a
sideways glance at dumb Syd across the room, happily sucking

down his eggs. Oblivious. Why did Harry insist on traveling with a guy like that?

"I have a proposal, Harry."

"Go on."

"I've got a place on the Eastern Shore where you could go and lie low for awhile. You could just disappear quietly. Let everything fold up, like the tents of a cheap circus. Without you around, everything collapses."

Harry said nothing. He was looking out the window again.

Ed wanted to get things wrapped up and get the hell away from Harry Tennyson. The place down in Easton would be perfect.

"Look, I can arrange for someone to pick you up tonight if you like. You'll get out of town fast and go down to my place in Easton. No one will know you're there. You can relax, enjoy the view, and nobody's going to have a clue as to where you are. From there, we'll see. What do you think?"

Harry looked at him with one eyebrow half raised. "Why're you doing this, Ed? I have my suspicions, but maybe you'd like to confirm them."

Ed shrugged. "Let's just say that it's in my best interest to see you survive. If you go down, I know I'm going with you. The way I see it, I have no choice—I've got to side with you."

"Spoken like an honest man," said Harry. "You sure you want to go down to Capitol Hill?"

"So, what do you say, Harry?"

Harry sighed heavily. He made no attempt to hide his emotions.

"Katherine's going on tour. The bitch . . . she's leaving me because I won't give up everything and run off to some fucking remote island."

"Maybe you should re-think that idea."

"Don't get cute on me, Ed. Katherine is no good to me right now. You were right the first time. I need to go it alone for awhile. Wait things out and see what's what. I like your suggestion."

Higgins relaxed a little.

"Yeah, I think I could use a vacation right about now."

"I want you to know, Harry, if there was any other way out of this mess, I would be there right by your side. You've been a good friend to me."

"Yeah, yeah. And you're returning the favor. Duly noted. I'm not gonna tank your career just because I fucked up a little. You did your best, and that's all I ever asked of anyone. Unfortunately they don't always deliver. Like Katherine."

The poor guy was really broken up about this hot little stripper. And here was a guy that had more women available to him than most sheiks with their harems . . . Katherine Louise must have been some kind of special dame. Or special fuck.

"I'm really sorry things aren't working out with Katherine."

"Never mind her. When can you have me picked up?"

"Eight o'clock tonight. And make sure you appear as if nothing unusual is going on. As far as anybody's concerned, you're going down South, maybe Atlanta, to check out some real estate or something like that. Nobody can know. Not even Syd."

"Really?"

"Not even Syd knows where you are," Ed repeated the words very deliberately. "Everybody knows you don't go anywhere without Syd. This will make it look very real. Delvecchio won't have a clue."

"You're taking a big risk here . . ." Harry let the sentence fade.

"Not as big a risk as siding with Vince," said Ed with an ironic little smile. "If he's serious about trying to take you out, I know I go down with you. Whether I planned it that way or not, I've become one of the bad guys. If I suddenly try to saddle up with the *good* guys, it's going to be a very short ride."

"You chose well," said Harry, knocking back the remainder of his coffee.

"You better get out of here."

Harry nodded and stood slowly. Syd had stuffed in the last of his toast and signaled for his check. Ed Higgins watched Tennyson leave the cafe and cross the parking lot to his black Chrysler. Harry slid behind the wheel and sat there for a few minutes, then pulled out onto Route 2 and sped away. Ed wondered what Harry The Lord Tennyson was thinking about at that moment. He wondered if his life was parading before his eyes. Wondered what the man was going to tell his wife and kids as he kissed them goodbye. Then he realized he didn't really care. As long as Harry Tennyson was far away from him, and wasn't talking, Ed Higgins' career wasn't on the edge of a cliff.

And Capitol Hill remained within his grasp.

Outside, Syd's bulky frame lurched across the parking lot to a black sedan, jumped in, then peeled out of the loose gravel in pursuit of his boss.

Ed Higgins, pleased with the way he'd deftly dodged yet another political bullet, paid the bill and left Belle's Diner wearing his confident, million-dollar smile. Things had worked out as best as he could have hoped. Harry Tennyson was voluntarily disappearing, and nobody was going to know his hide-out except the state senator . . . .

. . . . who could, if things got complicated, make sure Harry The Lord Tennyson disappeared forever.

Thirty

Harry Tennyson

Harry paced nervously across the Persian rug in the bedroom as Dolores continued to arrange pressed slacks and clean underwear in a suitcase. She wore a sickening half-smile. The one she reserved for times when the children were close at hand but she wanted Harry to know how much she truly despised him. He wondered why she would screw around with helping him pack if she was all that pissed off. You never could figure out how women really worked, could you?

"What are you so damned nervous about?" she quipped.

"Nothing." He stopped in his tracks.

"Can't you hurry it up? The car will be here in ten minutes!" Her smile tightened.

"I'm just making sure you'll have enough underwear to last you, dear. You never know when you'll need a clean pair of shorts."

A knowing smirk. The bitch. Harry wasn't the least bit broken up about getting away from her for a couple of weeks or so. He'd used Higgins' suggestion about the real estate deal in Atlanta. It wasn't unusual to be going on a business trip. She didn't buy it, but he didn't really give a damn.

Harry wasn't about to offer her any clues regarding his true whereabouts. Too risky. He didn't give a shit about her. Hell, Dolores' old man was planning to put a torpedo into him, wasn't he? No, there would be no thoughts wasted on sappy Dolores. She was a Delvecchio through and through, and not to be trusted.

But Harry *was* concerned about his kids. They were innocent in all of this, and in case he never saw them again, he needed to make sure they knew he would always love them.

"Where are the kids, Dolores? I wanna say goodbye."

"Doing their homework," was her terse reply.

As he walked down the hallway towards his daughter Shirley's room, Harry thought quickly about how to say goodbye without conveying that this could be final. Shirley was emotional like her mother, with sensory perception that promised to one day make her the envy of suspicious women everywhere. Her second best quality was manipulation.

"Hi, Daddy," she chirped, looking up from her math book. "Did Mother tell you about the class trip?"

"No, sweetheart. What trip?"

"To London." She sounded exasperated. "There's a class trip to London this spring and I'm just dying to go. What do you think, Daddy? We'll get to go to Buckingham Palace and the Tower of London. It'll be the ultimate cultural experience. Don't you agree? I mean, when will I ever get another a chance like this? Can I go?"

"Absolutely, Shirley. If you want to go to London, your wish is my command."

Her face lit up like a Christmas tree as she catapulted herself out of her desk chair and into Harry's open arms.

"I love you so much, Daddy. You're the greatest. Mother said you'd be a real meanie about this. You showed her." A smug smile.

"I love you, too, sweetheart. More than you'll ever know."

"I promise I'll bring back souvenirs for everyone and write you all dozens of postcards."

"That would be swell. Now don't let me interrupt your studies. Go on back to your homework. I wouldn't want to do anything to break your straight-A streak."

She planted a kiss on his cheek and returned to her work. Harry went across the hall to his son's room and knocked on the door.

"John?"

"Yeah, Dad?"

"May I come in?"

"Sure."

John Tennyson was a handsome boy and, at seventeen, he already had the broad shoulders and maturity of a full-grown man. Harry had high hopes for his son. He had brains and drive just like his father, and ever since a childhood accident which had resulted in a broken leg and hip-high cast, the boy had aspired to medicine.

A doctor in the family. What more could a father ask for?

"What's up, Dad?"

"Just wanted to say goodbye . . . I'll be leaving in a couple of minutes."

"Okay. When will you be back?" The boy's dark head dipped down and disappeared under his desk. He popped back up, huge dictionary in hand.

"Oh, I'm not sure. I've got some business down South. Shouldn't be too long though. Can you be sure to look after your mother and sister?"

"No problem, Dad. But Mom's been acting real weird lately."

"Really? In what way?"

"She talks to herself when she thinks no one's looking. Shirley caught her this morning out in the back yard."

"Don't worry about that. She's just got a lot on her mind. If she needs someone to talk to, you can be there for her. You're a good son, John." Careful. Don't let on too much.

"Okay, Dad. Or I can just call Grandpa Vince, right?"

"Sure. Feel free to call on Grandpa Vince at any time. He's family. Family should stick together." Harry winced at the irony.

201

A horn blared outside and Harry leaned toward the window to peek out. It was a beige Ford. Nondescript-looking. The driver's-side window was rolled down. An arm rested there.

"I gotta go, John. Be good." He reached out and touched his son's strong shoulder.

"Yeah, see you, Dad." The head was bent over the dictionary in desperate search of a definition.

Harry moved to the door and paused on the threshold.

"John, I love you." He didn't turn around to see the puzzled expression on his son's face. He knew it was there and that was enough.

Dolores had placed the suitcase outside their bedroom door. She sat primly at the vanity, polishing her nails. Harry poked his head in.

"I'm leaving now."

"Have a great time," she said with sarcasm.

"Dolores, this is a business trip."

"Then go take care of business, Harry," she said quietly.

On that cheerful note, he picked up his bag and headed out to the waiting car at the curb. The driver didn't pop out to take his bag and hold open the door, so Harry slung his valise across the back seat and hopped in next to it. There was no partition separating him from the driver, who smelled strongly of garlic.

"You all set, Mr. Tennyson?"

"Yeah. What's your name?

"Call me Jimmy."

"Okay, Jimmy, let's roll. Do you know where you're going?"

"I live near Easton. No worries, man."

"Well, let's hit it then."

They pulled away from the Tennyson home and Harry couldn't help looking back over his shoulder. The light in his bedroom was out now. He knew Dolores was standing there at the window, white lace curtains pulled back slightly, watching him drive away. In a week or so she would tell the children he'd walked out on them. She would reap loads of sympathy from friends and family. The kids would endure bad jokes in school for awhile. Then everything would settle down and he would be able to come back to town. He hoped. He would make it up to the kids somehow.

Lighting a cigar, he settled in for the long ride, and tried to keep unpleasant thoughts from his mind. Thing was, that's the only kind of thoughts he was having these days . . .

They traveled northeast towards Delaware, then back south towards Maryland's Eastern Shore—a mainly flat, featureless expanse of chicken and tobacco farms that was light-years from the colorful life Harry was used to. If Jimmy was any indication of the locals, Harry feared he might stand out like "a Chinaman at a Seder." He pushed the thought out of his mind. Jimmy blared country music on the radio and crunched grease-laden potato chips to the rhythm of the twanging guitars.

In the back seat, Harry shook his head. How in the hell had it come to this? He longed for his limousine and a glass of sherry. His nerves were shot.

He pulled a black, leather-bound book out of his briefcase and flipped it open to page one. It was a daily planner of all his appointments over the course of the last two years. He had a lot of incriminating names listed in that book. Delvecchio's name came up many times. Next to each appointment was a space for notes. In his own special coding, Harry had recorded the gist of each meeting. He could take a lot of people down with this book.

Earlier that afternoon, after the meeting with Higgins, he'd swung by the club. He'd waved Syd on home and snuck up to the office above the Desert Club to collect a couple of things. Didn't want it to look like he cleaned everything out. After all, he was just going away on business. But he took the black appointment book. He also took all signs of his dealings with Little Marvin. That included a file an inch thick on all the shakedowns with the police and the initial deal he struck with Marvin for the East Baltimore territory.

And a cardboard box full of reels of recording tape. Years ago, he'd run into Meyer Lansky and some of his people on a gambling boat on the river south of Philly, and the old pro had told him how important it was to make tapes of everything that was ever said on your home turf. Ever since then, Harry'd had a big Webcor reel-to-reel running in the storage closet just behind his executive chair. He'd wired in a switch under his desk so he could flip that sucker on and catch any conversation he ever wanted. You never know when a tape might come in handy, especially now that everybody was out to get him . . .

Jimmy interrupted his thoughts and the country music snapped off.

"I think we're being followed."

Harry's instinct was to swivel around to see who it was, but common sense got the better of him.

"What makes you say that, Jim?" Stay calm.

"White Plymouth. Been tailing us since the last town we passed through. A couple of guys driving. They look suspicious."

"Keep an eye on them. Can we dump 'em?"

"Well, I think we oughta consider changing our destination, Mr. Tennyson."

"Damn, and I was looking forward to relaxing on the front porch in Easton." The sarcasm was wasted on Jimmy. He didn't get it. Harry swore again under his breath and contemplated his options. There weren't many. "You got any ideas?"

Jimmy checked his Timex. "Well, if we catch the ferry at Lewes, we could hit the Jersey shore. Last one leaves in thirty minutes."

"Sounds good to me!" said Harry. "We gotta lose these goons."

"What do you mean?"

"Ever heard the words step on it?" Harry said, annoyance slipping into his voice. "I mean *hit it,* Jimmy. Don't let up until you see the fucking ferry."

The car lurched forward and the music snapped back on. Harry sneaked a look over his left shoulder and saw the Plymouth wasn't far behind them. It was starting to pick up speed. He reached down and opened his briefcase. He tucked the black book inside and slid his hand down the inner compartment until his fingers rested against the cool metal of the .38 Smith & Wesson. It was already loaded, but Harry hadn't shot it at a person in quite awhile. He smiled, hoping he wouldn't have to take the aim of his life tonight. He slid the gun into the breast pocket of his jacket and called out to Jimmy to cut the tunes.

"How're we doing?"

"I think I lost 'em. Nope, spoke too soon. Here they come now."

"There's an extra hundred bucks in this if you can ditch those assholes."

The car surged forward again and Harry sunk down in the back seat. He would kiss the ferry if he made it there alive.

"You're lucky I know these roads like the back of my hand, Mr. Tennyson. I got an idea."

"That's one more than I got, Jimmy."

They turned abruptly and sped west along a small country road. As they picked up speed, Harry could see the headlights of the Plymouth dipping along in the dark as it sped towards the turn. The idiot tried to take it too fast and the car spun out in the gravel. That afforded Jimmy some valuable extra seconds. He pumped the gas and shadowy corn fields flew by. A mile up the road he turned right, putting them back on course due north.

"The ferry's about twenty minutes from here. We'll make it," said Jimmy.

"They're still gonna be right behind us."

"Not for long. Trust me, Mr. Tennyson."

Jimmy jammed on the brakes and spun onto an even narrower lane that seemed to bob and weave straight through the crops. Harry had never liked corn, but now, here amidst the stalks, he loved it. Loved that it had a habit of growing so tall and strong and thick. The car had actually left the road and was plowing through the still-standing husks. Where the hell was this hick taking him?

They made several more turns, each taking them deeper into what felt like an endless checkerboard of farms. Then suddenly they popped into a clearing. The sky was blacker than the bottom of a gun, thought Harry, but the moon was lighting up the field like a giant desk lamp.

Unbelievably, the white Plymouth, with its jet-plane fins, lay broadside at the end of a narrow lane, blocking their path.

"Jesus Christ! Are you kidding me?!" yelled Jimmy.

Jamming on the brakes, Jimmy started to force the column shifter into reverse. Two guys jumped out of the sleek car with guns drawn. Muzzle flashes were accompanied by weak, popping sounds as the miles of open country refused to echo the sounds of the gunfire.

"Goddamn!" yelped Jimmy as a slug spidered the front windshield. He dived down towards the floorboards as the car idled in neutral.

Fuck it, thought Harry, as he threw open the back door, using it as a shield, and slipped out behind its hinged slab. The bigger of the two gunners was wearing a yellow vest. Using it as a target, Harry two-handed the .38 and squeezed off three quick shots.

Three misses.

Their return-fire peppered the car door as Harry drew down on Yellow Vest again.

His next shot caught the guy in the belly, knocking him back against the side of the Plymouth. In the moonlight, he could see a red flower starting to blossom against a field of yellow.

The guy was screaming and his partner gave up the shooting match to help him out. Harry pulled the door shut, and vaulted the front seat, half falling behind the big steering wheel.

"What happened?!" said Jimmy, still wedged in on the other side of the transmission hump.

"Get up and give me some directions!"

Harry grinded the shifter into first gear and popped the clutch. The car hurtled forward, veering away from the Plymouth at a sharp angle, as Harry shifted up through the gears. The two shooters stared at them like a couple of raccoons staring into a flashlight, until, at the last instant, the one guy raised his gun. But Harry had Jimmy's sedan cranking by then, and they blurred past the Plymouth at almost fifty.

With Jimmy yelling turns in his ear, Harry punched a hole

through the farm land night. Signs and telephone poles clicked by like he was passing a picket fence.

Harry looked behind them. Darkness. A green street sign flew by which read Lewes Ferry 5 Miles. Harry relaxed a little.

When they pulled into the ferry loading area, there was no sign of the white Plymouth. The ferry was just about finished letting a small line of cars onto the deck. Harry stuffed a hundred-dollar bill into Jimmy's outstretched hand and jumped out of the car.

"Thanks! I didn't really deserve this," said Jimmy.

"Don't worry about it. You did just fine."

Jimmy smiled a big country smile. "Me? What about you? You're a hell of a driver! Not a bad shot, either . . . . "

"All in a day's work, James."

"Looks like we fucked up," said Jimmy. "What do we do now?"

"I'm going to take this thing to Jersey for the night. You tell your boss, the senator, what happened, and see if you can get a different car and pick me up here tomorrow. I'll be on the afternoon ferry back to this side."

"Sure thing, Mr. Tennyson. We'll get you to that house one way or t'other!"

Harry boarded the ferry. He tucked his bag and briefcase under a bench and collapsed onto a hard chair nearby. There weren't many people on board. He figured to get a room in a motel near the ferry. Maybe call the senator.

The night air was brisk. In the summertime, this was actually a very pleasant excursion. But right now, tonight, the season was wrong and everything appeared surreal. The boat seemed old and unseaworthy. The salt air stung his eyes and face. This wasn't the way things were supposed to go. What the hell was he doing here, running scared like a fucking rabbit? Harry Tennyson never ran from anything in his life. He faced his troubles head-on.

But he'd never had troubles like these before. Now, not only was his livelihood crumbling around him, but his very life was on the line as well. His wife hated him. His mistress hated him. His kids didn't really know him. His father-in-law wanted him dead. And his lifelong pal, Syd, didn't even know where he was.

Syd. He'd been there in fifth grade when Harry kissed Lucinda Shiner behind the gym. On a dare. The whole class had been buzzing about it. Amazed she'd let him use his tongue. A little twist on the truth, courtesy of Syd. Then in high school, he'd taken the fall for Harry when he was suspected of cheating on a test. He didn't want Harry to further jeopardize his already flimsy scholastic record. God bless him. And, of course, he'd stood up for Harry on that ominous, rainy day in 1940 when he'd agreed to love, honor, and cherish Dolores until they were parted by death. Syd, always the strong, silent type, had held his tongue and smiled throughout the whole ostentatious affair.

And, best of all, Syd had finessed the thing with Katherine. Harry knew his friend secretly lusted after Katherine, but always the gentleman, Syd never let on. Only Harry, and perhaps Katherine, too, knew the real meaning behind those sorrowful kicked-puppy eyes.

Time kind of stretched out as the ferry muddled across the open water. Harry kept thinking about the guy in the yellow vest, wondering if he was going to make it, or if Harry Tennyson had finally "made his bones," had finally killed a man . . . .

THIRTY ONE

Charles Whittier

"Who are you here to see?" asked the desk sergeant, a broad-shouldered, black woman with loosely-waved, red hair.

"Deming. Detective Dwight Deming. He's expecting me." Charles looked at her with what he knew must be a weary expression. The trip to Central from his hotel was not that long, but he was not exactly on top of his game these days.

"Do you need to fill out a report?"

"I did that already. I just need to see Detective Deming."

"Have a seat over there. I'll page him."

Charles, feeling like a war-torn refugee with his facial bandages, stiff neck, and the damned cast, moved gingerly to a folding chair in the waiting area of the police station. People gave him the once-over. It was tough to distinguish whether their faces registered pity or disgust.

He felt like shouting out, *I was attacked! I didn't pick a fight with anybody. I wasn't roughed up for dealing. I was just attacked. An innocent black man, walking down the street, minding my own black business.*

But he said nothing. He sat and waited, passing the time by trying to read the faces and background stories of the various people that paraded into the lobby.

Twenty minutes later, Deming emerged from another room and lumbered towards him.

Charles met him halfway and followed him into an interview room.

"How you feeling?" asked the detective.

"I've felt better."

"Take a seat. Can I get you some coffee?"

"Nah. I just want to know what you've found out so far."

Deming lowered himself into a chair across from Charles and took out a pad.

"I've got possible Latino or Italian assailant, dark eyes, dark hair . . . " he paused.

"That's it?" Charles was incredulous.

"You didn't give me a whole lot to go on, Mr. Whittier."

"That's *your* job, isn't it? You guys are supposed to be out on the street asking around, searching for witnesses. I told you there was a foursome up ahead of me. Maybe they saw something."

"And just how do you suggest we find them? Do you remember what they looked like? Ages? Men, women?"

"We've been through all this . . ." Charles was frustrated. He also knew he sounded a bit ridiculous. Of course, there were only hundreds of other crimes far more important than his puny attack. Shit, he wasn't even robbed.

"Look, man, I realize this case is not exactly at the top of your priority list . . . hell, I'm sure it's not even *on* your priority list, but could you give me some peace of mind here."

"I'm not sure what you mean."

"I mean—am I okay out there?"

"I *told* you to watch your back."

"Yeah, but I was kind of hoping that was just a routine line. But I can't get it out of my head."

"Why don't you just say what you're thinking, Mr. Whittier?"

"Okay. Do you think I'm in trouble here because of my investigation into Harry Tennyson?"

Deming swallowed hard. Tried to shrug with great nonchalance, but looked awkward in doing it. He stood up, moved to the door. "Stay here for a minute . . . I'll be right back."

He disappeared into the noise of the precinct, leaving Charles to stare at the featureless, undecorated walls. When Deming returned moments later, he had a piece of paper in hand.

"Call this guy. His name's Applegate. Former chief of police. He retired about ten years ago, but he still has a lot of buddies on the force."

"How's this guy going to help me figure out why I got jumped?"

"Applegate wasn't exactly a close friend of Harry Tennyson's, but he knew him pretty darn well. But listen to me, Whittier—you didn't get any of this from me, okay?"

Charles nodded.

"Applegate's predecessor—Bobby Kilpatrick—and Tennyson were very tight, if you get my drift. There was plenty of talk that Kilpatrick lived in Tennyson's pocket."

"What's this guy Applegate have to do with it?"

"He succeeded Kilpatrick. The old chief died rather unexpectedly when he tried to 'eat his gun'—his own service revolver. Applegate tried to pin the death on Tennyson. I don't know if Applegate wants to talk about it, but he might shed some light on things."

"How old is Applegate now?"

"Christ, he's gotta be in his seventies, at least."

"I appreciate this, Detective Deming."

"Good. Now maybe you'll let me get back to my job." A small smile eked its way onto his face. "Just be sure you leave my name out of *everything* you say or do, okay?"

"Deal. I appreciate your help."

"I can't wait to read all about what really happened."

"You will, and it'll be a page-turner for sure."

"*Esquire*, huh?"

"Yeah . . . "

"That's that men's magazine without any spread shots, right?"

Charles winced. "Yeah . . . they don't use those."

Deming shrugged. "I'm a *Penthouse* man myself, but maybe I'll look you up, Whittier . . . "

They shook hands and Charles made his way out of the police station. He walked west two blocks through The Block, noting how shabby and bleak it appeared during the day. The marquee to the old Desert Club, without all the bright lights to jazz it up, looked as old and tired as the women who danced there forty years ago. In a matter of days it would be gone.

Hailing a cab back to the Stouffer Hotel, Charles sat back and made his plans. Maybe a short nap, then make the call to Warren Applegate. The painkillers were knocking him back a few steps, but a little shuteye should help keep him sharp.

The ringing of the phone nudged him out of what had turned into a very deep sleep. Groggy, Charles reached for the phone and dropped it. When he recovered the receiver, he spoke into it with mild annoyance.

"Yeah?"

"Mr. Whittier, please." The voice was commanding.

"Speaking. Who's this?"

"Warren Applegate, Mr. Whittier. Do you know who I am?"

Charles sat up straight in the bed.

"Yes, sir, I've heard of you. How . . . how do you know *me*?"

"Oh, I have some old buddies down at Headquarters who mentioned you the other day. Said you were doing a little research."

"Yeah, as a matter of fact, I was planning to give you a call."

"Oh, I know, young man. I know." Applegate sounded strong and confident, much younger than his years.

"So . . . do you think I could use you as a source?"

"Let's get together. We can discuss the subject."

"Great, where should we meet?"

"I'll be up at Loch Raven Trap and Skeet later this afternoon if you want to stop on by. I'll look for you around two."

"Trap and Skeet? Will I be able to find it?"

"If you're as good as I hear you are . . . "

"I'll be there, Mr. Applegate. And thanks."

Loch Raven Trap and Skeet lay off in a wooded site several hundred yards off Dulaney Valley Road near Towson, a wealthy suburb north of Baltimore. Surrounded by large-acreage homes and a state park that bordered a large reservoir, the area provided welcome contrast to the hard edge of the city. It was nice to get out of the traffic and the noise and back into relative safety again. Charles parked between a couple of four-wheel-drive vehicles and walked over to the shooting area.

It was two o'clock on the nose and as he approached the row of men preparing to take aim, he had no trouble picking out Warren Applegate. He was the only older guy there, but for a man in his seventies, he appeared strong and vital. Charles watched as the skeet were released and the men fired. Chief Applegate dropped one with relative ease.

When the round was finished, Applegate turned to take in Charles and his bandages. Recognition flickered, then he turned back and motioned for another round. Charles waited patiently, beginning to feel slightly uncomfortable standing around. He was about to walk back towards the parking lot and sit on a bench. Walking and standing seemed to aggravate the pain in his shoulders. Just then Applegate lowered his gun and made a big fuss over wiping the weapon down and laying it in the case.

Finally he strolled over to Charles and extended his hand. "Mr. Whittier."

"Charles will be fine. Pleased to meet you, Mr. Applegate."

"Thank you for your patience. C'mon over here. There's a spot where we can sit a minute. Looks like you could stand to take a load off. I heard about your mishap. Damn shame."

"How'd you hear about me?"

"Oh, I keep in touch with a few of the guys down at the precinct. They tell me you been digging into Tennyson's murder."

"Was it ever established that he was murdered? They never found a body, right?" injected Charles.

"Well, I think everybody supposes he was killed. God knows there were enough people who would've liked to have seen him dead back then."

"I see."

"Is that what your article's all about—Harry Tennyson, The Lord of The Block?"

"Not really. Supposed to be a run-of-the-mill history of The Block, then suddenly I start uncovering dirt on Harry Tennyson. You were close to him, right?"

The old guy kind of smirked as he popped the tab on a Pepsi he produced from his equipment bag.

"We were acquaintances. The chief before me was more than that. Old Bobby Kilpatrick. He did the dinner bit with the wives, cozying up to the politicians. Stuff like that."

"Do you know how Harry died?" Charles asked.

There was a long pause. Charles listened to the sound of the skeet biting the dust and waited for a reply.

"I think Harry was murdered for money. He was doing big business at the Desert Club and the gambling boats were a huge success, but there were rumors that Harry made an even bigger score buying and selling real estate through companies that nobody knew he owned."

"Really?"

"Yeah. His buddy, Syd, and one or two others were the only ones who knew the whole story."

"What others?"

"Well, Tennyson's mistress for one. Katherine Louise. And even though he didn't confide in his wife, I think Dolores Tennyson knew about the money, too. And you can bet if she knew, her father knew. I take it you've come across some of these characters in all your research," he said matter-of-factly.

Charles nodded.

"Yes, but I thought the money was coming from drugs. I thought Harry delegated the drug trafficking to Little Marvin Harper."

"We did too. But the more we dug into the whole operation,

the more we realized Harry was no drug dealer. He never liked it. Thought it was too dirty a business. Turned out he was right, didn't it?" Applegate smiled. "Yeah, by today's standards, Harry Tennyson was like a kid hustling lemonade on the corner."

"So the real estate was legit?"

Applegate shrugged. "Well, back in the fifties, things weren't as regulated. Lots of saps were buying housing lots in the Everglades back then . . . there were lots of scams, and I'm sure Tennyson was in on some of the best of them. He was secretly stockpiling the money, that's for sure. And as far as we could tell, he never touched it. Harry disappeared shortly before he would've been set for life."

"That's when he just disappeared."

"Bingo," said Applegate sardonically.

"What happened to the money?"

"Good question. We never found it. It disappeared with Tennyson."

"And Tennyson's body was never found."

"You already know that."

Applegate chugged down the last of his Pepsi, slowly shook his head, then continued.

"Tennyson went into hiding just before the grand jury indictments were set to come down. He told his wife and kids he was going on a business trip. No one ever saw him again."

Charles stood, offering Applegate his good hand.

"I appreciate your time and information. I'd like to find that money."

"I wouldn't talk about your intentions so boldly, Mr. Whittier. There're still people around that would like to get their hands on more than a million in cash."

"You mean I might be in danger?"

Applegate smiled, gesturing at the cast. "Look at you! You gotta ask a question like that?"

Charles felt embarrassed.

"Besides," the old man continued, "what makes you think you'll find what the police never could?"

"Intuition and hunger. I've got a good feeling about this. And if my luck holds true, this story's going to put me on the map."

"Well, good luck to you, then. Let me know if I can help. And Charles?"

"Yeah?"

"Don't forget what I just told you. I'd watch my back if I were you."

"I hear you."

"I mean it. Anytime you're dealing with that kind of money, there's bound to be someone else after the same thing. Just be aware."

"Thanks for the advice."

"It's gospel, Charles. Live by it. I did, and I'm a happy old man."

Charles shook his hand, climbed into the car and headed south towards the city. He sensed things were winding down. If he pushed just a little harder, maybe he'd have the ending to his story.

He just hoped it was going to be a happy one.

Thirty Two

The Article

Born and raised in Baltimore, The Lord married sweet Dolores Delvecchio before God and three hundred witnesses, then promptly aligned himself with his father-in-law, City Councilman Vincenzo Delvecchio. Harry had great hopes of cleaning up his image and gaining a relative who could smooth things over when feathers got ruffled. But Tennyson's marriage fizzled quickly into one of convenience, and his unhappy wife was forced to devote herself to homemaking and child-rearing as her husband hotly pursued and won the love of Katherine Louise. Eventually Delvecchio found out, and it was all downhill for The Lord after that.

Tennyson met Katherine shortly after she was hired as the new "ingénue" dancer at the Desert Club. They were the darlings of The Block . . . the sexy young girl and The Lord. She was an instant sensation, and I talked with her recently about her life and experiences as a big-time stripper. Now up in years, she is still an attractive, smartly-dressed woman with clear, blue eyes, and the pleasing remnants of a trim, firm figure.

"I had a body that wouldn't quit back then . . . " she laments with a proud smile. "They used to call me Hips because of the way I could move. And, of course, Harry loved that."

Katherine Louise, nee Mabel McCallister, is a quick-witted and very determined lady. She blew into Baltimore on a train, fresh out of the hills of West Virgina. The product of a bitter mother and sexually abusive father who produced seven unwanted children, she spent her childhood longing for a way out. When she could bear no more, she packed her small bag in the middle of the night and was gone.

Katherine rose to stardom on The Block quickly, grasping Harry's coattails in the process. She showered him with the kind of love and attention he craved, never asking too much in return. But deep down inside, she admits with a sad smile, she wanted to be Mrs. Harry Tennyson. But it was never meant to be.

Much of this history of Baltimore's Block reads like the script of a weekly soap opera. You have your heroine, a classy stripper, in love with the very married and very defiant nightclub owner, who just happens to dabble in slightly illegal activity on occasion, but always leans on the very righteous shoulders of his political father-in-law and comes out smelling like a petunia. Then you have your nemesis. In this case, it comes in the form of a short, black man named Marvin, who elected to take The Lord to task.

Little Marvin, as he was called, was a big-time drug pusher on the West Side of Baltimore in the fifties. He happened into the East Side business quite by accident. The Lord ran the numbers on The Block, and Marvin hit big. When Harry couldn't pay up, he "gave" Marvin a drug territory—East Baltimore, a white neighborhood, totally untapped. But determined, Marvin worked it and harvested a healthy business, trafficking his way to near-millionaire status. He never forgot that he was duped by Harry Tennyson, though. Harry thought he was free and clear. He continued to pursue his get-rich-quick idea . . . offshore gambling casinos aboard luxury boats. Little Marvin took stock and plotted revenge.

Thirty Three

Harry Tennyson

Harry rattled around Ed Higgins' Eastern Shore home like a shiny pinball at the Coney Island arcade. Actually, he kind of drifted from room to room in the upstairs apartment of the old house. He never had liked reading and the TV reception was terrible—one station from Salisbury. So there wasn't much for him to do except walk around and listen to all the comings and goings from the people in the downstairs apartment.

He walked out on the big back porch and watched yet another car pull away from the house. A breeze made it feel colder here, and there was a suggestion of water in the air. Harry lit a cigarette.

The black woman who rented the lower floor was very secretive about her days. Although she wasn't exactly Harry's type (a little too plump around the middle and not dark enough), he was beginning to want her. He couldn't help but fantasize about his white skin next to her dark flesh and their bodies moving in rhythm. He didn't know why, but black women responded better in bed than did the white girls. Maybe it was the jungle rhythms that were in their blood, or maybe it was—

"Mr. Tyler?" A woman's voice pierced his thoughts. She surprised him by slipping up the porch steps so that she stood below him on the landing, looking up. "Mr. Tyler, sorry to interrupt your daydreaming . . . "

Higgins had insisted he use the alias while hiding out. "Just in case," he had said. This whole scene was beginning to get on Harry's nerves. Having to stay holed up all day and night was bad enough. Not being able to use the phone to check up on his affairs—business *and* of the heart—was downright crippling.

"Miz Florence, she goin' to the market this evening. Needs to buy some supplies, and was wondering if you might be needing something?"

Harry waved her question off and asked, "Tell me, Rosie, what is it that keeps Miss Florence so busy?"

"It ain't none a my bidness, Mr. Tyler."

Rosie leaned against the railing with her arms folded across her chest. "All's I know is that some say she deals in the devil's work and others says that she helps thems in needs. I say so long as she pays me on time, I don't see nothing."

"That's the spirit, Rosie. See no evil, hear no evil, right?"

"Whatever you say, Mr. Tyler. Now, is there anything you'll be needing?"

He wanted to tell her he needed to get laid. He wanted to tell her he needed to feel the pavement of the big city streets of Baltimore. He wanted to tell her he needed a lot of things, but instead he said, "No, I'm okay. Thanks."

It was times like these he wished he liked to read. But the thought of picking up a book had always been abhorrent to him. So, instead, he idled the hours away by walking the length of his apartment. He practiced tying a bow-tie knot for awhile, then he polished his shoes, and he'd even managed to learn how to balance a cigarette on the end of his nose.

And, by dinner time, he knew how a prisoner must feel doing hard time in a jail cell. But the most important thing Harry Tennyson *knew* beyond all reckoning was that he had to avoid a prison term at all costs. So, from now on he had to keep his nose clean. If Higgins could get him out of this one, he was going to figure out a way to stay clear of trouble.

He walked back into the house and sat on a brocaded sofa that Rosie had called a "davenport." Thoughts washed over him like the retreating breakers of low tide.

He'd have to come clean with Dolores and wish her well. She hadn't been a bad wife, really. But it was time to let her go. He would create something new with Katherine. Yeah, Harry Tennyson was planning out a new life for himself. He had all that cash salted away and it was silly to not think about finally using it. He wasn't getting any younger, and the heat was not going to lighten up, not with Kilpatrick eating his gun like he did and Delvecchio no longer in The Lord's pocket. But money was power. It might not buy happiness, but it could buy time, and time was the great equalizer, wasn't it? A little time untangling this mess would be all Harry would need.

Harry stretched back on his chair, kicked his feet up on the window ledge, and took a deep breath. He marveled at the sky. All those stars as far as the eye could see. He was thinking that he still had a chance to keep going with the "good life" when he felt something ram into the house with such force the foundation shook. He heard the sound of imploding wood.

Downstairs, the front door crashed open.

"POLICE! Everyone stay where you are. Nobody moves and nobody gets hurt!"

"Holy shit!" Harry said as he tried to jump up and his chair fell backwards. His heart started beating faster. He heard screaming and a lot of running around downstairs. Without giving it a second thought, he peeked out the window. What had once been a quiet night was now a spectacle of lights as police cruisers swarmed the place like ants at a Sunday picnic.

"Oh God, oh please, oh God." Harry sat down by the window repeating his mantra. He managed to scramble towards the door, open it a smidge and peek down the stairs. The entrance foyer seethed with blue uniforms. Pure bedlam. Cops were throwing things around.

A voice on a bullhorn beckoned him. *We know you're in*

there! Let's make it easy on everybody . . .

God . . . please, thought Harry, get me outta this one.

Looking out the window, he saw some of the uniforms lugging out all sorts of equipment, filing cabinets, and what looked like an examining table from a doctor's office. A big, beefy cop was guiding Rosie into the back seat of a black-and-white. "Where's that killer, honey?" he asked.

Rosie screamed and cried as she said, "Please, Mr. Policeman, let me go. I don't know nuthin'."

As Harry looked down on the scene, he sensed movement beyond them. A woman in a white coat was running away from the house, heading toward the corn fields across the street.

A couple of the uniforms spotted her, gave chase, and dragged her down before she reached the road.

It was Florence. Harry would recognize that big ass anywhere. She kicked and screamed as they hauled her back to the nearest cruiser. "Stop it! Y'all hear me?! We have nothing here. Y'all let go of me!"

Good for you, Florence, thought Harry. She's buying me time.

"McKinley!" cried the guy on the bullhorn. "You and Carter go check out the upstairs and see what you find."

Harry scrambled around like a crab with a couple of legs missing. He had to get moving, to hide, but he had no idea where to go. These motherfuckers were cleaning out the house looking for him.

The window seat! Thank God for *Arsenic and Old Lace.* If the cops hadn't seen that movie, Harry might be safe. Harry ran over to the window and moved the solitary vase that rested overtop and placed it on a table. He managed to squeeze in, but it was a tight fit.

His heart racing, he listened as the cops clopped into the room and moved clumsily around the furniture. They'd be going through all his stuff, but if they never found him, they might figure him to have split.

"You think she's a whore, too?" Harry heard one of the muffled voices saying. The two lunkheads laughed as though the remark had been a particularly witty one.

"Looks clean up here. There's just a suitcase."

"Check under the bed?"

"Yeah, nothing."

And with that the room fell quiet. Harry didn't move a muscle. He would just stay in this damn box until he was certain they weren't coming back . . .

. . . and he was very surprised when the lid to the window seat lifted back to reveal Rosie looking down at him. "Mr. Tyler? What you doin' in there?"

Stunned, dazed, confused. All the words applied as he struggled to get conscious and make sense to himself. He didn't know how long he'd been there. How the hell did he fall asleep?

With some effort, he managed to stand up.

Rosie chuckled as she said, "Now, Mr. Tyler, how long have you been in there? Some man you turned out to be."

"How'd you know I was in there, anyway?"

She smiled. "Oh, I've been workin' for the senator for a long times. My chir'rens used to hide in that winnda-seat. I guess I jess natcherly looked in there . . ."

"What the hell happened here last night?" Harry asked.

"The cops finally found out about Miz Florence. She been doin' abortions. She be up at the jail house right now." Rosie shook her head.

Jesus, he couldn't believe it. He'd turned himself into a human pretzel for nothing. What kind of luck did he have, anyway? And how long would it be before it ran out? Did the flatfoots who'd been rousting his room look in his bags? Had they seen anything? What was the chance his name might come up in their reports? And how long would it take for these bumpkins to realize the Baltimore cops were looking for him?

Too many questions. Too many things that could go wrong.

Harry had decided right then and there that he had to get to Katherine and whisk her away somewhere. Somewhere faraway where they could start a new life. She had been right all along.

Why is it that they're always right? Harry marveled at the

thought.

"Rosie," he said, looking at the housekeeper, "I've got to use the phone downstairs."

Thirty Four

Charles Whittier

Charles listened as the big, brass knocker fell heavily against the door. He heard the sound of heels clacking on tile floor, then the door opened. Katherine Louise smiled broadly and stepped aside. "Well, hello again, Charles. I figured you'd be back." She slipped a pair of reading glasses off her nose and looked at him closely. "Got a few more questions?"

"Just a few . . . if you have the time, so do I."

"All I've got is time, hon. You planning to stand in the hallway all night? C'mon in and have a glass of iced tea with me."

Katherine Louise lived in a row house on Thames Street in Fells Point. It was garishly decorated. Lots of gilt-framed mirrors and paintings. The tiny living room featured ruby-red, velvet furniture nestled on plush, white carpeting. A replica of "the little piss boy" statue stood in a corner in the middle of a miniature pond. Charles found the pseudo-babbling-brook sounds annoying.

"So," she said, eyeing him up and down. She looked at his bandaged arm as she motioned him to the sofa. "What happened to you?"

"Oh, it's a long story, but the short version is I had to come clear to Baltimore to get mugged for the first time in my life."

"Oh, I'm sorry to hear that. Damn thugs are taking over the city. I swear I'm going to up and move to Florida one of these days. You look like you're in pain . . . hell, it's after five. Forget the iced tea, how about a drink?"

"You know what, I think I'll take you up on that. I wouldn't mind a gin and tonic."

"Coming right up. She turned gracefully on her two-inch heels and moved over to a mini wet bar in the corner. Charles noted that Katherine performed every task with calculated precision. The ice into the glass. Gin poured just so. Tonic splashed over the top with a bit of a flourish. She handed it to him and he took a deep drink. She must have been good up on stage.

"So how's your story going? Come back for a little more color?"

"Well, surprisingly, I've got more 'color' than I'd planned. I've uncovered a pretty juicy sub-story that's kind of taking on a life of its own. I think my editor's gonna kiss my feet when I throw this one on his desk."

"And how do *I* fit into this juicy sub-story?" Her red lips curved into a seductive smile that was not altogether unattractive on this older woman. "I am correct in assuming I'm part of the juice, aren't I?"

"Uh, yes, ma'am, you are . . . "

"So, are you going to tell me?"

"Well, it all starts with an old friend of yours."

Her eyes flickered with interest. "Go on."

" . . . guy named Harry Tennyson."

She stiffened ever so slightly. "Ahh. I knew sooner or later you'd dig up some dirt on old Harry. He was quite the character."

"Well, Ms. Louise, that's why I'm here. Last time we met, you gave me some real good stuff on the essence of The Block back then, but you never mentioned your affiliation with Harry Tennyson. Any particular reason?"

226

"Please, call me Katherine. If you expect me to lay my life out on the table for you, the least you can do is call me by my first name."

She seated herself on the chair nearest to Charles. He could see her plotting her next words. Perhaps a little too carefully.

"Harry Tennyson and I had a love affair," she began. "It lasted a couple of years . . . from the time I arrived in Baltimore to just before his disappearance. I s'pose you've heard all about that?"

"Yes, a little. But I was hoping you could fill in the gaps. Some people think Harry didn't disappear on his own."

"Meaning . . . ?"

Charles shrugged. "Meaning that he was actually murdered."

"Why would anyone have wanted Harry dead?"

Charles grinned in spite of himself. She was acting so naive, it looked painfully phony. "Well, it seems to me there were a lot of people who had their reasons . . . "

"Really? I never realized that."

"And then there was the money he was supposed to have hidden away."

"Oh, yes, the money . . . " Katherine sipped her drink, tried to act disinterested, and did a very bad job of it.

"He never talked to you about it?"

"No, he didn't." Katherine stared at him for a moment. "Who else have you talked to? Just out of curiosity."

"Well, most recently, Warren Applegate." He paused for effect. "And, of course, Harry's widow, Dolores."

A deep chuckle eased out of her.

"Ahh, Dolores Tennyson. I haven't thought about her in awhile. What a piece of work she was back in the old days. That woman could slice a person to bits with a mere look. She considered herself above everyone whose last name wasn't Rockefeller or something. I guess that was partly Harry's doing, but that woman gave us the damnedest time . . . "

"She knew about your affair?"

"Oh, yes. She knew. And it killed her. Harry was so caught

up in appearances. See, it just wouldn't have looked right if he up and abandoned the city councilman's daughter and her kids. So poor Dolores was forced to live with a man who didn't love her."

She walked to the corner of the room to an antique writing desk called a "secretary." She paused, looking at him. "He really *did* love me, though. And I've still got the proof, right here."

"Really? What do you mean?"

Katherine reached into one of the pigeonholes of the desk, pulled out a scrolled piece of paper held fast by a faded, pink satin ribbon.

"Harry gave this to me the last night I saw him."

"What is it?"

Katherine smiled wistfully. "It's a poem. He wasn't much of a writer, but he read it to me out loud. I was so angry with him, I don't think I paid attention to the words, the feelings, 'til later. When it was too late."

"I understand," said Charles.

"Here. Take it." There was pain in her voice. "Maybe it will help you tell the real story about Harry."

"Are you sure you want to give *me* this? I could just copy down the words," he said, feeling awkward.

"I've read it so many times I memorized it long ago. Take it."

Reluctantly, he placed the poem in his briefcase. "Thank you, Ms. Louise. I have a feeling there's a lot you can tell me."

"Perhaps there is. What do you want to know?"

Charles cleared his throat. There was no way to ease into this without sounding crass. "What can you tell me about the last time you saw Harry? What day was it? Where did you meet? What did you talk about?"

"My, my, you don't want much, do you!?" She reached down and pulled off her shoes. Pink toenails peeked through her stockings.

"Okay, hon, since you're so cute, I'll tell you about the last day I saw Harry Tennyson. I'll tell you *all* about it . . . "

THIRTY FIVE

Dolores Tennyson

As she walked through the doors of Hutzler's Palace on her way to the beauty shop, Dolores couldn't help but smile. She had regained control of her life.

It was nice to have a daddy who could help you out in any situation. Vinnie Delvecchio was connected. It was that simple. He knew so many people, it had been easy. Daddy had arranged for that wicked Katherine Louise woman to leave Baltimore and go on to bigger and better things. And that cheap trick from West Virginia had probably thought she was going on tour because she was *talented*! Dolores chuckled out loud. What a hick, she thought. When you are born trash, no matter how pretty the package, you remain trash.

And, thanks to Daddy, she knew *exactly* where Harry was, or better yet, where he *wasn't*.

There was a bounce in her step that hadn't been there in years. Ah, yes. Life was good.

She pushed open the doors to the beauty shop and was greeted by Lavinia, the shampoo girl.

"Good morning, Mrs. Tennyson," she beamed.

"Good morning, Lavinia."

"Well, it's nice to see you all smiles," Trudy said as she walked over to Dolores, took her by the arm, and led her to a chair. "How's that husband of yours?"

"Never mind about Harry. Got any good gossip?" she asked conspiratorially.

"No, nothing new really. The lady that gives me all the juicy dirt has been out of town. She's the fancy one that hangs with Blaze Starr."

"Blaze Starr? You mean the *stripper?*"

"Yeah, sure. Who do ya think?"

"And who is this other woman . . . ? Her friend . . . " The spark left Dolores' eye and she felt the muscles in her face tightening. "*Who* do you mean?" she asked.

"Her name's Katherine Louise," Trudy said matter-of-factly. "Hey, wait a minute, you met her . . . Remember?"

"I did?" Dolores was perplexed. Meeting her was hardly how she would ever describe the first time she'd seen her husband's floozy. "I guess I don't remember . . . "

"She's real pretty," said Trudy.

"So, she's out of town?" Dolores figured she should at least fake some interest in the bitch.

"Well, she was on tour. Washington, New York and like that," said Trudy as she reached down for a brush. "But she must be back in town . . . "

"Really . . . ?" Dolores tried to sound only mildly paying attention, but inside, an alarm bell had started ringing. Why would that hussy be back here?!

"Yeah, Miss Louise scheduled an appointment for tomorrow," said Trudy with a smile and a wink. "So ya know what that means?"

"What?" Dolores looked at her with naked suspicion. "No, what?"

Trudy tapped her on the shoulder. "It means I oughta have something juicy for you next week."

No, thought Dolores. I think this time it will be my turn. She knew she would have to call Daddy again.

Thirty Six

Senator Edward Higgins

The mantle clock struck 11 p.m. as Higgins poured himself a fourth Jack Daniel's neat. Why the hell hadn't Harry called? Hadn't been there a week and already there was trouble.

The guy was being damned inconsiderate. Here Higgins had put his ass on the line to help him out, and the guy couldn't even make a phone call? He was supposed to call in once a day. That had been their deal.

He'd sent Jimmy down to the "safe house" when it got so late he couldn't stand it any longer. Now he was waiting for his driver to call, as well as maybe Harry.

Maybe something had gone wrong. If it had, Ed didn't want to think about it. After that car chase through the corn and Harry shooting it out with the two goons, Ed figured it was all over. All over the papers, and the story would eventually leak out like the air in a cheap balloon. But when the radio and papers never caught on, and the dead shooter on the Eastern Shore never even got a couple of column inches on the back page of the *News American,* Ed knew Vinnie Delvecchio had been the man behind everything.

Hard to believe he would have his own son-in-law killed, but these were desperate times and politicians were desperate men.

The ringing phone interrupted his thoughts. Knocking back the rest of his bourbon, Ed grabbed the receiver. "Hello?"

"It's Jimmy," said the familiar voice.

"Jimmy, where are you? What happened to Tennyson?" Higgins barked.

"I'm down the place," he said in a very drawn-out voice. "There was a little trouble here."

"What?! What happened? Spit it out, you slow-talking moron!" Anxiety had him by the throat. "What the fuck are you talking about?"

"Florence got hit . . . "

"Jesus Christ, when?"

"Around 7:00. They hauled in Rosie, too, but she's back. She's okay."

"Fuck Rosie! What happened to Tennyson?! Did they get him or what?!"

Jimmy told him about Rosie finding Harry. "She said he made a few phone calls and then walked up to the corner store to wait for a bus."

"He say where he was going?" asked Higgins.

"I already checked on that. Nah, he didn't say nothin'. What do you want me to do now?"

Ed looked at his watch. He probably wouldn't get much sleep tonight. He exhaled slowly. "Give me a minute to think this one through, Jimmy . . . "

"Sure, Senator. As you know—my time is your time."

Shut up, you pinhead . . .

Ed tried to keep his thoughts in order as he analyzed what might be happening. He had an idea of what Harry might have in mind. Not that he could blame the guy for panicking after the police raid, but having Harry on the run was too risky.

Finally: "Jimmy, I need you to just sit tight until I make a few phone calls. I think I'm going to need you."

"You got it, Senator. I'll be waitin'."

Ed Higgins replaced the receiver and put his hands to his temples and rubbed. His head was pounding. His heart was racing. He had to think fast. Who was the only person Harry would try to contact? Katherine, of course. Now where the hell was she? He remembered Harry saying something about her going on tour and ending up in New York. He'd have to track her down, and quick. New York only had a hundred strip joints . . .

Then he had an idea. John Galiani. His old buddy out on Long Island who had shared his love of ethics and fast women at the University of Maryland twenty years ago. Now a prominent New York state senator, the guy boasted of various connections to not only the highest office in the land, but also to the grimy underbelly of New York City night life. Everybody called him "Senator," but Ed remembered him from his college days when he preferred "G-Man."

Despite the hour, Ed put through a series of calls that eventually gleaned him Galiani's private number in South Hampton.

The woman who answered the phone did not seem put off by the hour. Late calls were part of the job if you were in politics, and she was obviously used to the routine. A half-minute passed and then his old college friend's voice came through the line, strong and boisterous as ever.

"Ed, how's it goin', pal?" he bellowed. "I was just thinking about you the other day. I spied a couple of dames that were ripe for the picking, and I thought about good old Ed and his trademark one-liners that always reeled 'em in!" He paused for a breath. "Man, it's good to hear from you!"

"G, I need a favor," said Higgins.

"I hear you're thinking about Capitol Hill! So am I!" said Galiani.

"John, please, I need some help . . . "

Galiani must have sensed the urgency in his old pal's voice because his tone changed instantly. "Hey, I hear you, Ed. What's up? You sound like you're wound up pretty tight."

"I have a small problem, but I'm hoping you can help."

"Name it. I owe you, Ed."

"You still have wires to a lot of the club owners in Manhattan?" asked Higgins.

"I don't like to say I'm connected, but yeah, I know a couple guys here and there. Why? What do you need?"

"I'm trying to track down a dancer, a stripper. For a good friend of mine. Her name's Katherine Louise. She's a pretty big attraction down here, and now she's on tour with some big promoter out of D.C."

"Not that schmuck, Winslow!"

"I'm not sure. Who's Winslow?" Higgins asked.

"Ah, the guy runs a traveling whore show. Books his girls into classy joints, then cheats the agents outta their money. This girl, she's a looker?"

"Oh yeah, yeah. Harry Tennyson made her a star. I need to find her, G. It's a matter of life and death."

"You're not kidding, are you, Ed?"

"No . . . Any suggestions?"

A moment of silence.

"Well, you might try the Metropole. If she's with Winslow, that's where he likes to bring his best dancers. I know the owner. Guy named Marco Rotundo. You can use my name."

"Can I reach him tonight?" asked Ed.

"Yeah, but you have to use a special number. Let me look it up for you. I'm right at my desk . . . "

Ed waited, still going over his options. He hoped he could talk to Katherine. Tell her to reel Harry in. Tell him how much danger he was in.

Galiani's voice brought him back to the present. He gave him the number, then, obviously not wanting to know what kind of dirt Ed had fallen into, tried to change the subject. "So other than that, Mrs. Lincoln, how did you like the play?"

Ed had to laugh, and the tension eased back for a moment. "I'm holding my own. The political scene is changing, John. We've got to change with it."

"You sound like one of those beatniks . . ." said Galiani.

Ed chuckled. He wanted to get off the line, but felt obligated to schmooze the guy a little. Old habits die hard, he knew. "How about yourself, John?"

"Good. Real good. I've got money in my pocket. I'm having dinner with a new broad every night. And last night I was with a woman who gave new meaning to the word 'blow'. I can't complain."

"Neither can I," Higgins lied.

"Hey, sure, buddy . . . then what're you doing trying to run down a two-bit stripper? You knock her up, Ed?"

"No, nothing like that. She's screwing a guy I need to find, that's all. I appreciate the information. You're a pal."

"Hey, Ed?"

"Yeah?"

"If you have any problems, let me know. Gotta run."

"Thanks, G. You're still The Man."

Galiani laughed. "And don't you forget it."

"Never happen," said Ed. "Thanks again. I'd better start working the horn. It's getting late."

They said their goodbyes, swore to stay in touch, and hung up.

Ed dialed Rotundo's number immediately.

Some guy named Lewis answered at the Metropole, and after dropping Galiani's name, Higgins was on hold for a matter of seconds.

"Yes, Senator, what can I do for you? This is Marco Rotundo at your service. It's not often we hear from our friends down in Baltimore."

"Yes, well, I was hoping you could help me. John Galiani thought perhaps you might be able to direct me to the whereabouts of a particular young woman. I'm looking for a dancer scheduled to appear at your club at some point during a tour she's currently on."

"Be glad to help. What's her name?"

"Katherine Louise."

"Oh, that dame? Yeah, she's been here three nights The crowds love her, I gotta tell you . . . "

Ed smiled. Pay dirt on the first call. Maybe things weren't so bad after all.

"Funny you should call and ask about her . . ." Rotundo

continued.

"Really, why?"

"She just left the office maybe an hour ago. Said her sister called. Her mother's real sick back in . . . wherever she said—Virginia, West Virginia, I don't know . . . "

"Where is she now? Can I talk to her?"

"Nah, she said she had to split. I coulda killed her 'cause she was a real draw."

"Split?"

"Yeah, she packed her trunk and got a cab for Penn Station."

"She's taking the train?"

"That's what they run out of Penn, yeah . . . "

"I'm sorry to keep bugging you, Mr. Rotundo, but it's very important that I find this young lady."

"Hey, no prob. I know how it is when you get a hard-on for a dame. It's happened to me a few times. . ." The man laughed, but Ed was not in the mood to join in.

"One last thing, did you get an address where she might be going?"

"Well, I wasn't gonna let her outta here without that! I need that broad back here ASAP. She was great for the business, you know?"

"And . . . ?"

"Oh, yeah, let me check that address," said Rotundo. "Yeah, here it is. She's stoppin' at the Lord of Baltimore Hotel to meet up with her sister tomorrow. Then she said she'll be gone for a few days, but that I can leave messages at the hotel."

Higgins smiled at the ironic play on words as he scribbled the Lord Baltimore Hotel on a piece of paper.

"Thank you very much for your help, sir. I'll tell Senator Galiani."

"Hey, that's great, Senator . . . what did you say your name was?"

"Smith . . . " said Ed Higgins. "Senator Smith."

"Yeah, right. Well, take care, Senator."

"Thank you, Mr. Rotundo."

"Anytime. It's like I always say, a friend of John Galiani's is a friend of mine for life. Let me know if I can ever be of service."

Higgins hung up the phone and congratulated himself on his detective work. Not only was Katherine Louise headed back to Baltimore, she would be just three short blocks away. And Higgins was willing to bet his left nut that Harry Tennyson would be with her. He picked up the phone and dialed a familiar number.

"Hello?"

"Jimmy Beaufort," said Ed Higgins, "I have another job for you, and it's going to be pretty dirty . . . "

Thirty Seven

Marvin Harper

The phone rang and Marvin Harper answered.

"Yeah?"

"Boss, it's Bones."

"Talk to me."

"He's here."

"*Who's* here?"

"The man . . . the man you been lookin' for. Tennyson."

Marvin felt something grab him by the back of the neck, like a ghost had suddenly crept up behind him. He struggled to sound cool and only mildly interested even though his head felt like it had been plucked like a guitar string.

"Say what? You sure it was him?"

"Oh, yeah. Positive."

"Where'd you scc him? Where is he?"

"Jus' got off a bus at the Greyhound."

"A bus!" Marvin had to laugh. My, my. Our Harry had certainly come down a few pegs. "What the fuck *he* be doing on a bus?"

"I don't rightly know. All's I know is that he's *here*. I'm watching him *right now*. He be makin' a phone call."

"Follow him. Call me each time he makes a stop. We can't let him get away now."

"He's leaving the station. Talk to you soon."

"Bones?"

"Yeah, boss?"

"You done good. Real good."

Marvin smiled as he nestled the phone in its cradle. The ol' Lord gonna soon find out he fucked with the wrong nigger, he thought.

Thirty Eight

The Article

Tennyson was looking to key in on an idea that was fast taking hold. In Charles County, situated in Southern Maryland, there was a legal loophole that stood to benefit the state, Harry Tennyson, and his partners as well. It seems that just across the Potomac, in Colonial Beach, Virginia, there were piers jutting off the coast that extended so far out that they were technically out of state. In other words, Maryland owned so much of the Potomac River, it included a portion of pier that originated from the Virginia side.

Harry Tennyson situated his luxury floating casino at the end of that pier, with the help of Vincenzo Delvecchio and some wealthy financial backers, and waited for the go-ahead so he could start to turn a profit. In the fifties, gambling was illegal in Virginia. Folks were desperate for a place to go. Harry saw the need and was anxious to fill it.

Problems plagued the venture from the start, however, and when the governor of Virginia went head-to-head with the governor of Maryland over the legal logistics, Harry got worried. He was ready to make a go of things and the lawmakers *were causing him to lose sleep. Harry decided to do what he did best. He greased a few palms. He snapped a few pictures of state senators patronizing his club and his girls. Harry figured if he dug up enough dirt on enough of the so-called good guys, he could make things happen. He was right.*

Tennyson's gambling casino opened to an excited crowd with money to burn. Harry started to turn an immediate profit, and served nothing but top-of-the-line liquor from the finest crystal. He treated his customers like royalty. He was there at the opening, pressing the flesh and smiling for the cameras. Delvecchio, painfully aware of his son-in-law's unethical dealings, lurked in the background, wary of the consequences if something went wrong.

But this was vintage Tennyson. Whatever he touched seemed to turn to gold, and the casino business boomed steadily for a couple of years. A few times he even brought Katherine Louise down to entertain the gamblers. They would sneak out and rendezvous in the back of a limousine, then speed down the interstate back to Baltimore so Harry could get home to his wife before midnight.

But somewhere along the way The Lord got careless. Someone out there was watching, and very closely at that. Someone wanted to do Harry in in a big way.

Despite his efforts to blackmail the police and the politicians in Annapolis . . . .

THIRTY NINE

KATHERINE LOUISE

"I understand now, Katherine," Harry was pleading.

"Look Harry, like I told you before, it's too little, too late."

He moved around the suite on the 20th floor of the Lord Baltimore like a boxer with wobbly knees. They'd been going at this discussion or argument or whatever it was for almost an hour. Harry had even read her a love poem he had written for her in Easton. He was upset and so was she. Katherine knew it wasn't going to get resolved, and she knew it had been a bad idea to come back.

"I have it all figured out," he said. "Look, over the years I've stashed money away. We have enough to live out the rest of our lives."

"How *much* money?" Katherine took a few steps away from Harry and shook her head and raised her arms. "No, better not tell me 'cause I really don't want to know."

She walked towards the window and picked up a silver cigarette case from the table, opened it, and delicately raised a cigarette to her lips and lit it. "You don't understand, Harry. It's never been about money to me. It's been about being in love with you, Harry. It's about wanting to please you, and knowing that you wanted to please me, too."

"Sure, babe, that's exactly what it's about for me, too." Harry grabbed her from the back and slipped his arms around her waist. He pressed his crotch against her ass. This disgusted Katherine. It wasn't that she was a prude. Not at all. It was just that, Jesus Christ, this man had no idea about tenderness. How could she have ever thought she was in love with him? He was helping her stand her ground.

"Harry, have you ever seen me as anything else other than your whore?"

He turned her around so that she was facing him. Katherine kept her head low so he wouldn't see the tears in her eyes.

"I've *never* thought of you as a whore!" His face revealed true shock, and it looked silly on him. "Katherine, I think about you all the time. No matter what I'm doing I stop and think, 'What is she doing right now?' I'm supposed to be hiding out, laying *very* low right now."

He told her about the attempt on his life, and she almost ran to him, but remained aloof.

"But I took a chance and came back here to get you," he continued. "I love you more than anything else. I didn't even call Syd. I picked up my own car from the garage."

"Oh, well, now I *know* you love me." Katherine's voice dripped with sarcasm. "At least it's nice to know that after all this time together I finally rate higher than Syd. For a very long time I didn't mind playing second fiddle to your legitimate life. After all, I had time with you and it was enough. But now, well, now I've met somebody that makes me feel like I'm the most important person in his life. When we walk down the street together he puffs out his chest as though to say, 'Look world, look who's walking next to me.'" Katherine wriggled out of Harry's grasp and said, "And, you know what, Harry . . .? I like it."

Harry suddenly got very serious. He grabbed her arm and said, "You know I don't like it when you talk that way."

"Harry, I don't give a damn what you like and what you

don't like! You're on your way down, Harry, and you're not taking me with you. I've worked too hard."

"You worked hard!? What about me?" He grabbed her wrist, twisting it.

"Harry, let go of me." He pulled her close, glared at her, then slapped her face.

"Look, you little bitch, I *made* you! I can break you!"

"Just try it, Harry. By the way, how many people know you're in town? You can't do shit anymore, Harry Tennyson." He loosened his grip and Katherine used this opportunity to break away from his grasp. She ran towards the bathroom.

Just as she reached the door, he caught up with her.

"Please baby, please baby, I need you so much." He hugged her and cried into her shoulder.

"Harry, let go of me." Katherine was getting scared. She had never seen him act this way before. He was a mess. Thank God she was getting rid of him. But as she looked into his face and saw his tear-stained cheeks, she began to cry, too.

"It's for the best, Harry." She cradled his head in her hands and stood on her tiptoes to place a gentle kiss on his lips.

"You little conniving bitch!" he screamed, jerking away from her. He moved like some Karloffian mannequin, and it was clear he was having trouble keeping himself under control.

"Wh-what?" Katherine stumbled backwards away from him. "What's the matter with you, Harry?"

"You think you can play with me?" Harry had the road map of a lunatic mind penned across his features. "I risk my life to come and get you . . . all for you to tell me it's *over*? And you think you can give me some bullshit kiss goodbye and I'll just slump my shoulders and walk out of here?!!"

"Harry—"

"You're *wrong!*" He grabbed Katherine by the neck and picked her up like a stuffed doll.

"Harry, you're choking me! Stop! Please stop it!" Harry had Katherine pinned to the wall as she kicked at his shins, but he didn't react to the blows. She wanted to scream, but even breathing was growing difficult. Was he trying to kill her?

The thought short-circuited across her mind. And she

wondered if this would be the way she would die.

And then, just as suddenly, he stopped and started to cry again. Clearly, Harry had lost it.

If Katherine could manage to get to the door she would be able to escape this madman. He hugged her again.

"Come on, Harry, lets go over to the couch." Katherine had once heard that you never argue with a lunatic. She decided to play along with him, lull him off to a comfort zone again, and then make a break for it.

"Katherine," he whispered, "don't leave me. I won't hurt you again. It's just that you hurt me when you tell me it's over. You're all I have left." He leaned on her and she tried to guide him to his seat.

"Do you want something to drink, Harry?" Katherine asked.

"Yeah. Something cool," he answered. Harry rested his head on the arm of the couch and closed his eyes.

Katherine got up and started to walk slowly towards the bar. She circled the couch and slowly walked past Harry on the other side of the sofa as she made her way towards the door. She slowly placed her hand on the knob and began to turn the handle when suddenly a heavy hand slammed the door closed again.

"Where do you think you're going?"

"Harry," Katherine turned slowly to face him. "I was going to get you some aspirins."

"Liar."

"No, really, I was." Katherine slipped out from under his arms and walked away from Harry. Once she was a few steps away she started to *run*. Not just a fast move, but she broke into a full sprint toward the bathroom.

Harry leaped over the couch, gaining on her as she stepped through the door and tried to close it on him. He came across the threshold like a locomotive at full throttle bearing down on her.

His lead foot hit the bath mat and he slipped as it shot out from under him. As he pitched forward, he reached out for her. For an instant she saw a flash of surprise and a little-boyish look of help-me panic in his face. She almost grabbed for him, to catch his fall, to absorb and pull him into her, but she saw past his veil of helplessness to his eyes, where something dark and crazy lurked with pure dementia. In that moment of recognition, she lashed out with both hands, getting the full weight of her arms and shoulders into it, and rather than pull him in closer, she pushed him past her, even digging her hands into his jacket like talons for extra purchase.

His speed accelerated and the edge of the tub cut him off below the knees as effectively as a two-by-four. Harry levered over like the counterweight on a giant clock and flipped into the tub headfirst.

Tangling himself in the shower curtain, Harry went down hard. Katherine heard a soft, squishy sound as his head impacted on the hot and cold water fixtures. For a terrible instant, his entire body spasmed and his feet ratcheted against the floor like drumsticks. The seizure-like contortions suddenly stopped, and the room filled with a terrifying silence.

Enwrapped in the curtain like a winding shroud, Harry lay very still.

She moved closer to him. "Harry?" She nudged him with her toe. "Harry?" He didn't move.

Leaning even closer, she could see why he wasn't moving, and *why* he would, in fact, never move again. The ornate fixture for the cold water consisted of four spokes fashioned in the shape of gilded, fluted flower petals. They were long and came to a point, and one of them had pierced Harry's forehead like the head of a spear.

A surprisingly small amount of blood had leaked from the lethal wound into the tub itself.

Moving away from his body, she bumped against the wall and slid down to the cold tiles. It was time to cry in earnest, and she did this until she couldn't see. She cried until she had nothing left. That's when she knew it was time to make a phone call.

It seemed like forever before she heard the knock at her door.

"Who is it?"

"Katherine, it's Syd. Hurry up!"

"Thank God you're here." She was so happy to see him she hugged him and gave him a peck on the cheek. His face turned red. It amazed Katherine how such a big man could be so gentle. "Oh, Syd, I'm so scared. I think he's dead. I *know* he's dead!"

"He hasn't moved?"

"No, nothing . . . "

Syd walked to the bathroom, appeared unwilling to go in. He looked back at her. "Did you check his heart, his breathing?"

"Syd, I can't. I can't get that close to him . . . "

The big guy took a huge breath, letting it out slowly. Looking into the bathroom at the body all twisted up in the shower curtain, he spoke softly, with his usual respect. "Hey, boss, it's just me . . . . "

Forty

Syd Daniloski

He never realized that people felt so . . . so *light* after they were dead.

Syd struggled to get Harry Tennyson's body up and out of the bathtub, weaving past the threshold to the couch at the other end of the suite.

He'd turned on the big Philco radio to WBAL to wash the room with some sound. Katherine had been bawling ever since he'd gotten there, and he was hoping nobody would hear all the racket the dame was making and try to get into the room. She kept crying and half-moaning that she'd killed him. That and a lot of "Oh, Harrys."

Now what was he gonna do?

Had to get the body outta the room. Had to figure out what to do with it so that nobody was the wiser.

" . . . Oh God, forgive me . . . Oh, Harry . . . !" Katherine continued to wail in the corner of the room as Syd approached her.

"Katherine," he said in a half-whisper. "You gotta help me. You gotta get aholt-a yerself."

Ignoring him, she kept crying, staring at Harry in his arms.

"Katherine, knock it off! Come on now!" This time, Syd turned up the volume a few notches. The force of his voice seemed to almost hurt her. Shrinking back from him, she looked as though she'd been smacked.

"I'm sorry, Syd . . . " She looked like a little girl who'd been scolded. "I really am sorry. I'll be all right. What do you need? What do you want me to do?"

He tried to shrug as he stood there holding his former master. "I don't know, ma'am . . . We gotta do something with the boss. We gotta get him outta here."

Katherine took another moment to draw a breath, exhale, and let the action calm her. Then she looked around the room like a cat looking for a place to leap.

"I've got an idea, Syd. Put him on the couch for now."

Syd moved to the sofa and lowered Harry down on the plush cushions. He hated the way his old boss' arms and legs just dangled like wet noodles. It just wasn't right.

Meanwhile, Katherine was going into the suite's big walk-in closet and dragging out her steamer trunk. He watched her unlatch the big, brass hasps and start yanking out all her costumes. Feathers and sequins and satins in a rainbow of colors began covering the floor. It reminded Syd of how Katherine threw her clothes off when she was dancing, and he had to admit she was even emptying the trunk with a lot of style.

"This will do," she said. "Put him in here."

"Jeez, Katherine . . . You sure?"

"I can get another trunk," was all she said, so he guessed she was pretty sure.

Leaning over the couch, Syd hefted Harry into his arms again. Once more, there was that terrible lightness—that sensation that something no longer abided with whatever was left of Harry Tennyson. He turned, moved to the center of the room, and hoisted the body into Katherine's trunk.

Before he lowered the lid, he paused. He had a hard time looking into his old boss' face. It looked so different. Pale, slack, and his lips had an almost bluish tint to them. He'd never imagined he'd ever be the last one to see The Lord of Baltimore.

"Wait a minute," he said softly. "Katherine, I need a towel, okay?"

She moved quickly to get it for him, and he rolled it up into a long tube that he wrapped around Harry's neck and tucked gently under the head. Then he closed the trunk quickly.

"I, uh . . . just don't want his head to wobble around in there, ya know . . . "

She nodded, wiped at the tears in the corners of her eyes, and tried to busy herself by scooping up her clothes and stuffing them into her suitcases.

Syd thought of Harry inside the trunk. His eyes were closed. Forever closed. But there was no time to mourn his pal now. He needed to get Harry the hell out of here quick, and he wasn't looking forward to hoisting the trunk. Be nice if he could find a dolly. Standing up, he told her he was going down to the lobby to get one. She was staring blankly at the wall.

He went over to her, turned her gently, then shook her by the shoulder. "Katherine, you gotta stay with me here. It's the only way we're gonna escape this thing okay. Harry wouldn't want you goin' down on account of his own . . . uh, untimely demise . . . "

"What?" she asked blankly. It was finally catching up with her, the reality of everything.

"He'd tell you to snap out of it and save yourself, right?" Syd looked at her squarely. She looked kind of glazed-over, like a day-old donut.

She glanced at him sadly. "Yeah, you're right, Syd. I'll be okay. You go on downstairs and I'll try to go over everything here and make sure it's totally clean." Her hands fell somewhat helplessly by her sides. Syd gave her a stiff hug, then moved off to the door.

Something had been bugging him, and he abruptly remembered. Stopping short, he turned to face her. "Oh, yeah . . . where's Harry's gun? Did you see it?"

Katherine looked at him. Again the blank expression. Syd spied Harry's overcoat on a chair.

"Check his coat pocket over there." She lifted the coat and removed the Smith & Wesson from a pocket, holding it loosely by the stock as though it were hot.

"Good. Now you hang on to that. You know how to use it?"

"Harry took me target shooting a few times. I shot this very gun."

"That's good. If there's any trouble, you gotta protect yourself. Understand?"

"I don't want to shoot anybody, Syd."

"You will if they're gonna shoot you first. That's the only reason you need to use it, okay?"

She was silent a moment.

"Okay."

"All right. Now I'll be back in five minutes. Don't go anywhere."

He ducked out into the hall and looked both ways. It was very quiet. A room service cart was parked a few doors down, but that was hardly big enough. Syd took the stairs down, skipping clumsily two at a time. "Don't fall you big klutz," he said to himself. At the ground floor he entered the main lobby and eyed the front desk cautiously. The bellboys usually rolled over to the desk with their carts already in tow, but the lobby was quiet and there wasn't a sign of either a uniformed boy or a luggage dolly.

Moving through the double doors to the sidewalk, Syd spied the doorman, splendid in his epauletted coat, wheeling a dolly away from a departing cab. Traffic crawled past on Baltimore Street, ignoring them.

"Pardon me, may I borrow that cart?" he heard himself ask.

The doorman just looked at him. Apparently more of an explanation would be needed.

Syd cleared his throat. "My wife has purchased far too many new items during our stay. I'll never get out of here without one of these." Syd congratulated himself on his quick thinking.

The doorman began pushing it through the doors to the lobby. "Donna's on break," he said, "but I can help you, sir."

"Help? Oh, no, I wouldn't think of bothering you," said Syd.

"Bothering me," said the doorman with a sly grin. "Hey, how do you think we workin' saps make a livin', huh?"

Syd looked down at him, speaking as deeply and officiously as possibly. "That won't be necessary, really."

The doorman continued to push the dolly towards the elevators. "C'mon, man," he said. "This is a hotel, and I'm a member of the Loyal Order of the Palm."

"Palm?" Syd looked at him, confused. He hated not understanding what people were really saying to him.

The doorman smiled a gap-toothed smile, held out his hand palm up, as though waiting to receive a tip. "C'mon, do I have to spell it out?"

Recognition jolted through him and Syd dug into his pocket for some folding. Nothing but fives and a twenty. "Please," he said as he pushed a "finsky" into the guy's beefy mitt. "I insist."

The doorman's gaze fell down to inspect the tribute and he half-chuckled as he backed away and let go of the dolly. "You betcha, sir," he said. "Knock yerself out with that thing!"

Syd grabbed it and guided it effortlessly across the polished marble floor. He entered the elevator easily and without incident.

Jimmy Beaufort

Seated in a comfortable, old armchair, just inside the entrance to the hotel bar, Jimmy Beaufort watched with great interest as Harry Tennyson's right-hand-man negotiated the luggage dolly into the elevator.

Looks like The Lord was getting ready to gather up his fair lady and make a quick exit, thought Jimmy as he left a buck on the table and headed towards the sliding doors. They closed just as he got there, and he watched the little clock-like indicator above the lintel indicate that big Syd Daniloski traveled up to the 20th floor without any stops in between.

As the car trundled earthward again, Jimmy prepared

himself for what lay ahead by reaching into his breast pocket for his flask of rye. All he had to do was wait right here and catch them on the way down.

Brad Vance

The service elevator stopped at the fifth floor and a cute, little colored maid prepared to step inside, loaded down with clean towels. Inwardly, Brad Vance cursed his bad luck. Turning his face away from her and tilting his hat down as though he were touching the cap of his maintenance man's uniform like a gentleman, he slipped out of the car.

She didn't even look up at him as the doors closed behind her, but he didn't want to take any chances on getting "made." Nobody could get a good look at him. That was the first rule on this caper. Now he'd have to wait for the damned thing to come back and pick him up again. He was anxious to get up to the 20th floor—there was a score to even up.

Room 2053.

This time Delvecchio's inside information had better be the straight business. Not like that Chinese fire drill on the Eastern Shore when Sammy Burch got air conditioned. Brad tensed at the memory of the shootout. He'd been scared out of his ass because Delvecchio hadn't said anything about Tennyson packing his own piece. It was supposed to be an easy snuff, but Tennyson turned out to be a tough nut.

Brad wasn't going to let this Lord character catch him off guard again. No damned way. Delvecchio paid big to get it done right, so this time Tennyson would be saying the long goodbye.

Brad carried an open-top toolbox in his left hand. On the top layer, covered by an old rag, rested an Army issue .45.

Katherine Louise

Katherine had wiped away the last of the blood from the

bathroom floor and was busy scrubbing her hands.

Hot tears stung her cheeks, and she couldn't seem to swallow the enormous lump deep inside her throat. Harry was dead. A confusing torrent of thoughts carouseled in her head. It was an accident. She killed him. An accident. She *helped* kill him. He slipped and fell. No, she did it. No, the faucet went through his head. Yes. No.

The water was scalding her hands, but she had to make sure the blood was off. When she finished, she looked up into the mirror and was frightened by what she saw. Her eyes were rimmed by puffy, red lines. Her hair fell wildly around her head, and the collar of her dress had a dark brown stain on it.

Blood?

She ran to the bed and fished another dress out of her suitcase. She hastily wriggled into it and balled up the soiled one. As she stuffed it deep down into the suitcase, there was a knock at the door. Her eyes flew to the trunk.

Harry. Harry's in *there*. And he was never going to move again.

Another knock. A knowing, expectant sound.

"Katherine, it's me. It's Syd."

She opened the door and Syd wheeled in the cart. Katherine stood back against the wall and watched as he lifted her trunk with effort. She winced.

"Katherine, I'm going out the service entrance with this thing."

"Where're you going?"

"I got a place, I think. A neighbor of mine just buried his Saint Bernard in a pet cemetery in Rosedale. Maybe . . . Don't worry, I'll take care of Harry and the trunk, and no one will ever know. Here's the keys to my car. It's parked out back. I'll find Harry's and get rid of it."

She looked at him, nodded. She couldn't speak.

"What about you?" he asked. "What're you going to do now?"

She shrugged. "I don't know. I hadn't much thought about it, really. I guess I should go back to New York and keep up with my tour."

Syd nodded. "Yeah, that sounds good. Stay outta here 'til things cool down. There's gonna be a lotta questions and such around here for awhile. Best if you ain't here."

"Nobody even knows I'm in town----except my hairdresser—but she doesn't count."

"Good, then, here . . . " He handed her a key ring with a plastic fob in the shape of a busty, naked girl. "You take my car to Penn Station and leave it in the lot on Lanvale with the keys inside. I got a spare set in my wallet. Old trick I learned when I was in the motor pool in the Air Corps."

"Thanks, Syd." Katherine was amazed at how clearly he seemed to be thinking. It was not like what she'd expected from the guy everybody just assumed was a big lunk with a vacant room upstairs.

He smiled sheepishly. "Katherine, you gotta go on like nothing's happened, see? Yeah, that's the ticket. Go back to New York, do a few shows, make it look natural-like. If anyone ever calls asking you if you've seen the boss, you haven't. Got it?"

Katherine nodded.

"Good. You gotta be strong now. Very strong. Don't call me neither. I'll be in touch with you when it's safe."

She leaned forward and kissed his sandpapery cheek. "Syd, you're a real friend. I don't know what I'd do if you weren't here, if you weren't my friend."

"I— I know, Katherine. I would just die if anything happened to you. Harry trusted me all his life and I owe him in more ways than I can count."

"All right, Syd. I'll be all right."

"And you know, if Harry hadn't been, well, you know, your man, I guess I would've liked to someday, maybe. . ." He paused and looked away from her and his ten-o'clock-shadowed cheeks flushed for an instant. "Well, let's just say I always wanted a chance to really protect you."

Katherine felt the pain of his awkwardness, the simple poetry of his needs and his dreams. She was grateful that he'd taken charge. She was grateful she'd finally seen him as more than another soldier in Harry's brigade. Maybe Syd had fallen under the tremendous shadow of Harry The Lord Tennyson, but it hadn't been enough to extinguish him.

The twisted imagery of her last thought reminded her that there would never again be that looming, powerful shadow in her life. Her throat tightened again.

Syd was wheeling the trunk out the door but he turned quickly at the last moment to throw her a sad, half-smile. He was heartbroken over Harry. It was written all across his broad, kind face, but he knew he should try to be strong.

"It'll be all right," he said.

"I know," she said. "Because of you . . . "

He dropped his head a little. "Yeah, well, I gotta go take care of my friend. Goodnight, okay?"

Nodding, she eased the door shut behind Syd and his grim cargo. It was time to continue.

Marvin Harper

Little Marvin busied himself in the kitchen by peeling another colander of potatoes. The hotel banquet manager was one of his better customers for reefer and a little smack. When Marvin told him he needed to be in the Lord Baltimore tonight, the sap had a pressed white uniform laid out and waiting for him.

But *sheee-it*, the things a black man had to do to get even. Marvin thanked his mama's Southern Baptist God he'd never had to really work for a living. He glanced at the solid gold Benrus on his wrist. If he didn't make his move soon, he'd get stuck back here in the kitchen shuffling plates for some honkie convention. He tugged his white cap over his ears and eased out from behind the sink. Fuck the potatoes. Time to make his move.

Syd Daniloski

The elevator had reached the 20th floor and Syd positioned

himself behind the dolly, ready to push hard. When the doors opened, a maintenance man waited there. Surprised, Syd instinctively reached up and pulled his fedora lower, over his eyes.

"Can I give you a hand?" asked the maintenance guy.

"No thanks," said Syd, tensing ever so slightly. "You going up or down?"

The guy hesitated, but only for second. "Yeah. Up. I'll send it back down."

"Appreciate it. Thanks."

The doors closed and Syd breathed a sigh of relief. He looked down the hall towards Katherine's room and heard her door open. She emerged, coat and suitcases in her arms and hands. She looked nervously down the hall, and when she spotted him, turned quickly and headed the other way toward the main elevator.

"Good luck to you, Katherine Louise," Syd whispered as the doors opened again, minus the maintenance man. He took a deep breath and shouldered his friend and the dolly aboard.

KATHERINE LOUISE

After checking out, Katherine moved through the lobby as quickly as she could with all her baggage, even though she knew she should be taking it easy. She could hear the echo of her heels clicking, but they sounded as if they were coming from someone else. Through the dark lenses of her sunglasses she could scan the practically deserted lobby. No one even seemed to be looking in her direction.

As she stepped through the revolving door, the doorman smiled warmly at her.

"Need a cab, ma'am?"

"Oh, no thanks. My car's around back," she replied. Then hastily she headed down the block.

Jimmy Beaufort

Something funny was going on, that was for sure. The dame had just crossed the lobby and headed out to the street. Either Tennyson was still upstairs and they'd had a lovers' tiff, or even-money had Tennyson waiting for her in the parking lot out back . . .

Wherever Katherine was, Harry would be right there, stuck up her crack. That's what Higgins had said.

Better to take his chances following her outside. Sprinting across the lobby, he put his right hand in his coat pocket, only this time he wasn't reaching for his flask.

Katherine Louise

She was moving across the parking lot. Syd's new Chevrolet Belair hardtop was about twenty yards away, glistening in the early evening light. Suddenly, she heard the hurried rhythm of footsteps behind her. Afraid to turn around, Katherine increased her stride toward the car as her grip on the suitcases weakened.

But her resolve did not. In an instant, she planned her next moves. Even though Harry's gun was in her pocketbook, she had time to retrieve it because her purse was like a natural extension of her own body, hanging over her shoulder and across her chest by the strap.

The steps behind her grew louder—a heavy, thudding sound accompanied by the wheezing breath of a man, a big man. She made her decision in that final moment. Dropping the suitcases to the cobblestone, she unclasped her purse in an elegantly simple but efficient motion. She withdrew the gun and positioned it as she whirled around to face her attacker.

"Hey, hold it, lady!" The man stared at her, his hand frantically digging into his pocket as if seeking a weapon.

Without thinking, Katherine pulled the trigger. The report

from the muzzle was small and puny, more of a popping sound than the thunder she'd expected. But the impact of the slug at close range was enough to stop the guy in his tracks and send him stumbling backwards under buckling knees. His right hand fell loose from his coat, a chrome handgun fouled in his fingers.

He seemed to fall backwards in slow-motion as she watched him through a time-distended lens. Then suddenly his legs stiffened and his heels beat out a drum roll on the hard surface of the parking lot. Katherine stood frozen, watching his nervous system go into overload, performing a final dance step into eternity.

Then, without realizing it, she had stowed the gun, grabbed her bags, and was running. Reaching the turquoise and white Chevy, she dropped her things and fished out Syd's keys with the little, naked woman on the chain. She quickly tossed the luggage in the car, got in, and turned the ignition.

Finally, the engine kicked in and she was moving away from the scene towards an alley that fed on to Baltimore Street.

As she punched the accelerator, feeling the surge of power from the big-block V-8, she could still hear the staccato beat of the dead man's heels, and she knew it was a sound she would hear for the rest of her life.

Rick ScHMidT

Officer Schmidt stood in the parking lot behind the Lord Baltimore with Sammy Mays, a maintenance man at the hotel. They were both looking down at the corpse of a young, heavyset man in a trench coat. On his back, his eyes were still open, staring into a place nobody wants to see. There was a small, dark red entry hole just above the belt.

" . . . and let me guess," said Officer Schmidt. "You didn't hear a thing, right?"

Mays blinked his eyes. "Tha's right. Didn't see nothin' neither. Wouldn'ta seen *this* if it whatfor that I hadta take out this here trash to the alley . . . "

"You don't recognize him, do you?"

"No, suh," said the old man. "About the only thing I could recognize is that he was about the ugliest white man I ever seed."

Schmidt nodded. "You stay here, Mr. Mays. I'm going down to the call box at the corner and get some of the boys from homicide up here. I think they're going to want to ask you a few questions."

Brad Vance

Brad headed down the hallway toward Room 2053. As he approached, he saw a short Negro with a room-service cart standing outside the door. Brad slowed his pace and stopped about twenty feet away at 2057. He watched the waiter out of the corner of his eye as he prepared to knock. But before he could do that, the door to the room opened and a woman screamed.

"Shut your mouth, you dumb bitch!" he said. The waiter reached for the heavy pewter tray cover, but stopped halfway to the handle.

"Lord in heaven, boy! You scared me to death."

"Wha'chu doin' in there?" he asked, a little too mean and cocky for a Negro waiter for Brad's taste.

"My vacuumin', sugar. Wha'chu want?"

"They called for Room Service."

The maid laughed. "Not in here they didn't!"

"Say what?"

"Yeah, baby. You can take that little old cart on back to the kitchen. The lady in here, she done checked out already."

Brad watched the guy tense up in an effort to control himself.

"How long ago?" He grabbed the little woman and shook her by the big white collar of her uniform. "Where'd she go?!" The Negro maid tried to push him off and that only seemed to enrage the waiter more.

"You get your nasty-assed hands off me, you crazy nigger! What's got into you, boy?!"

"Shut up, bitch! I want to know where the peoples in this room went!"

"Well, I don't know," screamed the maid. "But if you don't get you hands off me, I'm gonna—"

Brad watched in shock as the waiter stepped back and cold-cocked her with a vicious left jab to the side of her head. Slamming against the door frame, she went down so fast it was scary. Then the guy lifted the tray cover off the cart to reveal a handgun that was half cannon on a bare plate.

This guy, thought Brad, was about as much of a waiter as John Dillinger. Something was out of control here and Brad knew he didn't want any part of it. He had been so caught up in the spirit of the chase, in the adventure, he'd never really faced up to the truth—he was playing with the big guys and sometimes they liked to play it real rough.

As he turned away from the door he was facing, he found himself turning back to catch one more glance at the short, crazy Negro with the big heater.

It was one too many.

"What the fuck you lookin' at, man?"

Brad shrugged. "Hey, listen, buddy, I'm just here to fix a leaky faucet."

"Maybe I fix a coupla leaks in you, white boy . . . " The Negro picked up the huge handgun and calmly pointed it at Brad's mid-section. Looking directly down the barrel, Brad felt like he was staring into the open end of a trash can.

Brad held on to his toolbox with his left hand, while keeping his right hand free. "Hey, I didn't see a thing, buddy . . . you havin' a tiff with some mouthy maid . . . it ain't none of my business."

The waiter moved a step closer to him down the hotel corridor, and Brad was sure the guy was stone-cold nuts-o. Some of the guests had probably already called the front desk, and security would be getting cops involved sooner or later. Nobody waves a gun around in the Lord Baltimore without drawing a little attention to themselves.

"Yeah, I'll bet," said the Negro. "I think I'll just—"

He suddenly buckled at the knee and screamed. Twisting down to his knee, he turned to face his attacker. Brad watched the waiter take aim with his magnum at the maid who had tried to take him out with the metal tubing of her vacuum cleaner.

Bad mistake, lady . . .

The Negro shot her at close range, and there was an explosive spray of blood and bone as half her shoulder disintegrated in a pink mist that airbrushed the brocaded wallpaper.

Brad ran for the nearest corner in the corridor, taking his toolbox with him. A second cannon blast behind him shook his eardrums as he edged past the corner molding. That he could hear it told him the shot had missed.

Footsteps padded in his direction. The crazy waiter was coming to finish him off for sure.

Pulling the old rag off the top tray of the toolbox, he grabbed the .45 automatic and held it out with both hands. The footsteps slowed, then stopped. *Come on, you crazy fuck!* Stick your big, blue melon-head around that corner. . . he thought.

But the guy didn't.

And the seconds ticked past Brad like redwoods falling in the forest at midnight. Then time became unglued and its passage lost all sense. Brad held his weapon out at arm's length, muscles tensing, foreclosing on themselves. Without realizing it, he levered the trigger enough to squeeze off the first round in the clip. The big slug tore into the wall across the hall, followed by the howitzer-blast of the waiter's gun, then footsteps running in the opposite direction.

I gotta be as nuts as he is, thought Brad, as he rolled into the hallway with his gun still held tightly in both hands out in front of him. Other than the maid who lay bleeding half in and half out the door to 2053, the corridor was deserted. He edged back to the corner, watching for any movement, wondering two things:

Was the maid already dead?

And, did he have any chance of still joining her?

Marvin Harper

Little Marvin cleared the fire stairs three and four at a time, all the while unsheathing himself from the kitchen whites. He had a flimsy, magenta, silk shirt underneath and with his black slacks, he was looking good. All he had to do was clear the building, he thought, and to the cops he'd be just one more flashy nigger on the street.

What happened to Tennyson?

The question rattled around in his head like a seed in a dried gourd as he continued to descend through the stairwell. His polished Florsheims were smacking on the concrete landings like leather strops in a barbershop, and his knees were aflame from all the shock absorbing they were doing. But there was no stopping now. He had to get out to the street and he had to do it quickly.

By the time he hit the first floor, his knees felt like jelly, but he forced himself into a wobbling sprint down a hallway that connected the laundry and storage rooms with the truck dock in the alley behind the building. There was a lot of yelling and screaming from the kitchen as he ran past it, and he knew he'd poked a big stick in this hornet's nest. Now it was time to split. Coming to an intersection of corridors, Marvin made a quick decision. It was either try to slip into the lobby and out the front doors during the confusion that was surely building, or go through the doors to the truck dock in the alley. His de Ville was parked up on Fayette so he had a long run to his ride no matter which way he ran.

Somebody was pushing through the double doors at the other end of the hallway, and Marvin stopped thinking about it. He pushed through the door in the opposite direction and stumbled over a container of industrial floor cleaner. Getting up, he ran for the exit to the truck dock. Incredibly, nobody had seen him yet.

But that was about to end.

"Okay, Bo Diddley, hold it right there!"

As Marvin cleared the exit and skidded across the dock,

264

he almost ran into a uniformed policeman coming in the opposite direction. Both men had their guns out, but Marvin's was swinging freely and the cop's was looking at him eye-level.

Marvin took a second to assess the situation, his eyes darting all around him.

"Don't even think about it, boy!" yelled the uniform. His voice was steady, no panic, no quaver. Marvin knew this guy meant The Biz.

"Ain't no problem, Officer," he said very slowly.

"Drop that iron. Right *now*!" said Officer Schmidt.

"Ain't no problem. Here it goes right now." Tossing the magnum away from both of them, he watched it clatter across the dock.

The cop kept his service revolver trained on him while he pulled a whistle on a braided cord from his pocket and blew loudly into it. The abrasively shrill sound shocked Marvin as much as the realization that there was still at least one cop in the city carrying a fucking whistle.

It worked, though.

Seconds later, there were more uniforms and two detectives at the scene. They cuffed him and twisted up his arms as they roughed him down to the alley and towards the cruisers.

"Well, if it isn't Mr. Pennsylvania Avenue himself," said the homicide detective named Doyle. Marvin had know him since he'd walked a rookie beat on Fremont years ago. "You're in hot water this time, Harper."

"Shit, you got nothin' on me!" Marvin glared at all of them.

"Oh, I think we do," said Frank Doyle.

Marvin let them goon him up the alley to a parking lot behind the hotel where he saw the medical examiner and an ambulance crew leaning over the sprawled body of a big, white guy.

"What's going on?" asked Marvin.

"Oh, well, we thought you might be able to tell us a little something about that when we get downtown."

"We *is* downtown, you dumb suckah!"

Doyle smiled. "Not as down as you think, son. Get him in

the car, Schmidt."

"Hey," yelled Marvin. "I didn't shoot that guy! I didn't shoot nobody!"

Forty One

Charles Whittier

Charles waited as Katherine Louise paused in her narrative, toying with the fringe on her tunic-style blouse. She looked uncomfortable.

When she didn't continue, he nudged her a little. "How did you find out what happened at the hotel after you'd left?"

She shrugged. "There were plenty of people telling their stories, their sides of what happened. Over the years I kind of pieced it all together."

"So what happened after you left the hotel? What happened to Syd? What about the body . . . Harry's body?"

Katherine's lower lip tightened. She tried to look directly into Charles' eyes.

"Do you think I killed Harry?"

He hesitated. What the hell was she asking him that for?

"I don't know. I wasn't there. But it sounds like you were just defending yourself."

"I often wonder if I hadn't pushed him past me, as he burst into the bathroom . . . if I'd just let him grab me . . . crash into me like he wanted to. . . "

"Ms. Louise . . . there's no sense worrying about it now."

She smiled at him like he was a little boy and she were tolerating some silly little phrase he'd offered up to her.

"Well, Mr. Whittier, I *do* worry about it. And there's never a day or night that passes that I don't relive it."

"No one ever figured it out?"

Katherine shook her head.

"I don't think anybody tried too hard. They had a perfect patsy in Little Marvin Harper. They'd been trying to put him away for years, and this incident would serve just as well as anything."

"You mean that they set him up?"

Katherine smiled. "Not really. They had witnesses on the maid's shooting. They figured what was another murder count going to matter?"

"You mean Jimmy Beaufort?"

"Right. And you can be sure Senator Higgins wasn't going to fight it. The faster they covered up that mess with his driver the better. He didn't want his name being mentioned in the same breath with any of this sordid business."

"And you. Nobody ever talked to you?"

"No one," she said, then shook her head as she stared off at the window. "I'd never really tried to hurt anyone my whole life. Then suddenly, in the space of a couple of hours, three people were dead and it was really all my fault."

"How do you figure?"

"I should have stayed in New York. None of it would have happened."

"What did you end up doing? Where did you go?"

"Oh, I drove straight to the train station, just like Syd told me to. I was running on autopilot, you know. I couldn't believe what had happened. I was thinking that they were going to pull me over at any second, but they never did. I hopped the train to New York and went back to the Metropole. I stayed there for a month. No one ever placed me at the scene of the shooting. I never mentioned it, and it kind of just faded away."

Charles bristled slightly at her chilling detachment.

"I didn't even see a dime of all that money he kept talking about." She was still looking off, addressing her remarks to the window.

"What happened to the money? Did it go to his wife, Dolores?"

"No, because no one knew about it. Harry told me it was hidden away. I never knew where to look for it."

"What about Syd? Did he ever tell you what he did with. . . "

"Harry's body?"

"Well, yeah . . . " Charles felt embarrassment, but only for an instant. The story was everything now. Push. Force it out. Go for the throat on this one.

"No," she said too quickly. Then: "Well, that's not exactly true. He told me generally how and where, but that, Mr. Whittier, is my one and only secret in all this. I'll take that one to my grave, thank you."

"Okay, I can understand that." Charles paused and finished his cooler of gin and tonic. "Is there anything else that I can include in the article about Harry? Was there anything *good* about him? Anything you treasure about him?"

She smiled. "Oh yes, there was plenty good in him. He took care of his family, and he was loyal to his friends from his growing-up days. He wasn't bad in the, you know, evil sense. He just believed in letting people enjoy themselves. He never thought there was anything wrong with gambling and sex. He was really a pretty good man . . . "

"I see . . . "

"Don't forget to read that poem. It showed Harry's compassion."

"Ah, I won't." Charles stood up. He noticed that she was alone with her thoughts. He'd kicked her off into some serious reveries, and there was no sense trying to pull her out right now.

"I can let myself out, Ms. Louise. Thank you. For everything."

"All right . . . "

Her words were trailing away from her like stale smoke, and he knew it was time to leave.

FORTY TWO

CHARLES WHITTIER

Carefully, he slipped the ribbon off the rolled-up, yellowing paper and looked at the carefully printed words.

You Are The Sunshine In My Days
You Are The Star That Lights My Night
You Give Me Comfort With Your Ways
You Make My Smile So Big And Bright

Charles shook his head and winced at the raging *clichés* and the utterly prosaic quality of the first stanza of Harry's love poem. He lay in his hotel room with notes scattered across the bed while CNN Headline News rattled on in the background, filling up the dead spaces.

Bad as the poetry might be, he liked it because it gave his piece a human touch and provided the link between Harry and Katherine, the past and the present, that made for good journalism. Still, he read the remaining stanzas out of a sense of duty rather than from any unconscious need to punish himself.

I Wish To Save You From The Madness
I Want To Take You From The Stage
I Can Give You Life And Gladness
Let's Us Turn To Life's Next Page

You Have Danced Upon My Dreams
And Never Knew The Most Important Thing:
Not Everything Is Always Like It Seems,
And My Love For You Doesn't Need A Wedding Ring.

Oh, God, that's bad! Julia would throw him out on Columbus Circle if he ever gave her anything like that. The sentiments were so banal and full of greeting card treacle, the rhymes so forced, that Harry must have used a shoehorn to make them fit.

And yet, there was something genuine about it. Something ... sincere.

Charles tossed the curled-up paper onto the pile of others on the forest-green bedspread. Something had made Harry Tennyson sit down and spend the time to cripple those lines of trite together. Charles would try to respect that.

After a shower, he called Julia and told her things were about wrapped up. Then he took a 10-minute taxi to the Polo Grill to splurge one last time before going back up to face his laptop and the final sheaf of notes. The article had taken on a life of its own, no doubt, but it was almost finished now.

Funny, Charles thought, how simple tasks like a shower, typing, and eating became major efforts with a busted arm.

When he ordered coffee and the waiter had removed the last of his dinner plates, Charles sat staring idly at the couples coming in for late-night, romantic dinners. It made him think of Julia and himself, and how fleeting it all was. How, not so long ago, Harry and Katherine were young lovers full of reckless passion and unfulfilled dreams.

His mind snagged on the final word. And amidst the

background hum of random thoughts, he realized that he could not get the idiot cadence and relentless rhyming of Harry's poem out of his head.

And then, with a smile that stretched his face to absurd proportions, he knew *why* . . .

At Sunny's Surplus, Charles paid the clerk and tucked his purchases into a backpack. "Didn't know you guys would be open so late," he said, trying to make conversation. He was anxious, but tried to give the impression of being lackadaisical.

The clerk shrugged with ultimate ennui. "'Til 10:00 every night."

"Well, thanks," said Charles as he ran clumsily from the camping-handyman-military surplus store to the curb. The arm in the cast was healing and itching and had become more of an inconvenience, causing him to run with a very awkward gait. His heart was metronoming at high speed and his breath was kicking like the old asthma attacks he used to have as a kid. He had to get back across town to The Block.

The darkness that hung over the city would be his only ally, and his only hope was that he was not too late.

Finally, a yellow sedan glided up to the curb, and his adventure had begun. He sat up on the edge of his seat with his backpack already in place, laden with his instruments of discovery, and waited with unusual and unfamiliar confidence.

The cab dropped him off on Gay Street, just around the corner from the garish neon of The Block and adjacent to the construction site boards that covered whatever was left of the last three buildings on the corner.

He'd known that Harry's Desert Club was being torn down, but hadn't kept up with its demolition progress. For all he knew, it was already gone, but he had to find out.

Standing in the shadows, he faced the street, where a phalanx of cars moved past him when the light turned green. In that one instant, he knew he was ignored and unseen. Charles slipped in between a gap in the boards, briefly catching his cast on a protruding nail, and found himself in the midst of chaos. The wrecker's ball had left things in broken piles, which in turn were being methodically sledged into smaller pieces for hauling away. The second floor and the roof had already been caved in. Ambient light from the street beyond the construction barriers cast everything in a yellowish-green glow. Combined with a sifting of dust in the air, it looked like a mist rising up from a Scottish peat bog. Charles stepped over a huge slab of stone and entered what was left of the Desert Club. There was really only one section left standing—the inner side wall where the big, polished mahogany bar lay there like a fallen tree.

Running his hand across the worn surface, he imagined the millions of hands that had touched that spot, and it gave him an unsettling feeling. Was his to be the very last? Carefully, using his good arm, he pulled himself up and over it, and hauled himself up onto the stage where the ghosts of a thousand naked women still lingered. He felt suddenly cold as he stood there in the dusty night. Cold, but not alone.

Time to get moving, he thought.

He knelt down and studied the polished oak slats of the stage, still tight and smooth—not like a lot of the flesh it had displayed over the years.

Slipping off the backpack, he eased a crowbar from its folds and looked for a crack or a split seam big enough to get started. The light wasn't great, but he examined the stage with the care of a country doctor, and he found what he was looking for—a place to start.

Charles knew he had to be cautious with his broken arm. Still, he could use the cast as leverage while putting almost all of the pressure on his good arm.

Resistant at first, the old stage slats finally surrendered to the force of steel and young muscle. As Charles worked up a sweat while breaking through the dance floor, his mind synced up his actions with a simple, insistent rhythm.

And a few lines from a very bad poem.

You Have Danced Upon My Dreams.

Not Everything Is Always Like It Seems.

As he pried and snapped and pulled away the slats of wood, making the hole bigger with each assault, Charles began to get a very good feeling about the work. Soon he would know if Harry Tennyson was just a bad poet or perhaps something far slicker . . .

When the hole was big enough, Charles pulled a flashlight from the backpack, flicked it on, and shined it down into the darkness. The first thing he looked for was anything moving, like a rat or something less identifiable. But it was simply still and dark—like a grave. He smiled as he imagined that in a very real sense, that was exactly what it was.

Still, as he lowered himself down under the stage, he felt none of the guilt or terror of a true grave robber. Rather, he saw himself as an archaeologist, given the mission of examining the mystery of the past through the pieces it had offered up to the present. His bad arm was beginning to ache, and Charles wondered if he had damaged it further. Forced into a crawling crouch, he scrambled around like a crab on a rocky coast. The beam of his light pierced the darkness with a tight column, revealing nothing outside the circle of its impact. Slowly he panned across the debris beneath what must have been a convenient place to store and stash things not ever needed again. Empty boxes, old movie and stage posters, wooden crates that once held bottled seltzer water, and a large box of women's high-heeled shoes littered the place. Charles had no idea what was beneath this level, although he knew most old buildings rested upon basements and not merely slabs. He didn't want to go banging around through primary flooring and end up crashing through to some murky below-ground chamber.

No, if there was anything here, it would be—

Right *there!*

The beam had reached the back corner of the stage where the two sides met. Wedged into the right angle was a long, metal box. If you weren't looking for it, you could easily mistake it for a dusty piece of lumber.

But Charles *was* looking for it, and that made all the difference in the world.

Shifting the flashlight to the hand of his immobile left arm, he pulled the box free of the corner and was surprised at the weight of it. It felt dense, substantial. In prior days, they called this a strongbox. Crawling as fast as he could, hefting the box with him, he made his way to the wound he'd created in the stage, and popped up into the night air, which had never smelled sweeter. He was oblivious to the throbbing pain in his broken arm.

As he sat on the edge of the stage, he realized the safest thing to do would be to wait 'til he reached his room at the Stouffer before trying to open it.

Yeah, he thought, and I'll just look as inconspicuous as possible lugging this heavy sucker through the lobby with a cast on my arm . . .

That's when he brought out the other tools from his pack—a hammer and a cold chisel, and a cordless electric drill. The best weapon, he knew, was a prepared mind. Surprisingly, the box wasn't as strong as it looked. And with one arm, neither was he. The piano hinge that ran across its length gave in to the chiseled hammer blows with very little effort. So little, in fact, that Charles wasn't ready for it, and the lid snapped free with such speed that it flipped off the stage, up-ending the box and its contents off the edge of the stage.

But Charles didn't care.

He was staring down at the dreams Katherine Louise had danced upon all those years ago: stack after stack of bank-wrappered, one-hundred-dollar bills . . . .

Forty Three

The Article

As the sixties wore on, much of what was colorful on The Block just seemed to go away. Maybe it was just attrition or a changing of lifestyles, but gradually there were no more headline dancers, no more glittering costumes. Musical accompaniment stopped and the orchestra pits were empty.

Two of the three blocks that made up The Block faded out of existence, and urban planners had their sights set on the few remaining clubs. The Charles Center–Inner Harbor Management, obviously viewing The Block with distaste, delivered the opinion that "it hampers the development of more respectable uses."

And if such local pressures weren't bad enough, The Block suddenly became an international incident. In a 1967 Moscow magazine article, a Polish reporter attacked The Block's decadence as an example of depraved Western culture. He portrayed Baltimore as a town of rampant vice where organized crime controlled the police through an intricate system of payoffs. Former Mayor Theodore R. McKeldin was cited by the reporter as an official who shut his eyes to police corruption and permitted *crime to flourish. McKeldin, a staunch, teetotalling Methodist, countered what he obviously felt was a red herring by wanly noting that "Personally, I have never entered any of those places on The Block."*

And, at the same time, some of "those places" were changing their business. Massage parlors began to appear around The Block area and other Baltimore neighborhoods in the late sixties and early seventies. By 1975, there were 24 parlors around town—three of which were on The Block. Attempts to increase the number of Block parlors were frustrated by a city-wide, vice-squad crackdown on massage parlors in 1976 and the continuous police pressure that followed.

As Baltimore rolled up its sleeves and dug into urban renewal, The Block stood alone, neglected, a wallflower at the dance. In 1974, Fanny Belle Fleming, a.k.a. Blaze Starr, sold her Two O'Clock Club. Later that year, other club owners from The Block went to visit Mayor Schaefer to find out where they stood. He advised them to fix up their clubs or risk having the whole area condemned.

As the 1970s ended and The Block moved into the eighties, changes occurred, which was in itself unusual, since The Block had changed slowly over the past 30 or so years.

The strip clubs got a face-lift, at least on the outside, with new, brighter, more livelier signs announcing the clubs' names. And some of the names had changed. Foxy Lady, The Circus, and Club Diamond appeared.

Inside the clubs, business went on as usual. The appearance of black dancing girls, which had really only gone beyond tokenism following the Baltimore City riots of 1968, was now seen as a regular staff item in all of the clubs. Mostly this was a peaceful evolution, but there were occasional problems.

By the late 1980s, the city ordered partial demolition of one side of The Block—the Villa Nova Club and east were to go. A new highrise office building went up. The Block, only one block long, got an entirely new sidewalk on both sides of Baltimore Street, including trees, brickwork, and protective metal grates. The Gayety Theatre building housed three new strip clubs (on Custom House alley) and an adult book and video store . . .

And the nineties? Recently, the Desert Club was demolished.

278

Four months earlier there was a surprise raid on The Block by six hundred state troopers. A lengthy undercover investigation culminated in the discovery that drugs and prostitution existed on The Block. Six hundred state troopers! Drugs and prostitution! Shocking, just shocking!

EPILOGUE

Two days later, early in the morning, he arrived at Baltimore Washington International fortified with painkillers. He was wearing a baggy pair of Banana Republic khakis and a loose-fitting fatigue jacket which the cast barely fit into. Everything had lots of pockets, which would allow him to carry all the cash on to the plane on his person.

The total came to $450,300. An unthinkable amount of money in 1957, and *still* a hell of a nut. He couldn't get the single thought out of his mind that it actually belonged to *him*. He kept waiting for somebody to run up behind him, tap him on the shoulder, and say: "Okay, hand it over, buddy . . . "

But there was nobody back there. And a more rational center in his mind knew there never would be.

Charles approached the security checkpoint and gave them his notebook computer for a routine check. The article for *Esquire* was completed and, while he still hoped they liked it and published it, he knew he would never have to write anything he didn't want to ever again. His career as a work-for-hire journalist was over. He would spend his time traveling and, of course, writing the novel that he and every other writer always believed they had in them.

Charles walked on through the checkpoint and into the corridor toward the planes. He was whistling and singing, mostly to himself, when the voice behind him made him pause, but not stop.

"Excuse me, mister."

Charles convinced himself the voice didn't mean him.

"Hey, mister, you dropped something. Is this yours?"

Charles froze, then turned slowly while he told himself to be cool, be smooth. Charles saw beside him a uniform, no, a young man in an army uniform. An officer and, certainly, a gentleman—a lieutenant. And in his hand the soldier had the pack of matches Charles had been given by Katherine Louise on his last meeting with her. One of the last original Desert Club matchbooks, with the pretty blond girl standing topless in a desert lake, a little oasis. Her breasts were protruding slightly—one of Harry's gimmicks—so guys could rub them and think of the girls in the club. Charles took the matches.

"Thanks, Lieutenant," said a very relieved and grateful Charles, and he put the matchbook deep in his pants pocket, rubbing them once more for luck. Then he continued down toward his plane, quicker now, and singing to himself from a Warren Zevon song:

Hurry home early,
Hurry on home.
Boom-Boom Mancini's
Fighting Bobby Chacón.

Such were his thoughts as he prepared to leave the city. So consumed by his thoughts and his own dreams that he failed to notice the announcement that someone else had finally gotten the hook.

Had he paused at the newsstand to pick up a *Baltimore Sun*, he might have seen a small article on the back page of the Metro section—little more than a footnote, really, that Katherine Louise had died suddenly of a stroke in her sleep the previous night.

Ironically, the obituary noted, she was scheduled to be buried on the same day that the famous Desert Club, where she had danced for so many years, would undergo its final demolition.

About the Authors

Bob Litwin has worked for the Federal government for over 30 years. He holds B.A., L.L.B., and J.D. degrees from the University of Maryland, and has taught writing courses at the College of Notre Dame of Maryland.

Chip Silverman, Ph.D., M.P.H., is Director of Chemical Dependency and Government Relations for Green Spring Health Services. Prior to that, he worked 25 years for the State of Maryland. He was Special Advisor to the Governor for Substance Abuse Policy and also served as Director of the Drug Abuse Administration.

During the past 20 years, **Chip and Bob** have written for the *Baltimore News American* newspaper, served as contributing editors at *Baltimore* magazine, and produced and hosted segments of the *Evening/PM Magazine* television program.

Chip has appeared in the films ... *And Justice For All*, *Diner*, and *Tin Men*; and the television series, *Homicide*. He is the author of the book, *Diner Guys*.

Raised in Atlantic City and Philadelphia, **Bob** has lived in Baltimore for almost 40 years. He is the winner of the National Bohemian Beer "Mr. Boh" Look-Alike Contest and he collects EC comics from the 1950s. His favorite hangout is the Midway Bar on The Block.